This is the story of one woman's conviction in the ancient science of Wicca or witchcraft, and the dedication of her life to removing the stigma attached to witches. Born into a well-known family in Calcutta, the young Ipsita began her quest when she joined the Society for the Study of Ancient Cultures and Civlisations in Montreal, Canada. In a chalet in the Laurentian mountains, where this group of women would meet, she pored over crumbling manuscripts holding secrets long forgotten and tantalizing answers to questions one is too scared to ask. Eventually, she chose to carry on with further studies in the ancient cultures, unraveling forbidden codes and deciphering obscure texts.

Ipsita Roy Chakraverti's life has been an amazing one. Time and again she has encountered the mysterious 'X factor' when the meeting ground between science and the supernatural – and she believes there is one – has been transcended by a force that defies explanation. Some of her strange encounters have been with the rich and famous – the scientist Homi Bhabha, Indira Gandhi and Elvis Presley. But equally there has been her work with the poor and persecuted in the towns and villages of India, those whom, as she puts it, 'if God forgets, the witch cannot.'

## Praise for *Beloved Witch*

'... the book is an ode from her to herself. But it does leave you bewitched.'

– *India Today*

'Chakraverti's absorbing autobiography is a valuable and historic document of one woman's journey with Wicca.'

– *The Hindu*

'It's an enjoyable, fairly engrossing read. The author is gifted with a simple, clear style and she clearly has a feel for the different energies that flow around us ...'

– *Outlook*

'The recurring theme is the great injustice done to independent, spirited women over the centuries who were branded as witches by hostile, insecure men.'

– *Indian Express*

'Chakraverti's absorbing autobiography is a valuable and historic document of one woman's journey with Wicca. A story as fascinating as any novel, written with perfect poise and balance.'

– *Indian Review of Books*

'*Beloved Witch* is made of sterner stuff ... her claim to being "intelligent" is justified.'

– *Business Standard*

'Written in a simple but hard-hitting style, the book is a statement to one of the guiding principles of her life – that every strong woman can be a witch.'

– *The Telegraph*

'*Beloved Witch* is a remarkable account of an extraordinary life told with honesty and lack of pretension.'

– *The Book Review*

# Beloved Witch

## AN AUTOBIOGRAPHY

Ipsita Roy Chakraverti

HarperCollins *Publishers* India

First Published in 2000 by
HarperCollins *Publishers* India
HarperCollins *Publishers* India, Cyber City, Building 10-A, Gurugram,
Haryana – 122002, India
www.harpercollins.co.in

1 2 3 4 5 6 7 8 9 10

Copyright © Ipsita Roy Chakraverti 2000

P-ISBN: 978-81-7223-987-9
E-ISBN: 978-93-5029-981-4

Illustrations on pages 1, 91, 153 and 255 by the Author

The information contained in chapter 12 "The Crystal Skulls" is based on
research by Chris Morton and Ceri Louise Thomas.

All rights reserved. No part of this publication may be reproduced,
stored in a retrieval system, or transmitted, in any form or by any
means, electronic, mechanical, photocopying, recording or otherwise,
without the prior permission of the publishers.

Without limiting the exclusive rights of any author, contributor or the
publisher of this publication, any unauthorized use of this publication
to train generative artificial intelligence (AI) technologies is expressly
prohibited. HarperCollins also exercise their rights under Article 4(3) of
the Digital Single Market Directive 2019/790 and expressly reserve this
publication from the text and data-mining exception.

*

HarperCollins *Publishers*, Macken House, 39/40 Mayor Street Upper,
Dublin 1, D01 C9W8, Ireland

*Those who came to me by day and gave me their hearts — I shall not forget them. But those who came by night and held out their souls — this book belongs to them*

Ipsita

# Contents

| | |
|---|---:|
| *Preface* | ix |
| **Part–I** | |
| **Return** | **1** |
| Lightning Strikes | 3 |
| The Mark of Vishnu | 17 |
| Strangers and Familiars | 23 |
| Learning About Lipstick | 31 |
| Mrs D | 36 |
| Secrets of Power | 43 |
| Wicca Summons Me | 52 |
| Unforgettable | 67 |
| The Prophecies of Luciana | 77 |
| **Part–II** | |
| **The Wheels Turn** | **91** |
| Pages From My Diary | 93 |
| Magic in Wood and Stone | 97 |
| An Encounter with Indira | 102 |

| | |
|---|---|
| The Crystal Skulls | 114 |
| A Strange Prophecy | 120 |
| A First Love? | 125 |
| Raising the Power | 136 |

## Part–III

| | |
|---|---|
| **Revenge** | **153** |
| Daggers and Uncles | 155 |
| The Witching Hour of Marriage | 175 |
| Jyoti Basu and I | 193 |
| The Witch-hunt Continues | 200 |
| If God Forgets | 208 |
| The Witches of Purulia | 215 |
| The Toast of the Town | 224 |
| Sweet Revenge | 235 |
| Some Witchy Diplomacy | 248 |

## Part–IV

| | |
|---|---|
| **Myths, Mysteries, Miracles** | **255** |
| A Witch by Any Name | 257 |
| The Tools of a Witch – And a Few Secrets | 265 |
| The Mystery at Konark | 271 |
| And at the End | 277 |

# *Preface*

This is a narrative like no other. A twentieth century saga which goes back many centuries. It is a story I have never related to anyone, though many have wanted to know. I have basked in my own knowledge and experience and held the secrets close. For I am selfish. I hold nobody in such great worth that I must share anything of mine with him or her. Why I am divulging many parts of my story now is because I feel I have accomplished a great deal of my purpose. There is a sense of satisfaction in talking of one's achievements and victories. If others profit by reading what I have to say, well so be it. But that is purely coincidental. I do not write this story with the intention of helping or convincing others. I respect and care for very few. Neither would I convert others to the path of Wicca. I have always held my art close to me.

Many centuries have passed since I first started delving into the mysteries left behind by our ancestors. The ancient crafts. The ancient sciences and wisdom. It started way back, from the time that the beautiful witch, Luciana lived and disappeared. It carried on when she returned and the work started or rather, began again — when I, Ipsita, commenced my studies with the extraordinary Carlotta, in the chalet in the Laurentian Mountains in Canada. My search for forgotten truths has led me into unparalleled situations where the human animal has been stripped of all protection and pretension. I have looked into the darkest crevices of nature's well-guarded secrets and learnt of things which the orthodox would deny and yet fear. And that is another thing. All along, I have been completely without fear. I have gone where the quest has taken me, in distant lands or in my own country, India. I have gleaned wisdom from the old trees on Mount Royal, from the megaliths of Brittany and from the mysterious rocks of the temple of Konark at Orissa.

I know for a fact that other dimensions exist, that we have other senses, which are in constant communication with higher planes of knowledge and being. The inanimate lives. The dead do not die. We are immortal.

Orthodox society has often had to bow to my will and my theories, firstly, because it could prove no other and secondly, because it could not ignore my credentials. Society sets its standards in the physical and material world. I pose a challenge to it because I am of it and yet, a rebel in its midst. I can play its games too, but beat it. And yet, I know that there is no need for arrogance. Material power is attractive, necessary, but meaningless in the long run. What I have actually striven for, is a few pickings from the vast harvest of truth which lies beyond, and if I continue to use my arrogance against society it is because I deplore its hypocrisy.

In the following narration, I have written about my journey into the ancient world of Wicca. Wicca, which was later turned by men and organized religion into the ugly word 'witchcraft'. I call it ugly because by distorting the meaning of the word, thousands of innocent women and a few men have been tortured and killed through the centuries, in all lands and times.

Today, in India, the scourge still continues, especially in rural areas. Even in this century, countless women who refuse to fall prey to male lust for flesh or money, are branded 'dayans', and workers of black magic. They are tortured, paraded naked through village lanes and stoned or beaten to death. The perpetrators of these actions, seldom receive their just legal deserts. Of course, in a society which batters and bruises its women, physically and mentally, in home and work place, every woman is a witch. They are perhaps no longer dragged to the stake, as in medieval Europe, but they are killed in the cradle, neglected and abused at home, battered as brides, and molested by employers.

But more of that later. Revenge is easy. Too easy. One must play with the mouse before the kill. And Wicca believes in subtle moves. The secret smile. The narrowed eyes. The knowing nod. And then the sure swoop. Wicca waits. It can afford to wait. The enemy eventually makes a false move. I know, from experience.

Of course this story is more than just a story of retribution and old debts repaid. I have taken the reader into the intoxicating beauty of Wiccan ways. The close rapport with nature. The celebration of the senses. The mingling with the Elements. The understanding of minds. The learning and the wisdom. The inner detachment and then the power. For this is what true Wicca or the Way of the Yogini, as it was once called in India, is all about. I have always maintained that it is a cerebral and an aesthetic way of life. Wicca is not for everybody. You may not choose it. It chooses you.

In this my story, you will find no dates with which to gauge the passage of years. Events and well-known personalities are mentioned. From that you may wish to place time, as you would understand it. For me, it has very little significance. Mention has been made here and there, of summer and winter months. To Wicca, chronological or calendar time is meaningless. The river flows on, sometimes straight and rough over the rapids, sometimes slow and meandering. I learn and I experience. The seasons change. That is all. That is the only 'time' I am aware of. I evolve. Dates pass me by. Some I remember. Many I don't. They are merely the points of interest on the shore. The river flows on, strong and swift. But the core or the soul remains the same. One life 'ends', another 'begins'. But I am here. I shall always be.

In my history, I have divulged as much as I have wished to divulge. It is not expedient that all should be revealed to the world when it is not yet ready. I have obligations to a discipline and to a way of life and I do not babble in the market place. Many names have been camouflaged because I do not believe all identities need to be revealed. The story is intact and accurate as it is — without spreading out all the cards. If some perceptive reader should perchance alight upon the true persona of an individual I have written about, I would advise him to keep his knowledge to himself. Let it suffice that he knows. Or thinks that he knows.

Many faces from the past swim up to meet me as I write. Wise spirits, strong ones with the knowledge of the centuries. Carlotta, Karen, Julia — and of course Luciana. Today, as I write about them and reveal so much about their secrets and their way of life, I feel a certain elation. I have kept to the ancient tradition and yet I am breaking away from it. I feel no qualms of conscience — for I am a free and wild one. I write what I wish with strength and with the knowledge that in this life there is no right or wrong. One's own conviction and understanding make the difference. Then of course, there is the question of arrogance. I know I have that. But as I always say, arrogance is a virtue worth possessing.

*Ipsita Roy Chakraverti*

The Winter of My Remembrance
India

# I
# Return

*'One does not reckon with natures like these, they arrive like fate… they arrive as lightning arrives, too terrible, too sudden, too convincing, too "different" to even make it possible to hate them.'*

— Friedrich Nietzsche

1

# *Lightning Strikes*

You know what reminds me of myself? Dark skies slashed with lightning. Forked lightning. Thunder which rumbles like deep-throated laughter. Rain which swirls along the dusty roads of Indian villages. Present but elusive. And yes, winds — strong, tearing, uncaring winds which know their own will and their way.

For these are a part of me. Ipsita. A child of the Elements. I understand them just as I understand the age into which I have been born. I have only to look into a person's eyes to know what he is, what he wants. And I do not like what I see.

The November-born are often called Elementals. Children born of mists, amethyst skies and approaching storms. They belong too to the mystical blues and turquoise greens of the deep seas. They sport with the crests of waves and laugh as they tumble over and around them, scattering pearls of froth and transience. For they know that they are born to ride high but that in the end, it's all a game. And they know how to play that game to perfection.

I remember the hour of my birth. It was the third day of November. The night had been covered with a fog which seemed to rise from the ground and swirl around the Beltola Road lamp-posts and the imposing gates of my grandfather's house. I had chosen to be born in his house. For he was an important man, the mayor of Calcutta and a much feared and respected criminal lawyer. Everyday, he dealt with the worst, the darkest, the most degraded side of human beings and he thrashed the truth out of them. I liked that. That was the only way to deal with the scum. I admired Nisith Chandra Sen for who he was. A very strong man who cared for nothing and nobody. He often sheltered Indians who were fighting for the country's freedom. The British hated Nisith Sen because they couldn't intimidate him. Neither could they buy him off with a promised peerage.

The night's chill was upon my mother and she pulled the silk quilt around her slim shoulders and shivered as she bit back the pain of my coming. My return, actually. There were three doctors present to usher me in, a man and two women. The time was exactly 3.15 a.m. by the silver timepiece on my mother's bedside table. That magical time between darkness and dawn when humans can ask the Goddess for their hearts' desire and their wishes are granted. That time when a sleeping person suddenly wakes and wonders who called out to him from the shadows.

Like any infant suddenly thrust from a warm womb into a cold room I showed displeasure. Somebody remarked that it was lucky to have three women in the birthing room apart from the mother. The nurse's hands were calloused, not like my mother's. I had chosen a lovely mother, an aristocratic lady of great beauty She had waited for me for many years. I knew she deserved a daughter like me.

In fact, it is true that our parents can be chosen. We choose to return either to fulfil their needs or to work out our own, perhaps both. I needed an influential family into which to be born. I needed the 'background' which means so much in this country for it was in India that I would have to start my work. I knew that I would move to the international arena, but that would come later.

I had loved and respected this man, now my father, in other lives. We had always met in turbulent times and I had always gone to him for advice and protection, for he was then what he was now. A good man and also a successful one. And I knew that in this world goodness and success are hardly ever found together under one roof.

I had much to learn from Debabrata Chakraverti, for he was scholarly and full of wisdom. The eldest of four brothers and three sisters he had to struggle much in his early years to support a family which looked to him for their wellbeing.

His father, a man of piety and many ideals was respected in Calcutta society for his plain living and high thinking. But Bepin Chakraverti was a disillusioned man. At a time in old Bengal when love, religion and one's life's work were practically cut out for one by parents, society and economic status, long before one had learnt to walk, my grandfather made his own decisions. He turned to the Brahmo faith of the great reformer, Raja Ram Mohun Roy, because he could no longer accept the worship of colourful idols and the ritualism which accompanied it. He believed it refused to let people see or look at anything beyond the clay and the stone. He openly denounced its bigotry and deplored the meaningless and cruel social customs which were upheld in the name of the Hindu faith.

His own cousin Sushila was a victim of this. Married and widowed as a child, she lived the life Bengali-Hindu society expected its widows to live. Sushila's lovely, long, dark hair was mercilessly chopped off and her head shaved at a time when other girls were winding strings of jasmine into their plaits. She was draped in a shroud-like borderless, white length of cotton cloth and was told that was to be her garb for the rest of her life. The Hindu religion laid down strict norms regarding the diet of a widow. Sparse meals to be taken twice a day. Countless fasts to be kept. No meat, fish or eggs. Nothing which would strengthen or arouse. The senses were to be deadened and dulled. No foods which bore even the slightest red hue. For red was the colour of marriage, of vermilion in the hair of married women, of adornment and passion. And for the Hindu widow in Bengal, all celebration must stop. No levity. No laughter. A separate cooking pot for she would not henceforth eat with the rest of the family. Because Sushila's husband had died, she was an outcaste along with Bengal's countless other widows.

Raja Ram Mohun Roy had brought about reforms to the extent that widows were no longer forced to commit sati. There was no forced immolation of these hapless women on their dead husbands' pyres, but they lived a living death. Bepin Chakraverti was disgusted with the Hindu dictates which were ordained by man. God, surely, had no part in this. Bepin told his uncle, Sushila's father, that he would get his young cousin remarried. He offered to negotiate and talk to a friend of his in college, whose elder brother was considering matrimony. Sushila's father turned on him.

'Bepin, have you gone mad?' he shouted. 'Do you know what you are saying? Do you want my community to boycott me? Besides, do you think any boy from a good family would come forward to marry a widow? No. Sushila must accept her fate.'

'But Uncle,' Bepin protested, 'Sushila is only fifteen. She's a child. What will she do with the rest of her life?'

'She will pray and count the many names of her gods on her rudraksha mala,' replied Sushila's father. 'She will try to lead a good and devout life, so that she does not suffer widowhood in the next life.'

My grandfather saw himself through college on the strength of scholarships and wanted to be in the world of academics after he graduated. He kept journals but never published his thoughts. His last post was as principal of Brahmo Boys' School in Calcutta, a chair reserved for men of integrity and scholarship.

By that time he was a staunch Brahmo and often delivered sermons at the Bhowanipur Brahmo Samaj, in a large hall with a wooden pulpit up front and row upon row of straight-backed pews stretching across the floor to the long doors at the back. There were stairs winding up to a gallery at the side, with more chairs of polished wood, solid, secure and firm. Bepin Chakraverti was an excellent orator and spoke with conviction about the One God, the Supreme Brahma, the God without form. People flocked to the Brahmo Samaj to hear him speak. In time he accepted the offer to become the Acharya or priest of the Brahmo Samaj but he wasn't there to try and convert anybody. His prayer to God was simple. Lead us from ignorance into knowledge, lead us from darkness into light. Lead us from death into true life. His relationship with his God was straightforward and simple.

People often tell me that I have witchery in my tongue. That I am very persuasive. Maybe I have inherited it from him. The only difference is that in his time, people wanted the truth, the light. Now they yearn for other things. Who wants the light of God when there's darkness to be had? I believe in giving people what they want. They deserve no better.

In his personal life, Bepin was a man in conflict. When in college, he had struck up a friendship with a classmate, Mrinmoyee. She came from a family that believed in educating its girls at a time when girls were groomed to be just that — girls. Daughters spent their time indoors, learning domestic skills. If there was money in the family, a few tutors stepped in, carefully screened and supervised, so that they would not make improper overtures. They taught a bit of English, some history and arithmetic. The really rich could afford to bring in an English governess. The slightly less moneyed settled for an Anglo-Indian. For a female of good family to step out of the house on her own was improper and brazen.

Mrinmoyee's father, Dhrubajyoti, was a professor of philosophy at Presidency College. A cultured and forward-thinking man, he had decided to let both his daughters have a college education. And so it was that Bepin and Mrinmoyee met. Both intelligent and dreamers, in their own ways, they were soon drawn to each other.

Mrinmoyee's family had a comfortable two-storeyed house on Amherst Street in north Calcutta. Not too large but spacious enough for the parents and two young daughters, a maid and a cook. The girls spent most of their time in the upstairs sitting room cum study. A sunny room that overlooked a patch of garden and then the busy street beyond the brick wall. The wrought iron gates were kept shut most of the time because street urchins crept in to steal the lovely roses that Dhrubajyoti grew and tended with such care in his garden. Come March and the first nor'westers, and the roses would scatter their petals in the fierceness of the winds. Then Dhruba started the planting of the mogras and jasmines which would blossom with a fragrant profusion of white and intoxicate the house with the coming of April and 'poila Baisakh', the Bengali New Year.

The family was not rich but they had warmth and most important, they had conviction. Bepin was always welcome in the house on Amherst Street. There, in the study, he and Mrinmoyee spent many hours talking about their futures over an elaborately carved rosewood desk. They came to an implicit understanding that they would spend their lives together. They were to graduate shortly, and Bepin decided it was time to talk to Mrinmoyee's father.

It had been a severe winter in Calcutta that year and the sun shone with a welcome warmth on Mrinmoyee's hair, parted in the middle and caught at the nape of the neck in a coiled bun, as she stood at the window in the study. Bepin had said he'd be there at tea time. That afternoon was an important one for my grandfather. He was telling the girl he hoped to marry about his future prospects, half diffidently but with hope. He paused. He waited for her to say something.

Mrinmoyee remained silent; attention fastened on the roses which she had arranged in the bowl on the centre table. Bepin said he was afraid she wouldn't be comfortable on a teacher's salary. The corners of Mrinmoyee's mouth trembled with a smile. She knew a lady of breeding did not show emotion. She said she'd be very comfortable.

That was in December. The following January, Bepin's widowed mother, a pious woman, went on a pilgrimage. She wanted to take a dip in the holy Ganga at Nawadip, during the sacred occasion of Makar Sankranti when the sun changes its position or its 'house' according to the astrologers. It is the time when the Ganges is alive with absolution and consolation. It also promises salvation to those who believe.

Bepin's mother was a strong woman. She had been widowed young and had brought up her only son with courage and with some moral support from her own family. Her in-laws had forgotten her long ago. It was her evil stars, they said, which had caused their son to go before his time. Bepin's mother had said nothing. Her grief was her own. Besides, a debate on the subject would not bring him back, the husband she had adored. Bepin's mother was determined that her own small savings and what her husband had left her should be spent on her child — on making him a man.

Her small house in Jhamapukur in Calcutta was always quiet. She spent her days in praying to her gods and repeating their names on her wooden rosary made from rudraksha seeds. She hoped that if she prayed hard enough, in her next life she would again be married to the husband she had lost in this life. Her son buried himself in his books. He graduated with honours in English and a gold medal.

Bepin's mother stood in freezing waist deep water in Nawadip. The sun was slowly climbing from the east, scattering shards of a mystical bronze into water and sky. Sacred chants and the fragrance of incense pulsated in the air. Dark figures, half shrouded by the darkness and the mist stood on the shore and in the water, whispering prayers, fearfully and yet with hope.

My great-grandmother scooped up water from the river of a million hopes and prayed to the sun — even though according to the Hindu scriptures, women were barred from invoking the Sun God. The Gayatri Mantra was not for them. It was a strong magical chant to be mouthed only by the menfolk. Too much power was bad for women — especially widows. But Bepin's mother lived the scriptures on her own terms. As she repeated the mantra thrice, she raised water from the sacred river in her cupped hands and offered it to the Sun God, to Surya Narayan. The copper turned to a blazing vermilion gold. Then she turned around and for the first time noticed the woman standing beside her, lost in her own prayers. It was Sarala from her childhood days whom she had grown up with, with whom she had shared confidences when she had got married at the age of twelve. Sarala who had recently lost her husband. They had been out of touch for some years now. She would not have recognized the plump woman with the shaven head and the white muslin saree had it not been for that familiar mole on the left cheek.

Her husband had never made much of his practice in medicine in the districts, and they had not been well off. But Sarala had always been a simple, straightforward soul. She made do with what she was given, never complaining. Sarala was blessed with a daughter, Pramila. They were an orthodox family and it was understood that Pramila would get married young. So she was not overly educated. She had a tutor for two years, but he had left because of her temper and her disinterest. At home, she had been taught sewing and cooking like other girls, but boredom had made her sulky. She had developed a sharp tongue too, which she frequently used on her mother.

Sarala worried about Pramila's marriage, especially after her husband's death. Now here was a boon from Surya Narayan himself. An answer to her prayers. She had heard about Bepin and what a scholar he had become. Sarala approached Bepin's mother as they stood together in that river water, cold, with a thousand sins washed away, and said, 'We were friends long ago.

We have both seen life. We have much in common. The bonds of friendship never break. Do me a favour now. Accept my fatherless child as your daughter-in-law. It is a strange destiny that has brought us together today. Promise me, as we stand together in these holy waters, that you'll accept my Pramila into your house.'

My great-grandmother promised. Partly because she was a compassionate woman and the plight of Sarala had moved her. But she had been thinking of Bepin's future for some time now and this seemed to be a sign from the Divine, sent at a sacred moment. So Bepin's mother promised that come the month of Phagun in the Bengali calendar, her son would bring home Pramila as his bride. Unfortunately in those days, promises were not broken, even if they were made for someone else. Bepin's future wife had been chosen with the sun as witness and Bepin was expected to honour his mother's word.

She told him about this at breakfast the day after she returned home. For a moment, his face went pale. A cold resentment at the unfairness of circumstances welled up within him. Then he looked at his mother's face, austere and ascetic, chiselled by trials, hardships and too much prayer. He used to keep a small, silver cross in his pocket, attached to his watch chain, which a Christian teacher had once given him. Fingering it now, he only said, 'Oh Mother, if you only knew the great wrong you have done me.'

Nonetheless Bepin Chakraverti was a good husband to Pramila Sundari and a caring and dutiful father to his children. Mrinmoyee never married. She never gave any reasons for her decision but went on to become a celebrated professor in a well-known women's college in Calcutta. Bepin and she often ran into each other in Calcutta's intellectual circles. They were always happy to meet and enquire after each other's wellbeing. As for Pramila, Mrinmoyee was courteous and pleasant whenever they met but nobody knew what she really thought of her. Pramila on her part, was not one to conceal her dislike. She had not lost her sharp tongue and often accused her husband of secretly nurturing a lingering infatuation for Mrinmoyee.

But life had not finished playing its games with these three people. Mrinmoyee's life centered around her college, her students and her library of books. She had few friends. Her parents had died and their house in north Calcutta had been sold long ago. She was to retire from her professorial job in a few months' time when she had a stroke. The left side of her body was totally paralyzed. The doctors advised constant and careful nursing if further damage was to be arrested.

When Bepin heard what had happened, he rushed to her side. One look at her pale, drawn face was enough. He ordered a guest room in his own home on Monoharpukar Road to be turned into a sick room and within a day Mrinmoyee was shifted there. Pramila was indignant but unable to protest too much. After all, everybody said this was the compassionate thing to do.

For the remaining months of Mrinmoyee's life, Bepin stayed by her side. She slept most of the time in a semi coma but at times she was amazingly lucid. At such times he read to her: the newspaper, or Tagore's short stories and poems of faith which had become Brahma sangeet, or the hymns of the Brahmo faith.

Mrinmoyee had taught my mother Roma in college, and my mother loved and admired her. She helped to nurse her in these last months while the other women in the house kept away. Two of my aunts, Bina and Satyabati, Bepin's daughters were in sympathy with their mother. They moved around the house, tight-lipped and disapproving. Only the youngest daughter, Lilabati, ventured into Mrinmoyee's room now and then. Lilabati was handicapped and very close to her father. She also found comfort in my mother's company. When Mrinmoyee died, my father performed her last rites at the crematorium.

I am quite sure Bepin must have suffered, but surely not more so than Mrinmoyee. Even though what happened later was very strange. But that is the way Surya Narayan rides his chariot. It is the way to power and detachment. I learnt about detachment too — but in a different way.

## Pages From My Diary

And yet there are those who would not be detached, who prefer the musk of love to the ascetic power of detachment. Very few would renounce the forbidden pleasures of the senses. Not I. And I know not of anybody today, who would renounce the lips and the limbs of the beloved. Especially if the one lusted for, belongs to another. What joy there is in possessing the object of another's desire. Ah. Therein lies sweet victory.

### Spells Of Love — And the Sweetness of Evil

If the truth be told, today we require lust spells, not love spells. For love is dead. But who cares. Long live lust. Candlelight and romance have been snuffed out. Good riddance, I say. But thank God, er, I mean the Devil, that witchcraft lives on. For you, my friend, crave to make him — or her — your slave. To hell with morals and ethics and rights and wrongs. You never cared much for that mush anyhow. Her body and soul — that's what you desire. A curse be upon you, but here's the magic formula. You have wrested it from me — and I tell you, I have lusted with many and left them pining. And if you can do the same, you are the true son — or daughter — of Darkness.

First and foremost, my advice to my sisters. Let yourself not go to seed. Let your mirror not show a sad and pale face. Sexual vitality is of the essence, my friend. He will not care for your tears. Visit the parlour of beauty if you trust not your own balms and oils. Men adore the glow on the cheek, the shine in the tresses, the tautness in other places — if you know what I mean. And if you are a true sister of mine, you will know how to retain it.

Now come into the dark den of sinful lust and hear me out, my precious.

## Spell No. 1 (For the Fair Sex)

The phases of the moon, when love spells work best are either on the first night of the new moon or on full moon. Fridays are specially effective. Wear scarlet silk and keep a charm or token of silver with you. Then in a large silver bowl or chalice, filled with clear water, float seven roses of the purest red. Make sure of their hue. That is important. Now take a knife with an ivory handle. Even pale wood will do. Dip the blade in the water and swirl it in a clockwise direction. As the roses spin, say in a whisper or as loudly as you will —

> I stir the waters of my desire,
> Your flame will burn ever higher,
> Come to me leaving all,
> Come to me as shadows fall,
> Break the ties that bind you down,
> Let others cringe — or let them frown.
> I crave you with my body's flame.
> Come to me with praise or blame.

Now, that's a powerful chant for all lovers — young and old, single or adulterous, bold or sneaky. Say it thrice. The results will be explosive.

## Spell No. 2

And here's another one for you — my sister in distress. You want him to distraction. You adore his money, mansion and Mercedes — but he gives the slip saying he loves another, or that his wife won't give him a divorce or that he's not the marrying kind. So here's what you do.

Retire to your bedroom, all alone on a full moon night. Lock the door and latch the windows. Draw the drapes. You must have the utmost privacy. Take a shimmering, sparkling crystal bowl. Fill it with water and float seven pink roses and six yellow ones. Put on that wicked song, 'Music of the Night,' and one by one take off your garments till you stand in a silken shift. Then bend over the bowl, close your eyes and visualize his face. Say his name aloud and raise from the bowl, the bloom which first touches the fingers of your left hand. Hold it aloft — touch it to forehead, eyes, lips and breasts. Then open your eyes and say these words of power.

    Him I would have to be my slave,
    Let him cry, rant or rave.
    I care not for his wife or dame
    I care not for a virtuous name.
    Him I must have to marry me.
    Him I must have. So must it be.

Then take the rose and put it under your pillow. In a brass or copper bowl, burn a pinch of camphor and as the flame leaps up, burn a piece of paper, twice folded, on which you have written your wish. As the Element of air hears your plea — the powers will be set into motion.

    The moon is bright
    Good hunting, my lovelies.

Have you ever heard of what storybook witches call poppets — or puppets? These are small dolls made of cloth, straw or wax. And sympathetic magic is done with their help.

They can help to bring the two of you together in an endless clinch. This, my sisters and brothers in magick can be quite a thrill, unless your own spouse happens to be caught poppetting too.

Anyhow, make two rag dolls with an old bedsheet. The poppets should be just thirteen inches high. No more than that. They should be stuffed with herbs consecrated to Venus — dried rose petals, blackberry leaves, rosemary, motherwort and vervain.

Clothe the poppet representing him in a dhoti-kurta, kurta pyjama, suit and tie or whatever. Draw a face onto it. If he has other assets, draw them on too.

Clothe the poppet that is you. Come on, you can shed your clothes once the magic works. It won't be long now.

Then give his poppet some distinctive signs, other than the ones just mentioned. If he happens to be a journalist, paste a bit of newspaper onto him. If a doctor, draw a stethoscope. If a politician — give him a little suitcase full of paper money.

Now, comes the magical part. Take a length of red ribbon and cut it in the multiple of the number seven — that is, it may be fourteen, twenty-one, twenty-eight or thirty-five inches long. Finally, bind the poppets together front to front. Before doing that, lift each poppet and call it by name. They will be too mesmerized to respond.

Next, the books say, wrap the poppets in a napkin or handkerchief or piece of used bedsheet. Used linen is usually very effective — specially if it is marked with lust. Finally hide the poppets in a secret place. Perform the magick on a Friday — the day sacred to Venus and to Freya, the Norse Goddess of love.

You must repeat the ritual on two subsequent Fridays. Use the same dolls. Unless you want to be tied to someone else by then. In that case just change the poppets. Give away the first one to somebody who is into swapping partners. Witchcraft is practical and adapts itself to modern day tastes and predilections.

**2**

# The Mark of Vishnu

I often marvel at the way I have planned and lived my life. A wide and wonderful tapestry, woven with dark and silver threads. The colours of Wicca. I have spun magic into my own loom and spangled the lives of those who have touched mine with mystery and adventure.

But make no mistake. I have always come first. No altruistic motives here, no by-your-leave unselfishness. Ever since the time that I was old enough to convey the fact that I was special, and that I possessed extraordinary powers, I have used them mercilessly — as long as they didn't create problems for me.

As a child I was adorable. Everybody said so. When I look at pictures of my young self, I see eyes that are dark and limpid, piercing intelligence hidden by the soft look of innocence. A down-curved mouth, hiding contempt but mistaken for shy petulance. I hardly ever shed tears. I knew that this world needed strength, not namby-pamby daisy chains. But that doesn't mean I grew up hard. Far from it. I was a chosen child of nature — of elemental storms and the aurora borealis. A creature of shimmering lights and unknown depths. It amused me when visitors to the house patted my soft cheek and said, 'What a sweet, shy little girl.'

I think my grandfather Nisith Sen, had instinctively hit upon the truth of my being when he named me 'Ipsita' — the Desired One in Sanskrit. I smile today many years later, when I reflect on the irony of that meaning apropos of what I have been and what I am. Many have desired me, many others have tried to possess me and what I stand for. Nobody has succeeded. Nobody can. Lightning passes through you. You do not aspire to hold it.

I was never afraid of the dark or of walking into empty rooms at night. I loved the rumbling of thunder and the clashing in the skies. Once an old sadhu had come knocking for alms at our door, and when I went to give him fruit and some sweets, he turned pale — with fright or delight, I confess I did not know. 'Oh, my daughter,' he asked my mother, 'May I read the palm of this child?' My mother was at once suspicious and protective. She did not see any reason for familiarity — holy man or not. However, not wanting to be too abrupt or rude to the mendicant, she took my hand and was about to turn back into the house with a namaste on her lips, when he touched his own forehead and said with something like awe — 'That mark, my daughter. Your child has it. The sign of Vishnu. When she frowns it is all the more prominent. Look at it. My own guru had seen it on a great man once. A high personage. But that a girl should have it. Strange are the ways of Prabhu.'

My mother gently shut the door and turned to look down at me, standing there with a pucker between my brows.

'Always be careful of the motives of people, darling,' she warned me. 'You never can tell what they really want'.

I touched my forehead and smiled. 'Ma, why should he be so surprised that a girl has the mark of Vishnu?' I asked.

'It's our society, my child. Girls are always pushed aside. Second best.'

'Were you disappointed when I was born? Because I was a girl?' I asked her.

My mother Roma was the best. I couldn't have chosen better. A patrician to the core, descended from the family of Keshub Chandra Sen in Bengal. 'Disappointed? With you? I always wanted a daughter. You know what an old family astrologer once told me? He said, "Roma, your one daughter will be worth a thousand sons." I believe he was right.'

I was an only child but never lonely. I don't think I would have wanted to share my parents' attention. And I think an ordinary earth child would have been miserable being my sibling. Comparisons would inevitably have been made and comparisons are odious. I think I had some cousins here and there but in the course of time, I saw less and less of them. We never had much in common. I did not live life in drab colours or shabby hues, and I had no patience with those who dabbled in grey and white. On their part, initial bafflement turned to dislike. To their parents I was a threat. I eclipsed their offspring and they detested me for it. Ultimately I stood alone. I did not have and do not own any 'relations'.

I knew I had qualities which other children did not. I knew the Elements, the nature spirits and other worlds were close to me. It did not make me vain or unpleasant. The knowledge just set me a bit apart from others — that uniqueness which is there till today, and which I know will always be there.

They say that memory is short. That the tides of time wash over and erase everything. But that is wrong. It's so untrue. It hasn't taken from me the memories of Devi of the dark eyes, who worshipped the Goddess at the temple of the sixty-four yoginis in Orissa and who fell in love with Surya at Konark. I shall relate her history in due time. And what about poor hunted, haunted Luciana, learned and beautiful noblewoman and rebel — called a witch, who fled her tormenters from Austria to a castle on the Rhine, to disappear forever? I always knew that they were a part of me. When I looked into the mirror, their eyes gazed back at mine. I held their secrets close. When the time was right the world would have their knowledge, which was not really lost at all. Of course, I was still a child. I would have to bide my time, to weave the past into the present. That would be the best part.

---

When I think of Kako I still get a warm feeling. And I want to hug her secrets to myself. I still wonder who or what she really was. Beautiful dark Kako with the black eyes. I did not think it strange when Kako visited me at dawn, with the first streak of sun, or at midnight when the moon searched for Hecate through a world dark and silver. She would sit at the window and knock cockily, her head tilted to one side.

I was in Calcutta that autumn and I remember my birthday was very near. The Goddess Durga had just departed for the Himalayas with her entourage. The pujas were over. Rummaging through a trunkful of old books in my room, I heard her tap. Softly at first.

'Tap-tap'. Pause. 'Tap-tap'. Pause.

I stopped leafing through an old Dickens classic and looked towards the door, leading into the adjoining living room. It was silent with the tranquillity of afternoon after lunch. Nobody there. A sudden thrill went up my spine. I got up from where I had been sitting on the maroon and yellow patterned carpet and heard it again. The tapping. It was urgent now. Impatient. The sound came from the window overlooking the compound downstairs. The three o'clock sun was still warm but a wind blew in through the light paisley-printed curtains. I turned slowly towards the window and she was sitting there staring at me.

Life is constantly springing the most amazing surprises if we only have the inner eye to see them. Kako was about to step inside but then thought better of it and waited imperiously for me to come to her. I parted the curtains dappled by the sun, and looked at her, face to face. I knew at once that she had come with a purpose. This was no ordinary messenger. Kako — the name came spontaneously to my mind, parted her long shiny crow beak as if she was about to speak.

The washerwoman who lived in the outhouse in the compound below, was lashing clothes against a slab of granite. The striking of wet cloth against stone, sounded like a whip. The cruelty of desire. Of man's unfulfilment. Of frustration. But Kako was happy. Maybe it was because she did not have human wants. Her sleek darkness was unruffled by the winds outside, which blew dry, brown leaves across the stone slabbed sill. Kako was an observer. Dispassionate but interested. Uninvolved but not withdrawn. The ideal teacher and friend.

I think she was my first guide. Long long ago, in Vedic times, in Bengal, the seeress Khana used to divine the mysteries of a man's life by the speech of crows — their cawings and their silences. Their risings at dawn, their flights and the rustling of their wings. Khana was a mystic, a shaman, a witch. A great prophetess. She was also married and had a husband. Her father-in-law, a diviner by profession grew jealous of her skills. He would become furious when her tongue uttered truths unseen and hidden to him. So Khana chose to be a dutiful daughter-in-law before all else. She slashed off her tongue. The truth fell silent. The crows spoke no more, and all discord stopped. Kako wept when she told me this story. I read about it much later when I was grown.

※

I took as my 'blood' only my grandparents and my parents. The only women I truly admired were Shovana, my maternal grandmother and my mother, a woman of unusual beauty and character. Roma was born in an age which witnessed the Indian struggle for freedom — a movement which strove for political liberation and yet which gave its women personal freedom with reluctance. Roma was a graduate, spoke impeccable English and Bengali, wrote in both and possessed an inner fire, like her mother. Shovana with the fair delicate features, the royal blood of Mayurbhanj and the silence which women in her time maintained. She spoke very little and translated her emotions into lovely, flawless embroidery. The strength and the fire flashed out only when she lifted those heavy, fringed eyes and looked with displeasure at an errant child or servant. She loved them both alike.

Roma was a modern woman. She never cut her long hair but she did pencil those naturally arched eyebrows. My father in his days of courting my mother, once told her that her high cheekbones reminded him of Greta Garbo. Roma merely smiled. But she remembered it and laughingly told me one day, seventeen years later, as I stood in front of the mirror, combing my hair, 'It's such a satisfaction to have a good-looking daughter. Your beauty will wear well, darling. Let's hope that one day you have a daughter with her grandmother's looks and cheekbones.'

I love arrogance in a woman. It is the one quality that sets her at par with the Goddess.

3

# Strangers and Familiars

When I was ten years old, my father was posted as India's Permanent Representative on the Council of the International Civil Aviation Organization, (ICAO) in Montreal, Canada. It was a high profile, diplomatic posting which suited a man of his talents. A graduate from London's Imperial College and a postgraduate scholar of aerodynamics from Glasgow University, he was one of the pioneers of modern aviation in India. I was proud to be his daughter. That brilliant mind. The distinguished looks. The speeches at the United Nations. The respect which came his way. The letters of appreciation from Congress ministers in Delhi. 'You have kept India's flag flying high,' he was told. I relished it all. I also knew that this was the right setting for me. A jewel can shine brightest in a clasp of the finest gold.

My father was asked to serve two terms on the ICAO. He divided his time between Montreal and New York, the headquarters of the UNO. I went to school in Montreal, a city with an old world, French charm and the modern bustle of any cosmopolitan metropolis. Montreal with its apple orchards near Snowdon and its quaint trolley cars on St. Catherine Street. On one side of town stood the imposing and luxurious Windsor Hotel and on the other, McGill University, which cultivated some of the best brains in the continent.

Those were the years when I became acquainted with a few exceptional minds of our times. Some came as friends and guides. Others profited from knowing me. It was only right that we should meet. I needed to understand the greatness of other souls, their purpose for being.

Among those who came to our home was Dr. Homi Bhabha, world renowned atomic scientist, who was visiting Montreal. Over dinner at our house I watched with fascination as the lamp light shone on his glossy, dark hair while he talked of things beyond my understanding. His aquiline, almost hooked nose, absorbed me. It almost seemed as though it was the one physical feature that accounted for his brilliance. I remember staring at it over the Wedgewood soup plate with spoon poised in hand. As I stared, a haze suddenly seemed to come from somewhere and settle in front of him. I wondered vaguely if the candles on the table were smoking. Where was the mist coming from? But this was neither smoke nor mist. This was different.

Dr. Bhabha was asking about snowfall in Montreal. Was it always so heavy? That morning he had been very impressed with the 'snowblower' he had seen on St. Catherine Street. My mother was offering him 'luchi' and 'alur dam' — both Bengali delicacies. Their voices seemed to reach my ears from far away. The maid came in to clear away the soup plates. Their clink and clatter subsided and another sound came to my ears. The snow had come again, falling with urgency as the wind drove it against the already frosted panes. I shivered involuntarily in the centrally heated room.

Slowly, very gradually Dr. Bhabha's face faded from before my eyes and another man, another face seemed to be superimposed there across the table. I heard a voice say, 'I am Heinrich.' Then I heard a word like 'Hurt' or 'Heart'. What was it? A very foreign sounding name. It came to me in a flash. Of course. It was 'Hertz'. Heinrich Hertz? Come again as Homi Bhabha? Before me lay a cold, grey country. A laboratory. A scientific work place. Winter. A man huddled in an overcoat with a fur hat came in. In some part of my mind I was aware that it was strange that Dr. Bhabha should have been talking of snow a few minutes before. The man in my vision rubbed his hands together. Was it the cold or had he just discovered something wonderful? He went to a table strewn with papers and apparatus and sat down. The expression in his eyes was elated.

How mysterious are the ways of the other dimensions, and our other senses — the ones which take us beyond the facade to the truth. The ones which we often ignore but cannot deny. Hesitantly, I asked Dr. Bhabha if he knew a man called Heinrich Hertz. Bhabha turned to me indulgently. 'Could it be Rudolph Heinrich Hertz, Ipsita?' he smiled. 'Oh yes, I know him, or rather I should say, know of him.'

'Is he very famous? Is he a scientist, like yourself?' I queried.

'Yes, he is very famous. But he died long ago. In the late 1800s, I think. He was a German physicist who was a pathbreaker in establishing the existence of electromagnetic radiation.'

'What did he look like?' I persisted, my gaze drifting to Bhabha's impressive nose.

Dr. Bhabha burst out laughing. He had caught the direction of my stare. 'A nose like mine, would you say? I really don't know, Ipsita, but why these questions? Do you think a good nose makes for a scientific temperament?'

I looked down at a spicy morsel of fish on my plate and started cutting it up into small pieces.

That was long ago. The child which was Ipsita often did not fully comprehend the messages and clues which came to her mind like the rays of the sun slipping through the fresh green leaves of springtime. But my inner self, the conscious I, was more than aware of the wonder surrounding me. With it came gratitude to an unknown benefactor. Slowly and imperceptibly a sense of joyous power crept into me. Joyous, because there was nothing sinister about it. Nothing clawing, nothing grabbing or imposing.

※

I had a natural affinity with four-legged creatures. They liked me because I understood them. About this time something happened to confirm this. A young Canadian boy had written to Jawaharlal Nehru, telling him about his fascination for Indian elephants. He ended his letter requesting Nehru to send one to Canada so that all the children could become acquainted with an elephant from India. Nehru complied and Ambika, a baby elephant arrived in Montreal bound for the zoo at Granby. It was a bright sunny day when Christopher, the nine-year-old writer of letters and Ambika met. She peered at him over the edge of the truck which had brought her to the zoo from the docks and he looked up proudly in blazer and cap while the dignitaries and important persons who had gathered for the presentation ceremony took their seats. The mayor beamed at everybody. The press clicked their cameras.

I had been asked to perform an Indian dance on a stage constructed for the occasion on the large lawns where the function was being held. Musicians specially brought in from Delhi, played afternoon ragas. A hush fell over the crowd as the ramp was lowered. Ambika's mahout, flown in along with her, walked down grandly and extended an arm towards her. Ambika stood stock still and eyed him sullenly. 'Ayo Ambika,' he cajoled. 'Sab baithe hai,' (Come Ambika, everybody is waiting) he coaxed. The elephant refused to budge. Christopher looked disillusioned. The mahout shifted uncomfortably.

I was standing on the dais, waiting for my cue to commence dancing, but as mahout and elephant faced each other with hostile expressions, something drew me down the steps and I walked towards the truck and Ambika. My anklets tinkled and my dancing finery shimmered with silver and gold zari. Perhaps I reminded Ambika of someone back home. I went up to the mahout who stood prodding her with a short baton.

'Keep still,' I told him. He looked at me disapprovingly but my father's daughter could not be ignored. Sulkily, he obeyed. I stood at the bottom of the ramp and looked up at the young animal, so far from the familiar sights, faces and smells of home. I sent her a thought. I was used to sending out thoughts to animals who needed me.

'Come on, Ambika. This is an adventure,' I silently told her. 'Show them, don't let India down. You are being called an ambassador of goodwill.' Ambika stopped rolling her eyes and stared at me. I kept looking at her and directing my thoughts. She swung her trunk from side to side as if deciding what to do. She looked towards the crowd, then slowly raised her trunk in salute. Everyone cheered. Ambika acknowledged the applause and started her slow and stately descent down the ramp. The mahout bowed to the mayor and joined his palms in a namaste. Ambika slapped his behind with her trunk. As she passed me, she stopped for a moment. Our eyes met in a friendly, sisterly way. Then she walked on to her new life and her new friends.

Even today, I like dogs and horses more than I do people. Their silences, their patience, their fears, their insecurities and joys are all so transparent and sincere. If one looks into their eyes and picks up the waves, they speak more articulately than people.

I have had dogs as devoted, household pets and also as strays. Wild beings who have wandered into my garden and refused to go. Jackie was one such. She came one winter morning to my husband's government residence at R.K. Puram in Delhi. She was black and white and had the most limpid brown eyes. Hardly two months old. She communicated her story to me. Her mother was gone all day, foraging for food. Jackie and her siblings were left to fend for themselves. I loved her at first sight but couldn't bring her into the house because my own dog, Lucky, a small white Lhasa would never have allowed it. So Jackie was accommodated on the covered porch in a blanketed basket with bones and biscuits to keep her company. Her tail told it all. She was happy. She spent the whole day roaming the neighbourhood, or sitting out on the lawn in the sun.

Maybe, inspite of her love for me, there was a free spirit in her which made her crave the outdoors. She hated being on a leash or tied up. At such times, she'd howl and shout. But come nightfall, she would retire to bed like a lady should.

Till the night that the neighbours had a wedding in the family. Jackie was one for lights and excitement. That night she wandered out and became a target for humans who decided to stone her. As it is, many thought a street dog was having it too good. It was common knowledge that Jackie had been adopted. The next morning she was in pain with a severely injured back. I knew it was no use. It hurt to see her. I fed her some biscuits and I knew she understood. Then I took her to the vet and had her put to sleep.

The next day, as I sat in the study reading, Jackie appeared by my side. She looked just like her old bouncing self. I put out a biscuit on the carpet and went back to my book. When I looked again, it was gone. It certainly wasn't the ants and Lucky was out in the garden. Jackie, even in her astral form wanted to prove a point. She took the biscuit to show that she was there. She was a great one for tricks.

In the other dimension, Jackie lives with a family that adores her. I think it proves how, in the great design, the incomplete is made complete — even for dogs.

## Pages From My Diary

Who knows? Maybe Kako had come to me as my familiar. Perhaps Jackie was meant to be my familiar. Perhaps even Ambika could have been persuaded to become a familiar. A somewhat large one, true, but then, in today's society the bigger the better. From bosoms to bank balances.

In witch lore, the familiar is a 'familiar spirit' — usually a pet or a domestic animal given to the witch by the Devil himself. That at least is what the inquisitors said before burning a woman. I suppose it justified the action and gave the roasting a nice, tangy sauce. The pet was dragged forward with the woman accused of witchcraft and it was announced that he leaped over fences and secreted himself into places the witch could not access. Dogs, cats, mice rabbits, bees — all were named in witch trials. They were supposed to have the most telling names, like Suckin', Great Dick, Fattin and Vinegar Tom. It was alleged that they lived by feeding on human blood from the witch's teats. In the seventeenth century, such teats, which could have been anything from moles to warts to polyps were the chief 'proof' that a woman was a witch. It was said that the familiars craved human blood, because the 'little devils were so mightily debauched' that their bodies were subject to the 'continual deflux of particles' — and therefore 'they required some nutriment to supply the place of the fugacious atoms.' This explanation was actually published in a scientific essay, circa 1681 by a Henry Hallywell, Master of Arts, Cambridge University.

Until quite recently all university curricula fell under the jurisdiction of the Church — and served its dictates. Today, it makes me laugh when so-called enlightened society, pales at the word 'witch'. It gives me pleasure to see them either tremble with guilty fear — 'Can she read what I have done?' or lick their lips in greed — 'What can we get out of her?'

Never mind, my sisters of old. My revenge is yours. Those who tormented you, tortured you, slashed at you, tore you — are today crawling at my feet. What would you have me do with them? You are there in spirit, and I, the High Priestess of your Magick speak for you. And they come with outstretched arms for favours — or mercy. The wheel has turned.

4

# *Learning About Lipstick*

To me, Montreal in those days was a place close to the Elements. The winters were pristine, pure and pagan. The summers smelt of wild flowers. There was a lilac bush beneath the bedroom window at our house on Lavoie and honeysuckle on the wall outside the study. Every spring, scores of dandelions carpeted the green slopes across the street.

There were two large apartment buildings there, red bricked with white trimmings and modern glass window panes. In one of them lived Edda, a girl in my class. She had soft blonde hair and lived with her mother and grandmother. A generation back they had been Estonians. The two women were big-boned, gaunt and efficient. The grandmother looked after the cooking and the apartment while the mother worked in an office in Snowdon. They worked hard to make a success of their life in

Canada. Edda's father had either left them or had died, I was never really sure which. But they talked very little of him. I thought they were very strong women and I liked them. They exuded confidence and the adventure of living. When I stayed back on an evening on a supper invitation, it was fun. We sat around the kitchen table while Edda's grandmother dished out large portions of lamb, carrots, potatoes and Brussels sprout — all boiled together in a pot with a sprig of basil thrown in and salt and pepper to taste. She would cut us out fresh, uneven chunks of bread with butter to mop up our plates.

I was sure that one day Edda would be like her mother and grandmother but at the time she was slim and girlish and laughed a lot. For the first time, I had a 'best friend', and for a few years, she helped me to lighten up, to become aware of a more fun-loving side to myself. As a teenager, I had a tendency to be stern. I saw no reason to smile unnecessarily. Edda provided that reason with her nonstop chatter about how essential it was to have boyfriends and a love life. We were just fourteen. She'd talk about the kissability and durability of various brands of lipstick and the chipability of nail lacquer. She sat next to me in class and combed her curls in between classes — sometimes during. She said she'd give anything to have long legs like mine and told me gravely that Billy Atchison who sat across the aisle from her had been eyeing hers since maths class. She found our English teacher, James Heywood very attractive even though he clearly had dandruff. She was very disapproving when Mr. Heywood chose to marry the maths teacher Miss Cameron from across the hall. She told me Miss Cameron must have 'trapped' him. I wasn't really sure of the implications, but I nodded. Edda was smug but even more disapproving a few months later when Miss Cameron, now Mrs Heywood clearly showed signs of approaching motherhood. 'Really, the things women do to get ahead,' Edda told me. I nodded sympathetically.

In those days, Indians were still a rarity in the US and Canada and hence social interaction was mostly with the whites. Contact with other Indians was restricted to a few dozen students and research scholars at McGill University in Montreal, and the diplomatic crowd in Washington and Ottawa.

My parents entertained and were entertained five days out of seven. I remember warm, gracious dinners at our house, with lace and crystal on the table and Indian music playing softly in the background. My mother was a dazzling hostess, moving among her guests dressed in rustling silks of magenta and amber. Knowing the right things to say. Putting people at ease. In summer, there would be a gardenia in her thick, coiled chignon. The diplomatic set adored her. They said she brought the splendour of India into the long, cold winters of Canada. Pride shot through me when I heard them sing her praises.

It was at one of these parties that I was introduced to Madame Corinne Lemont. A French Canadian writer, she came from literary stock and her husband was a noted professor of physics at the university. They had a daughter, Roslyn, who was studying at Columbia. I took an instant liking to Corinne. She had dignity, a quality that cannot be put on, that rare combination of simplicity and sophistication. Tall, slim with a chiselled profile, she reminded me of a pale cameo engraved into expensive ivory. At our first meeting, amidst the clink of glasses, the sporadic sounds of mirth and banter in the many languages of the world, it was difficult to have a real conversation. But a few days later, Corinne asked me over to her neat Georgian style house near Mount Royal. It was the beginning of a new chapter for me.

It was over lunch on a Thursday in October that Corinne and I sat across her elegant, French Provincial dining table set for two. There was a fresh green salad in a large wooden bowl and hot broth in glazed blue pottery soup bowls. Admitting frankly that she was a good cook, Corinne brought forth a trout grilled with thyme, lemon and fresh coriander. For dessert she had thought of an innovative peaches with maple syrup. Onto her own peaches she poured a dollop of Cointreau and smiled when I looked hopefully at the bottle. 'Have some more maple syrup,' was all she said.

That afternoon, we sat and talked of many things. Corinne told me about her youth spent in Paris — her beginnings there as a painter and writer. Her years before that at the Sorbonne where she studied literature. Her walks by the Seine and Christmas Mass at the Notre Dame. At the time I had visited Paris only once, and only for a few days. I soaked up all she had to say like a parched sponge.

She talked about her family and her work, throwing in colourful little details — like a writer would, I thought. After dessert, with coffee cups in hand, we moved to her comfortable drawing room dominated by a lovely Aubusson rug and a crackling log fire. On the mantelpiece were photographs of Corinne's parents, her husband and her daughter framed in silver. An upright piano was placed near a window, now overlooking autumn foliage of russet and gold. Corinne sank into a snug looking hearth chair next to the fire and I perched on an Egyptian leather hassock with Oriental motifs. I looked at the logs, glowing and spitting, then turning into sparks, splintering and tumbling into so many radiant pieces. The warmth from the fire was soporific. She suddenly asked me if I had read about the worship of the sun in ancient India.

'Not much,' I replied truthfully. 'Maybe a little bit here and there. Why?'

'No particular reason. You are a great reader and you are from India. I just thought....'

Somehow I felt I had disappointed her. 'I'm very interested in the subject,' I tried to cover up. Corinne smiled. 'No, it doesn't matter. Eastern religions and traditions are so rich. I don't think one can cover it all in a lifetime.' The fire burnt with a rich, red glow spreading rays of immeasurable warmth and comfort. I gazed into the centre. Something within me was moved and also very impressed. 'You seem to know a lot about these things, Madame Lemont,' I said.

'I have been studying about the myths relating to the sun in ancient cultures. I was trying to understand how much the sun meant to the ancient Indians in Vedic times. It's so fascinating.

If you go through the fifth book of the Rig Veda, you realize that even though mention is made of the seven horses of the sun and his regality — it is the divine energy that is the focus rather than his anthropomorphic form. I just wondered if you had read anything on the subject.'

I swallowed. My smart-aleckiness was now out of its depth. I felt drawn to her knowledge. I felt I knew something of it from another time, another place — but I couldn't put my finger on it. I couldn't get the relevant data.

Corinne sensed my frustration. She observed me for some moments over her cup, then got up and softly put it down on a fluted peg table.

'Ipsita, come with me next Tuesday to a tea meeting.' It was a simple friendly invitation. That's all. But a thrill of some old forgotten memory coursed through me.

'Where to, Madame?' I asked.

'A friend of mine, Mrs. Delario, has these group discussions at her place every Tuesday afternoon. I think you would find one interesting, and you might also profit from it.'

It might have been my imagination but I thought there was an amused gleam in her eyes as she said that.

5

# Mrs D

The next few days were no different from others. Busy days, autumn days. The chill of winter setting in. Preparing for exams before the holiday season was upon one. Northmount High School was an imposing building about four blocks from Lavoie. The staff were friendly and interacted well with the students of whom a large majority were Jewish.

I excelled in two rather differing subjects — English and algebra. The first was a doorway through which one could peer into the working of people's minds. Language for me was a lever, a tool with which to pry open the locks of the inner being. I think I enjoyed algebra because it was like a puzzle to decipher. There were mysteries to unravel. Codes to crack. There was a challenge in it, and I was naturally attuned to challenges of any kind.

On Tuesday afternoon, Corinne Lemont picked me up in her shiny, ivory coloured Chevrolet and we sped across town towards Mrs Delario's rather sedate residence at Lachine. This was a bit of a suburb but not quite. The expensive houses which stood here had an air of understated good taste and aloofness about them. They spoke of sophistication without mentioning the money which went into their building and upkeep.

Mrs D's house overlooked the river and had a country house look about it. Mrs D was Spanish. Her husband was an army man who came from a political background. She had studied law at Madrid University but never practised. She was a good wife and supportive of her husband's career. But she had another hobby. She had made an in-depth study of the ancient civilizations of the world — specially their esoteric philosophies and traditions.

The doorbell rang and echoed somewhere in the warm, lamp-lit interior of Mrs. Delario's house. I remember a maple tree near her front door rustling in the late afternoon breeze, gently scattering leaves of gold and bronze which brushed my hair and settled at my feet. Corinne and I waited for the door to be answered. The maid, a silver-haired woman in a grey and white striped uniform, smiled as she ushered us in and took our coats. Corinne nodded to her and we opened a door to the left of the foyer and found ourselves in a large room.

The first thing that struck me was the books. Row upon row of them, lining the walls. Leather bound, paper bound, clothbound. Old tomes and modern novels. A veritable library of knowledge and information. Our steps were cushioned by the thick, dark blue carpet. The table in the middle of the room was longer than an average dining table, and polished so that the reflection of the flames from the fire in the hearth opposite, danced as if on a copper surface. Eight women sat around the table. A straight figure with auburn hair which shone russet in the mellow light of the room, occupied the head of the table. An alabaster lamp stood near her shedding a soft glow on the book she was reading. She looked up briefly as we entered and with a slight nod indicated that we should be seated. Corinne and I took two chairs at the other end, one on either side of the table.

Mrs D continued reading. It seemed to me that I had walked into a meeting of university dons. There was an air of infinite erudition here. Of more than knowledge. Wisdom. The table at which I sat seemed to speak of something monastic and mystical — and yet there was something sensuous here also. The comfort of the room. The firelight. The vases full of late autumn roses. This certainly wasn't one's conventional kitty party. The women around me looked elegant and distinguished. There were no whispers of frivolous gossip. No titters of inane laughter. But at the same time, there was no prim, self-righteous smugness on these faces around me, only a friendly interest as they greeted Corinne and me. A natural camaraderie prevailed, yet there was an inherent aloofness and dignity. I was intrigued and fascinated.

For the first few minutes I let the atmosphere of the room play around me and I savoured it. The logs in the fireplace crackled and the flames cast shadows on the walls and on the faces of the women. There was a comfortable smell of resin and pine in the air, mixed with the dry mustiness of old books and furniture polish. I sat back in my chair and looked at the woman at the head of the table.

So this was Mrs D. A woman who was to be my guide on a path few people have the courage to tread. Mrs D who sat there, reading from a book on the Way of Tao. This was no middle-aged guru. This was a woman of the world. A woman whose face reflected the confidence bestowed by rank and privilege. But there was no avarice here, no gluttony for more. Her quest was obviously of a different order. She was a scholar who lived her theories. It struck me that she would make an excellent administrator or counsellor. Here was a blend of the worldly and the spiritual. That is a combination which is rarely found.

It grew dark outside. The elderly maid, Mrs. Jennings came in to draw the curtains and brought in our tea on a beautifully carved silver tray, set with china cups and saucers in a floral design. She also brought in thin slices of bread, warm from the oven and biscuits with honey and raisins.

Mrs. D had finished reading and stood up. She was tall. Till then I had been too busy observing her face. I now looked at what she wore. A thick silk cape of black fell around her shoulders. It was caught at her throat with what looked like an amethyst. It glowed in the lamplight and sent out a streak of purple as she undid the clasp and removed the cloak. Under the cape she wore a simple blue silk frock with black velvet at the throat and cuffs. Her walk was brisk and decisive. She rubbed her palms together and held them out to the fire. For a moment she stood with her back to us, shoulders regally thrown back. Her auburn hair had streaks of gold in it, or maybe it was silver and looked gold in the firelight. She turned suddenly and looked directly at me.

'Well, Ipsita, so you have come,' was all she said by way of introduction.

It is strange how certain meetings are just meant to be. Preordained. I knew there was a reason for my going to that house in Lachine that afternoon. It wasn't just to attend a tea meeting of the Society for the Study of Ancient Cultures and Civilizations. It wasn't just to meet some successful, well-turned out women. It went beyond that. That day I was taken to a place and to a person who would help me become the personality I was meant to be for the world. Mind you — there is a difference between the people we are for ourselves and what we are meant to be for others. Our work in the world is decided by the personality which emerges from the secret confines of the private individual. Sometimes the public persona becomes so strong that it merges with the inner being and together they create an entity akin to a super breed of the living.

The next meeting, and the meeting after that, took me into the winter solstice. The snow lay knee-deep and the trees, bare of their autumn splendour, now stood glistening with frosted branches. Icicles hung from the eaves of Mrs. D's house when I rang her bell. Corinne had stopped chaperoning me after the second visit. I was now on my own. That evening the discussion was on the mysterious Candelabra of the Andes mountains and on how it could have got there. A woman called Karen spoke on her experiences during an expedition she had undertaken with an explorer, Richard Hartman, the summer before.

I had made a few friends in the course of the last two meetings, in the way that we exchanged smiles and nods and a few notes if needed but I still did not know all their names or who they were. A few faces looked familiar. I had seen them in the press. A woman I particularly liked for her quick smile and wit was Jean S. I was sure I had seen her in magazines and on television. Perhaps the screen. She was noted for her gamine good looks as well as her acting and singing talents. The first day I had been startled to see her. Later I had asked Corinne about her.

'Was that Jean S? The actress?'

'Yes,' was all Corinne had replied.

'I would never have thought her to be interested in meetings like these!' I said.

'Like what?' Corinne was quick to take me up on my slip.

'Well, you know, sort of high-brow. Intellectual.' Corinne had a smile tucked away in her eyes. 'You mean actors and actresses have no intelligence?'

'No. It isn't that.' I was fast verging on embarrassment. 'I mean you would hardly expect the star of a Broadway musical to be discussing Chinese philosophy in Lachine.'

We were driving home in the clear, star-studded Montreal night and Corinne leaned over and switched on the radio. Eartha Kitt was singing *Under the Bridges of Paris*.

'Ah. That makes me nostalgic,' Corinne sighed and turned down the volume, 'But yes, to come back to what we were saying. Why can't Jean discuss Chinese philosophy in Lachine?'

By this time I was looking forward to a change of topic. I felt I had been caught out in a bit of adolescent snobbery.

'Tell me, Madame Lemont,' I said, 'How many members do you have in this group?'

'Seventy-five,' she replied.

'Do they all come from Canada?'

'No. Not all are Canadians. Some are from the US. Quite a few members are from Europe. Meetings are sometimes held in Paris or Rome.'

'How about the Middle East?' I persisted. I was really interested by now.

'Well,' Corinne replied, 'We did have a very valuable member from Egypt till last year. Ayesha, an expert in Egyptology, connected with the museum at Cairo.'

'What happened to her?' I had read the book *Lost Horizon* long ago. I felt I was entering a world similar to that. There was something infinitely beautiful yet strange here.

Corinne was speaking slowly as if wondering how much to divulge. 'Ayesha had lived a long life, you see. She felt she had completed her work here. She felt drawn to other dimensions.'

I felt a chill run down my spine. 'You mean she opted for death? She killed herself?'

Corinne's reaction was unexpected. She threw back her head and laughed. 'No, no, my dear. None of us believe in suicide. Nobody would have herself done off with either. We are strong women. Mentally Amazonian. No, what I mean is that when the spirit and the mind achieve certain levels of evolution, not only can you see the dimensions beyond but you can enter and leave them at will. You don't have to attack the poor body in order to do that. Ayesha chose to travel to a realm which she found more attractive. She chose to leave her body behind. She wanted renewal. She has achieved it.'

'How do you know?' I was spellbound. 'Do you communicate with her?'

'In a way. Sometimes. But certainly not through ouija boards. And not through seances either,' Corinne stated.

'You aren't afraid of death, then?' It was more a statement on my part, not a question. But Corinne replied. 'No. Life and death are both adventures. One leads to the other. But there's not much difference between the two. Both are positive. Both are existence. There is no oblivion.'

I observed her profile as she drove, eyes focussed on the road ahead. 'How about the Far East? Do you have members there?' Somehow it seemed to me that the mysteries of life and death were very deeply connected with the eastern part of the world.

'No,' Corinne said. 'We don't as yet. Maybe in the future. Our society is not that old, in years at least. It was started about eighty years ago by a French woman. An elderly professor of mathematics who took up the study of metaphysics after retirement. We have a lovely "clubhouse" in the Laurentians. I'll take you there one day.'

6

# Secrets of Power

That summer, I made a trip into the old country. I had made a few trips before this, to Kaughnawaka, the Red Indian reservation near Montreal. My guides were Minihaha and her grandfather. Everybody called her Doris, but I knew that her grandfather, who still wore his feathered headress for the tourists had named her Minihaha — Laughing Water. He was called Chief Thunder Cloud because of his size and his reputation as a formidable adversary. Now, of course, the days of fighting were over. The white man had won and in his magnanimity had built reservations for the Redskins — and there they lived. Whatever thoughts they had, they kept to themselves.

To the white intruder, they tried to present an ordinary, mundane front, making a living by stitching bead pouches and leather moccasins for the tourists. They were silent, secretive people. Even in the evenings, as they made a bonfire and danced around it, slightly crouched as if to spring, they looked like figures from a past, forgotten race. Dark eyed, with gaunt faces, they held their secrets close. They smiled at the tourists and stood by their sides to be photographed. But their souls were old and unsmiling. The real enigma was untouched.

I visited Kaughnawaka whenever I was free, because I found the place, set amidst green forests, great rocks and hard soil, strangely energizing. Minihaha and I had struck up a friendship from the very beginning. She looked after a small souvenir shop and lived with her mother and grandfather at the back of the structure — a wooden log cabin, straight out of the wild west. Minihaha was in her twenties and very pretty. Her blue black hair swung in long plaits down to her waist and she wore a beaded leather chaplet with a single feather. She was a chief's daughter. Her father had come from Arizona. He had been a Hopi and known the old ways, she told me. He had died when she was twelve.

Minihaha's soft deerskin skirt was straight cut with a fringe at the hem. She wore a plaid linen shirt tucked in at the waist. Without a trace of make-up and with her glossy black hair combed smooth, Minihaha had a striking face but her eyes were her best feature. Long, amber brown, with the darkest lashes, they glowed with feline beauty in the sunlight. She didn't smile much though. Neither did her eyes. They were quiet, watchful.

'You are most unlike your name,' I said to her one day. 'You are the most sombre friend I have.' She allowed her eyes to crinkle for a second.

'We smile from within, my friend — if there be reason to smile at all. Otherwise, it is best to be silent and watch.'

We were walking down an earth track with tall pines on either side. They stood like sentinels in the mist, which had not as yet fully lifted, even though the sun had shifted to a forenoon slant.

'Mini,' I suddenly asked, 'What exactly do you watch or rather, watch for?'

'Sheeka, the dark wolf,' she replied, without pausing in her fast, lithe, sure-footed walk.

'Sheeka?' I asked. 'I don't understand.'

'Sheeka lurks around corners. Lyda, the white wolf is fierce and a predator, but she is straight as an arrow and her eyes are direct. Sheeka is sly. She descends upon one if one allows the spirit to be negligent and careless.'

'What does Sheeka do?' I persisted.

'Sheeka makes one's mind go grey. One becomes forgetful. Then the darkness sets in. The body is affected. Sheeka devours like the Cave of Darkness which swallows the Great Sun Father at certain times.'

'But the Sun Father is not eclipsed forever, Mini. Surely one can defeat Sheeka.'

'Yes, if one is alert — and doesn't waste time in too much talk.' Minihaha allowed herself a rare and lovely smile revealing perfectly set, pearly white teeth.

In the course of time, she taught me many things about the old race, the original inhabitants of the land.

'Where did your people come from?' I asked her one day.

'Why should they have to come from anywhere? They were here. Always here. They lived with the soil and hunted the bison and the boar. They grew corn and swam in the great rivers. And the Earth Mother taught them her secrets.'

'What secrets?'

Mini looked at me and at a point beyond me. Her face was clouded with many thoughts.

'The Earth Mother tells her secrets to her chosen ones in her own way and in her own time. One doesn't ask to be told.'

I remained silent for a while. 'Do you know the secrets Mini?' I had to know. Many thoughts and visions were crowding into my mind. I was being led to something. I knew I had to follow.

'I know some,' said Minihaha.

'Do you know for example, how to renew yourself from earth energies?' I asked.

Mini looked at me with those long silent eyes. She spoke cautiously, carefully weighing her words.

'Yes. There are old and sacred ways. The ancestors knew. They passed on the knowledge to only a few.'

'Teach me some of your ways, Minihaha,' I said.

'That is not for me to decide, Ipsita. That is between you and the Earth Mother. If she so wishes it, you will learn.'

And so it came to pass that that summer vacation, I spent my days with Mini and her family. They were warm, wonderful people — but with an inner silence. One had to know how far to tread — and one had to tread softly.

Mini and I shared her small log bedroom. It was sparsely furnished with twin bunks and a rough-hewn pine table near the one window. Two straight-backed chairs were brought in as an added comfort and Mini and I sat there drinking our coffee from glazed clay mugs in the early morning. For the other meals we would meet in the kitchen, at the back of the cabin and converge round an old potbellied stove. Their meals were simple but utterly delicious and hearty. Garden fresh carrots and peas and turnips thrown in with diced lamb. Seasoned with celery stalks and rosemary, fresh from the small patch of garden Mini's grandfather looked after.

I stayed with them for one whole month. In the afternoons, Mini and I looked after the small souvenir shop. The evenings were our own. As the sun set in a ball of fire, making the maples and pines on the distant horizon blaze for a few moments in pure glory, we'd sit on the porch of the cabin and talk till all was dark and the stars were out in the vast and endless sky.

One evening we talked of power. What it meant. True power. Sources of power. How to find them. And objects which could be made and used to draw in the power. Mini's grandfather went into the cabin and brought out things he had made or which had been given to him and to his ancestors. Beautiful little objects, which he let me hold and feel and experience and know.

'Understand them for yourself, child,' he told me. 'Your mind must always be free as Eki the Eagle. Experience from your own heart. Wisdom comes from within.'

There were pebbles and stones of many colours caught in delicate nets of silver and copper. There were small, parchment shields, covered with intriguing signs and writings. He held out a long white eagle feather, which gave out sparks of light in the dark — and in a copper box there lay two or three of the loveliest crystals that I had ever seen. They glowed and sent out glimmers of yellow and blue when I picked them up and held them in the hollow of my palm. Mini's grandfather smiled.

'I am glad you like the gems of Yellow Woman. These are used to ward off her bad temper. She is whimsical — like a storm in the desert sands.'

I looked up. 'Sir?' I asked.

'To the native North American Cochiti tribe, she is a predator, a force which devours. But to some people, Yellow Woman may show a smiling face, and be a bride, a benefactor or a heroine. To the Keres she signifies the total woman. You see, yellow is the ceremonial colour that belongs to women.'

'And these crystals?' I asked.

'They are wedding gems. As long as you hold them without fear, the Yellow Woman can do you no harm. You are the master.' The crystals glowed in the light from the porch lamp.

'Have you had them long?' I asked the chief.

'Yes. Very long,' he replied.

'How did you come by them?' I asked.

The old man smiled. 'I picked them up one night on the hill near Punished Woman's Lake in South Dakota. It was after a screaming-coyote like storm. Lightning flashed over that hill that night and one could see the trees and the rocks for miles around. The light was pure white and it slashed like a dozen swords.'

'Where is Punished Woman's Lake, chief?' I asked, intrigued by the name.

'Well, it's quite a story, child. Years ago, early settlers came upon these huge, larger-than-life statues of a man and a woman, at this place. There was also a huge effigy of a man in the middle of cairns and shallow pits. When the Sioux Indians who lived there then, were asked about the figures, they replied that they knew nothing about how the figures got there. They said they had always been there. They had heard a story about them though. The woman had run away with her lover, from the husband she had been forced to marry. The standing figure was the husband who had chased them and slain them at that spot.'

'And these crystals you found there, do they have any power?' I asked him.

'Of course, they do, child. Yellow Woman came in the form of lightning and gave them power. And I have given them power by saying the chants of Father Sky and Mother Earth over them. They can heal. Or they can destroy. But then, power always has two faces, does it not?'

'Can they hear us and grant wishes?' I persisted without really thinking. The stones seemed to roll in my hands, or maybe it was my imagination.

'They give power. That is all I know. It is up to you to use it to your best advantage. It is easy to get power. To know how to keep it, that is the difficult part. To know how to make it work for you. That requires wisdom from within. That is where Yellow Woman waits to make us falter and fall.'

Mini had gone inside the cabin and she came out now with mugs of soup sprinkled with rosemary. It was delicious and comforting.

'These crystals, sir, how do you empower them — or make them work?' I asked Mini's grandfather.

'I smudge them with the smoke of cedar, sage and sweet grass,' he said. 'And I talk to them in the language of the sky, for you must remember that they are the children of lightning.' He suddenly lifted his face to the darkness above us and sent forth a long-drawn-out plaintive wail like a wolf baying at the moon, or like a creature of the wild yearning for its ancestors. I had been sitting on the porch steps with the stones beside me and they suddenly rattled. Mini's grandfather had stopped his invocation to the unknown as suddenly as he had begun it and now seemed almost angry as he looked at me.

'You have been given the gift. Be aware of it. Remember, it is easy to achieve power. Hard to use it.'

---

Mini and I would go for long walks into the woods of pine and elms on the reservation. We would follow the tracks for as long as they went — straight or twisting. Mini would be mostly silent as was her wont — and then speak abruptly about something, as if she had already told you all about it. Like when she suddenly asked me if my shoes weren't too tight and hard for the sun dance.

'The sun dance,' I asked mystified. 'What about it?'

'You know. You were asking me about the ways to draw in energy from the Mother Earth, only a few days ago.' She had this aggravating habit of saying no more.

'Yes. Well, tell me more,' I coaxed.

'You need to wear soft moccasins — like us. Through the hide of the deer you can feel the earth. Or you can be barefoot. But then the soil is full of stones. This is the spot, you know, where three trees form the shape of a teepee.'

'You mean, a triangle,' I said. 'We are in the middle of one?'

'Yes. This is a sacred energy spot. The elders have tested it and you will find it to be so yourself.'

I was excited. 'What do I need to do, to draw in the energy?'

'First, draw in your breath and hold it, like this. Then let it out. Now lift your right knee and bend over a little.' Mini demonstrated the movement as she spoke. 'Now, let your hungry left side take in the food of earth through the foot of the left. Feel the spirit travelling up, through your leg to the rest of your body.'

She did a kind of circular dance within the clearing in the woods. Incredibly light. Her slim body slightly bent forward. One foot swiftly following the other.

'You see, the toes soak up the energy faster. So it's a toe-heel movement. And it has to be swift,' Mini instructed me.

I tried to follow her steps. It felt incredibly good. I didn't care whether or not I was doing it exactly as it should be done. I just knew that there were amazing vibrations all around me and underfoot. Undeniable energy in that triangular space, in the moving air and in that soil of the Mohawk Indian — ancient soil which held the secrets of centuries.

'Let your feet touch the earth lightly,' Mini reminded me. 'And move from left to right, then right to left with ease. Lift your knees higher. Look down at the earth. Take in your breath spirit and let it out without any jolt or jerk. Be one with the energy.'

As she danced round and round, with an almost hypnotic repetition in her movements, I could imagine the earth essence rising to meet her, renewing every nerve, cell and sinew in her.

## Pages From My Diary

When we sit at dusk on the porch, Chief Thunder Cloud often says words which I feel must constitute the wisdom of the ancestors. He will suddenly utter something apropos of nothing in particular, then puff at his long pipe and sit staring into the darkening sky. Yesterday I asked him about the old shamans of his tribe. Could they harm anyone? All he replied was, 'The truly powerful never kill or harm anybody themselves. They make the person concerned kill himself. That is how evil people are destroyed.'

I liked the sound of that. Today, I told him about the sun dance Minihaha had taught me. He seemed pleased and happy. When I asked him about earth energy he said that the Red Indians believed that the Mother Earth could rejuvenate us with her energy. The earth is a great storehouse of energy. Merge with that source he told me, and you shall be whatever you wish to be. Then he said something very intriguing.

'There are secret spots around the world where once the great chiefs danced for power and the spirits of the dead warriors reside. What you have learnt today will remain with you. Now I will tell you something further. Stand on a spot where you feel the spirit resides. Then crouch and dash your two arms behind you expelling your breath. Draw energy up from the earth as you breathe in. Close your eyes. Steal that energy. In your mind's eye see a yellow coil of fire ascending. That is what the wolves guard. It must be stolen. Make no mistake. The wolves know these spots and you can too.'

I knew I would remember.

7

# Wicca Summons Me

When I returned home at the end of the month, I found that Corinne had phoned while I was away. There was a note from her also. It said simply that the members of the circle had liked me. If I felt I could contribute something in terms of knowledge to the group and learn something in return, I was welcome to join their group — as a member. It added that Mrs. D would like to meet me.

I was aware that I was being offered a rare privilege. Alongside my natural arrogance there was a practical sense of things as they were. I knew that these women were scholars and possessed an intelligence of an exceptionally high order. This was a select society with a wealth of information — and I was being invited to study and discourse with them. It was true that I had my natural talents and was better read than most girls my age. But to hold my own with the members of this circle was not going to be easy. I was willing to give it my best shot. It would be worth it. What I had seen and heard was just the tip of the iceberg. Of that I was sure.

There was something else. I wanted to acquaint Mrs D with my brilliance. I think all exceptional and vain individuals are constantly seeking to impress those they feel threatened by. And I suspected that unlike my parents who loved me, and my friends who admired me and were slightly afraid of me — Mrs D didn't give me much thought. That was something I couldn't accept.

It was after breakfast on a Sunday morning that Mrs D summoned me to her house. I was just going through the comics, when the phone rang. My parents were still at the table, finishing their tea. I sauntered over to the phone and picked it up.

'Hello. Ipsita?' It was a brisk voice. Just a hint of an accent.
'Yes,' I replied.
'This is Carlotta Delario. You remember me, of course.'

It was a statement, not a question. She was completely assured. Confident that one did not forget Carlotta Delario.

'Yes. Of course I remember. How are you Mrs Delario?'
'Call me Carlotta,' was the brief command. 'Now, when can you come over? Make it ten. I have to have a brief discussion with you.' There was really nothing for me to say, except, 'I'll be there, Carlotta. At ten o'clock.'

She was sitting in her small study when I reached her place, a bit out of breath, for I had hurried. I usually took time to dress and do up my hair. Today I had rushed. I had worn a beige suede jacket with a blue skirt. I knew the colours just didn't go together. Well, it was too late for that now. Carlotta looked up briefly from a letter she had been writing when I was shown in, and said, 'Sit down.'

She did not smile but her voice was friendly. I sat down rather stiffly on an antique Spanish rectory chair with mahogany arms. I remember thinking apropos nothing at all that it was a very dignified piece of furniture.

'Corinne must have informed you about my wishing to include you in our group. Do you feel you will make it worth your while by joining?' Her hands were folded in front of her on the desk. She was looking at me intently.

'Yes, Carlotta. I am really very interested. Of course, I realize I shall have to do a lot of reading,' I said. 'But reading has never been a problem for me.'

'Have you formed any idea at all about what our goals or purpose may be?' Carlotta had a faint smile on her lips as she asked me this.

'Self-improvement? Delving into forgotten traditions and cultures?' I found myself groping for words when it came to a question like this.

'Yes. But something much more than that, don't you think? After all, you must have realized that this is not an ordinary study circle. Our members are exceptional women — each one of them. I would say they are like crew members on a truly fantastic voyage.'

I could feel each nerve and fibre in my body tingle as she said this. But Corinne was continuing to speak. 'You see, Ipsita, the difference here is that we don't merely study about the incredible and the unknown. We live it. We experiment with it. We become it.'

'How do you do that?' I managed to ask this mysterious woman sitting before me.

'At the beginning, it is a laborious task. It is seemingly mundane. We sift through mountains of information. Old theories and philosophies. Fact and folklore. Myth and history. Then we bring our "findings" into our "laboratory" and we experiment with what we have found in the old and crumbling pages. We use the tools of our forefathers. The same apparatus. The discoveries are often startling.' She almost whispered the last word and then repeated it. 'Yes, startling.'

I realized in the course of seasons, what Carlotta had meant. The studies, the discipline, the explorations into the tangible and the intangible, set free the mind into the limitless. Life became one vast experimnet, an adventure. The universe opened out, timeless and ageless. One became a participant in the unravelling of countless enigmas and yet one learnt how to be a spectator in this human drama. Viewing it all with the detached interest of a scholar. And in the final analysis, I think that is how we should lead our many lives, as players and scholars. Involved yet detached.

When I first saw the wood and stone chalet in the Laurentians, I thought of the Temple of Tikal built by the Mayans. The difference was that the chalet stood on a two acre plateau of rolling greenery and deep woods with stone steps leading up to it. It flashed across my mind that here was a pagan place of worship. The land was charged with invisible but palpable forces.

The Native Americans always said that these mountains were once a part of a great volcano. And volcanoes are a part of mystical rites and secrets. It is said that volcanic rocks and stones should never be carried away from where they lie for that angers the Goddess of the Volcano. And it seemed to me that this old chalet was a part of that great mountain. That it had always been there and always would. There it stood, solitary and apart from all signs of human habitation. The house could not be seen from a distance for pines and birches and maples grew thickly on all sides. But before you started climbing the steps, if you looked straight up, you caught a glimpse of it between the trees. A two-storied building, made of stone and timber, dating back to the 1800s. It had not been restored in recent times, and the stucco walls were crumbling in places. The beautifully carved wooden eaves were cracked and chipped. It was a house with six gables, and in the centre was an exquisite rose window with tracery.

The group of about twelve or thirteen of us would meet there on pagan festival days — or otherwise several times in a month. We would gather in the central hall downstairs with the high ceiling and the wooden rafters. A large fieldstone fireplace dominated the hall furnished with a long, worn refectory table with straight-backed chairs around it. That room had tremendous power. It was there that I first saw Luciana — in the astral form, for she had been dead for many hundreds of years. It was in that room, I think, that I first decided to take the torch of revenge from her hands and carry on.

※

From ceiling to floor, the walls of the great hall were lined with books, old tomes and crusty manuscripts, gathered over the years and preserved with care and long, black dried tobacco leaves. I learned from the librarian, Margaret Shoreham, by profession a practising neurosurgeon, that that was one of the best ways to keep the bugs away from these precious, yellowed parchments and papers.

'It's an old way,' she said. 'It was used in the East. You must be knowing about it.'

'Er, yes of course,' I muttered and buried my head in an old volume.

There were three learners including myself. We were not as yet dignified by the term initiate. There was Jessica, in her twenties, a research scholar in chemistry at McGill. A brilliant Jewish girl, her family owned a furniture business in Montreal. Then there was Cindy, a tomboy with red hair and the proverbial freckles. Her parents had come over from Ireland about five years ago and were now settled in California as prosperous growers of oranges. She was studying at Loyola. She had an infectious grin and made comic comments about the Teachers. But Corinne had told me that the Irish were 'fey', natural mystics. Cindy certainly didn't look like a mystic. But then, to use a cliché, appearances are often deceptive. I was to one day become a witch. And I certainly didn't look like one.

## Pages From My Diary

Summer

Today, Carlotta called me into the hall after morning study. Usually we all troop into the garden after that and help Dupont with digging the beds and planting seedlings and bulbs. This morning, Carlotta said she had something important to say to me. I was slightly disappointed because I enjoy working with the soft black loam and the fresh green shoots. They smell of high mountain reaches, gnarled bark and wild flowers. But Carlotta must be obeyed. I wondered what she had to say. Like me, she is difficult to read. The others I get around. Karen has taken me under her wing. Margaret is fun to be with when she isn't making me sort out library books. Mrs McComb reminds me of an old-time grandma. She's a rare person. Strict on the outside, soft, verging on the sentimental within. A real mathematical genius — she does all our accounting. Also watches the stars and planets and constellations at night through the chalet telescope. Knows where to look for each one. I once asked her if these sparks in the skies rule our lives — and she replied that they do, if we let them. Life is a constant battle between them and us. But intrepid Scotswoman that she is, she said, 'In the end, we win, Ipsita.'

This optimism is something they all have in common. Then, there's Jean S. She's not a Teacher as yet but a senior member. Jean is glamorous and famous but totally unassuming. Something in me sometimes says I have a lot to learn from her. Jean says profound things in the most flippant manner. She'll flick some ash off from her cigarette (no, smoking is not permitted in the chalet, but she'll sneak around the garden shed and wink at us). As the ash plops down and crumbles away, she'll say, 'That's worldly fame for you. Fun while it lasts but don't count on it to be around. Besides, it leaves a bad taste in the mouth.' With that, she'll wag a finger at us and say, 'Never smoke.' Then she'll be off with a bounce, look back and whisper loudly, 'Tell them I came and no one answered. I kept my word she said.'

## The Next Day

When I went into the great hall today, I found the core circle there. Carlotta, Karen, Corinne, Margaret, Mrs. McComb, Julia and Lorraine. They were seated around the upper end of the table. My first thought was, 'I must have been found out.' I had a guilty conscience — or maybe not so much guilt as fear of being found out. Yesterday, I leafed through one of the 'Forbidden Books' — the ones under lock and key, when Margaret was in the garden giving instructions to Dupont. There are whole volumes of vellum bound parchment with strange signs and writing in the corner cupboard. I had been dying of curiosity for some time. Yesterday, the opportunity to open that cupboard came to me. Margaret had forgotten to take the keys with her. They were left on the table. I picked them up and opened the cupboard not really thinking of what would happen if I were to be found out. This wasn't like me. But I seemed to be propelled. I picked out a maroon, vellum bound volume and turned the crusty pages. Suddenly I came upon a sketch done in black ink, of a woman's face. The ink had faded but the woman's features were clear. It was a beautiful face. Strong but haunted.

Next to the drawing there were written in the same ink twelve or thirteen questions in old English, regarding a pact with the Devil. They seemed to be addressed to her. Had I stumbled upon an old witch trial? The questions were bizarre and obscene. About her body, intimate questions, audacious questions and about sexual intercourse with the Devil. I put the book back. I truly hoped Margaret wouldn't find out what I had done. I felt strange, slightly sick, as though I had suddenly got a chill.

Now, Karen was looking at me with amusement. Mrs. McComb looked concerned. When she was concerned her Scottish brogue became pronounced, as it was now. 'Therre, therre, girl. No need to look worried. This isn't an exam.'

I sank down on a hard-bottomed chair and folded my hands in front of me. I thought that would make me look subdued and proper. I looked down at the old table at which we sat, worn, scratched and repolished over the years. Somebody, at some point in time, had carved a little sistrum in one spot. I had never noticed it before. Now Carlotta spoke and asked me what I had been doing that morning.

'Cindy and I, we've finished polishing the old silver utensils in the dining hall,' I said. A lot of emphasis is put on work at the chalet. Constructive, physical labour, along with study. Carlotta nodded. Karen spoke. She always has an efficient, brisk air about her. She was an only daughter in a family of five brothers. Her father had been a general and her husband was a major in the US army during World War II. She herself had served in the nursing corps and had seen frontline horrors. This has not made her either bitter or resigned. It has just turned her into a better fighter whose spirits are always high.

Now she said, 'You've come to a time of choices, Ipsita. In the last year that you've been studying with the group, which subjects have you related to the most?'

The Teachers never believe in a preamble. Coming straight to the point is one of their traits. It's true I have learnt a lot here. The curriculum has been hard but fascinating. Like a journey through mystical realms. I have read rare books on ancient histories, people, their cultures and philosophies and traditions. The Celts, the Druids, the Way of Tao, Egyptian myths and esoteric beliefs, Hindu mythology and magical texts, the Goddess culture of ancient times. And yes, a little bit about Wicca — that strange, fascinating pagan way, practised by our ancestors from time beyond memory. Carlotta was watching me closely. She said, 'Yes, you have worked well. What do you feel about your own progress?'

'I have read about as much as I can remember, Carlotta. But there's so much to absorb and understand. I'm sure I've just scratched the surface.'

Carlotta nodded. 'I am glad you understand that. In the first year you merely scratch the surface of subjects. Just to know what they're about. That's all.'

'When do I begin my actual study?' I asked.

'You have begun your "actual" study many centuries ago, as strange as that may sound to your conditioned ears. The wheel has started turning. It will stop only when the purpose is fulfilled. Maybe you have already realized the purpose. This is not merely a college of higher studies. It leads you to that awareness. So.' She broke off abruptly. 'Do you wish to continue with us? Or you can always look back on your past year of study as very useful leisure reading.'

I gulped slightly. Is that what this slogging amounted to? Leisure reading? My eyes still burned from long hours of reading into the night so that I could discuss topics with some understanding at group meetings the next day. I had spent hours trying to fathom diverse philosophies and paths. Trying to remember names. Trying to decipher ambiguous signs and charts. Trying to sift the real from the trite.

'Well,' Margaret was smiling. 'Do you wish to continue?'

'The way is difficult,' Carlotta put in.

'I would like very much to continue,' I said.

'Which way would you like to go? Now that you know a bit about many!'

'Yes. But they all meet at the same point. So they're all the same in the final analysis, aren't they?' I hoped I had said something meaningful and profound.

'That may be,' Carlotta replied. 'But the roads wind through differing country, rivers and mountains. The soil, the air, the vegetation, the clime differs. You must know which terrain will suit you better. Which will you adjust to sooner? Do you see what I mean? Above all else, there was a Path you were meant to walk on. Recognize it, just as it knows you.'

'Yes,' I replied. 'I understand. At least I think I do.' And suddenly I knew. That face in the forbidden book. Those eyes which often looked back at me from the mirror. They were one and the same. The woman of Wicca. Millions of others like her. Fire and torture. Those haunted eyes. 'I choose Wicca,' I cried out. 'I want to go back and find out all about that pagan way. What was it? Why did men name it "witchcraft"? Why were women accused of being Wiccans and burnt and tortured? Why was Joan of Arc called a witch? I want to know why men were so afraid of these women? Yes. Yes. I choose Wicca.'

There was moment's silence after I ended my impassioned speech. A silence which rang through the room and in my ears. I looked at the Teachers and was suddenly aware of my outburst. I had the modesty to look down at the table before me and could feel a warmth suffuse my cheeks. It wasn't necessary to be so loudly assertive — even if one had convictions. I glanced up and noticed that Karen, with great seriousness was writing into a scribble pad. That was a sure sign that she was trying hard not to smile — or laugh? Mrs McComb was nodding her head to show support and was looking concerned. Margaret looked proud of me. Julia looked at Carlotta.

Carlotta rose from her chair and held out her hand. I took it.

'So be it, Ipsita. You have chosen your Way.'

When we were there, the learners, that is, Cindy, Jessica and I, spent most of our time in reading and wandering about the sprawling, wooded grounds adjoining the chalet. Now and then we'd tire of books and revert to talk and subjects which were often on our minds — clothes, make-up, parties, the opposite sex, film stars and their love affairs. But we were discouraged from herding together overmuch.

'Think your own thoughts. Read for yourselves. This is not the time or place for talk or chatter,' Carlotta would say. 'When you're away from here, attending to your workaday worlds — there's plenty of time for gossip.'

We felt chastened and subdued by her words, spoken firmly in low tones. Mrs Delario never shouted or raised her voice. She stayed for days on end in the chalet, even after the rest of us had come down to the city. My own intuition told me that that was the time that she renewed herself and communicated with the elemental forces which sustained her. For there was no doubt, Carlotta was no ordinary woman. Either through tapping some secret vein of knowledge or through a quirk of natural forces she had come upon answers which the human race was seeking. Even then I was convinced that I had been chosen to receive the answers to those secrets from her.

One day my suspicions were confirmed. It was a Sunday morning and the other members had left for the city the night before. Carlotta was to remain till Wednesday. We had had a session on the secret symbols of ancient Egypt and Carlotta had said she would prepare a test for us for the coming weekend. In that way I suppose it was like school. We assembled, we studied, our guides and Teachers delivered their lectures and we asked questions. There were seniors and juniors amongst us. Once a fortnight, we had 'exams' by discussion. Carlotta put questions to us. We gave her our point of view. We were encouraged to speak our minds openly and to view a theory or a philosophy from many aspects.

That particular Sunday, the maid, Mrs Jennings, who came up to the hills with us to attend on Mrs D, was in the kitchen making breakfast. Dupont, the elderly gardener, was pottering around in the shed outside. I was in my room upstairs — a large room with furniture and drapes from another era. I was planning to go down to the city by the three o'clock bus that left from St. Jerome. As I sat and waited in my room, I gazed at an oil painting on the wall. It was a seascape faded and old — but magnificent in its depiction of tumultuous waves and an approaching storm. I got up from the chair I had been sitting on and went up to it to see if I could read the artist's name. But the name had either faded or someone had painted over it with a light brush.

Suddenly there were steps on the stairs. A light tread. Must be Mrs Jennings, I told myself, coming up with Carlotta's breakfast. Her room was at the end of the wing and looked out onto the distant slopes on the eastern side. I had been in her room only once — when she had summoned the learners to lay down a few ground rules. The room was small with windows opening out onto the skies and the distant hills. An old four-poster bed stood in the centre of the room. Apart from that, there was a lady's boudoir table with a round mirror and drawers, a wing chair in rose silk upholstery and a matching rug in dusty rose. A mahogany armoire stood against the wall which had no window. The room reminded one of an eagle's perch on a high cliff — a kind of flying-off point for someone powerful. The room was so above everything. One could not think trite or petty thoughts there.

The steps had reached the landing and were now coming towards my door. There was a knock and a voice said, 'May I come in, Ipsita?' Before I could answer the door opened and it was Carlotta herself. It was typical of her. She expected no delays. No refusals.

'Carlotta,' I said, startled. 'Do come in. Is there anything for me to do? You should have just sent a message.'

She kept standing on the threshold, watching me. 'Come to my room. I would like to talk to you,' was all she said.

'Now?' I asked.

'In about fifteen minutes,' she said and closed the door behind her.

I packed up the few clothes and books I had brought with me, kept my suitcase by the door and walked a bit uncertainly down the corridor to her door. What could it be? I felt something like a schoolgirl in front of the principal's office.

Carlotta was sitting in the wing chair and motioned me to sit on the bench in front of the boudoir table. I sat down facing her. 'Ipsita,' she began at once, 'you remember our little meeting of six months back?'

I searched my mind. What meeting? What had happened there? Was she testing me to see how well I remembered information? She was smiling slightly. 'Where we asked you what you wanted to study and research.'

It all came back to me then. But that had been months ago. I thought the whole thing had been relegated to the shelf for further consideration. In the meantime, I had been happy to just be. Just studying. Reading. Communicating with nature. And being. That was an art I was learning.

'Are you of the same mind? Do you want to learn Wicca?' Carlotta was asking.

My heart jumped. I felt a surge of power and elation.

'Yes, Carlotta. I am of the same mind. I want to learn Wicca.'

'But think of the implications,' she said. 'Society calls it witchcraft. It is a study, mysterious but misunderstood. Are you willing to undertake it? You are a young girl now. It seems novel and challenging. It seems colourful and curious. But later? Won't people in the world wonder why a girl with your background and talents should have wanted to study a subject called "witchcraft"? Think again, Ipsita. It has many pitfalls. You may even be called a witch one day.'

I raised my chin defiantly. 'So what?' I asked. 'I find nothing wrong in that.'

'People are ignorant and superstitious, you know. Are you that strong to be unconcerned about what people say? They might ask if you have a broom and black cat.' She was teasing me now. But it did make me stop and think.

'I don't care about people,' I replied.

'You will be living in society, after all,' Carlotta went on. 'You may regret this later on. You must also ask your parents' permission. You are not yet twenty-one years of age.'

'I shall ask them, Carlotta. But I know they have confidence in me. They have been watching my work the last year. They have seen my books. They are happy with what I have been learning. They will not object. If I am strong, they are stronger. If I want to learn the Way of Wicca, they will understand and support me.'

'You are a determined young girl, aren't you?' Carlotta smiled. 'What about when you want to get married? Some young man may misunderstand and be too frightened to marry you.'

'Carlotta, whether I study Wicca or not, that is going to be a fact of my life. Most young men will have an inferiority complex when they get to really know me. I know I am more intelligent and better than most.'

Carlotta's face suddenly became serious. 'On the path of knowledge, Ipsita, beware of that feeling ... justified or not. However, I must tell you, you are making excellent progress in your studies. And yes, you are suited to study Wicca. The path is rocky but you were meant to walk on it. You have work there. But be careful. That is all I will say for now.'

I felt a certain triumph course through my veins. Praise from my Teacher was proof that she had recognized my brilliance. I was the Chosen One.

'Next week,' she continued, 'I shall give you the first instructions for the initiate. There will be a short ceremony. Let us see how you take it and what you make of it. I am against any form of ritualism. But I believe that sometimes rituals and ceremony bring direction and committment into the life of a young person who has started walking on the path. Specially the Path of Wicca!'

'Will Cindy and Jessica be there too?' I couldn't help asking. Carlotta frowned a little. 'Ipsita, you have the gift. You have also been given a fine mind. One just hopes you will put it to good use. It pains me to see your arrogance and inflated sense of self-worth. You ask me about Cindy and Jessica not out of concern for them, but because you want to be assured that you are ahead of them.'

I blushed. She had seen right through me. 'Don't worry,' Carlotta said. 'They will be initiated on the days that are appointed for them — on the Ways they are marked to travel on.'

I rose to go. I knew she was displeased with me. I would have to learn that in the Way of Knowledge, there is no first and last. Just as there is no beginning and no end.

8

# *Unforgettable*

I had the good grace to feel a bit humbled on the Tuesday evening that Mrs Delario and six other Teachers of the Circle officially took me into the fold. It was a summer evening in the chalet. I remember the vases stuffed with roses and lilacs and the group sitting around the refectory table in the hall. A feeling came over me that I didn't deserve this honour, this warmth and friendship — a new sense of humility that was quite alien to me. I felt shoddy because Cindy and Jessica were there and beaming with genuine pride, for me. Jessica gave me a little silver rose — 'To remember this day,' she smiled. Cindy had baked a cake shaped like an 'I'. 'For Ipsita,' she explained, ' "I" for Ipsita.' We all laughed at her excitement. But for a moment I looked at Carlotta and our eyes met. There was no accusation there. They were detached eyes.

But I knew. So far the world had really centred around the 'I' in my life.

The Circle was splendid in their ceremonial attire. Carlotta wore a long, rustling black tafetta skirt and an ivory lace blouse pinned at the throat with an extraordinary cameo. The sleeves were long and close. She looked imperious and completely the aristocrat that she was — from another time and place.

The other women seemed to be out of some picture book. Long black skirts, blouses in chiffon or silk, sleeves long and loose, caught at the cuffs with jewelled pins. They looked regal.

There were thirteen of us that evening. That was how it was supposed to be. For a while we sat around and chatted in the hall. The warm late afternoon breeze blew in and was pleasant. Dupont could be seen through the long windows, crouching over the flower beds. There was peace and a feeling of wellbeing in us. Nature was close. There was power all around us. I could tell.

The funny thing is that power comes into our midst and sits with us wearing a mask of ordinariness and we do not recognize her. We are too busy looking for her in the wrong places. That evening we sat and talked of familiar things. Karen's son was coming home from college for the summer holidays. Julia had missed the sale at Eaton's and was put out. Lorraine's cake baking session had fallen flat. Too little baking powder — or the oven was too hot. Jean's last movie was doing well at the box office but her leading man was taking the credit. She laughed. Sandra maintained that she wasn't in love, but her boyfriend was — with her that is. She had decided that that was a good enough reason to get married. Come December. She knew she'd make him a good wife. Debbie had won the chess championship — but that was to be expected.

Then it was dusk and Margaret got up and switched on the lamps. There was a very large old clock on the wall that sounded with far reaching echoes as the hand struck the hours. It struck seven now and the chimes rang out, solemn and inscrutable. We rose, suddenly quiet. In a body we followed one another up the stairs and down the corridor, towards an inner room away from the gabled façade. This wing lay on the western side, away from Carlotta's room.

As far as I knew, this room was always locked. The juniors called it the 'mystery room'. Cindy had once sneaked up to the door and had stood outside listening. She had sworn to us that she heard the whispering of many voices, all speaking together. Or it might have been the wind, she had admitted. But her probing mission had ended when our elderly Teacher, Ellen McComb, who had a rare sense of humour, crept up behind her and laying a cold finger on her neck, whispered 'Whoohoo'. That sent Cindy screaming never to return to those cold corridors.

I had heard that the room was used on special ceremonial occasions or when somebody needed guidance. Guidance, from whom or from where, I never asked.

Carlotta was at the head of our little procession and we stood around her now, quiet and expectant as she took a brass key from a silk pouch at her belt and fitted it into the lock. The key turned with a click and I held my breath. What would happen in there? What would I feel? Would I be different when I came out? I looked at Cindy and Jessica. They both looked very pale.

'Come Ipsita, follow me,' Carlotta was saying. 'The others will come behind us.'

I inhaled and nodded. She held the door open and we walked in. The others were close behind. From somewhere faraway, I heard the door shut as the last member entered.

The room was fairly large. A dim light shone around though there were no lamps that I could see. I wondered from where the faint white glow was coming. Then I looked up and saw the source. The stars. Tiny bright specks were shining down through an hexagonal area of glass ceiling which rose like a spire in the centre. This was amazing. It was apparently invisible from outside. I realized that we were somewhere in the heart of the building. Karen, Margaret and the others were now briskly setting about the business at hand. Two lamps in the form of wall sconces were lit and I looked about me. Walls of dark wood panels and a grey stone floor. There was no carpet here. There may have been windows but these were now covered with heavy, dark blue drapes. Straight-backed wooden chairs lined two walls. The room was austere but contained a magic and mystery one is unable to put into words.

Then I looked to the centre of the room and I stood transfixed. There, on a grey marble stand, about four feet from the floor was an object incredibly, exquisitely beautiful. A huge crystal bowl with a myriad facets reflected the lamplight and glittered and sent forth arrows of a thousand colours in all directions. I looked up and was aware that the bowl was placed directly under the glass atrium.

A grey stone chair, roughly hewn and carved with arms, stood at one side of this marvellous object. Carlotta stood in front of the chair and motioned for us to spread out and seat ourselves. I was to remain standing beside her. I suddenly noticed that the other end of the room contained a high table of polished wood. On it were laid out objects which glowed and shone in the subdued light from the lamps. But Carlotta was speaking.

'Today, my friends, my daughters, we meet in this room of a thousand crystals, because we wish to invoke the power and the blessings of the Goddess. On other days, we work, we labour and we study. We live in the world. Today we come a little away from that world. We aspire to that which most people fear ... and yet crave. Truth, knowledge and the power that that brings. We wish to tread on land yet unknown. We seek to remember that which has been forgotten. And before we begin the journey in earnest, we must in our hearts at least, prostrate ourselves before that Power which is above everything construed and constructed by man. Man has made religion, philosophy, ritual and dogma. But our quest is for that Power which is within us and yet all around us and above us. Call it what you will. Since we are women on a wondrous journey — we call it the Goddess Power.

'If any of you feel uneasy about the ceremony of initiation about to take place, you are free to leave — with all goodwill from me. That includes you too, Ipsita —' and she nodded to me.

I glanced at her and suddenly I blinked. I drew in a breath sharply and grasped the handle of the stone chair for support. Was something the matter with me?

Carlotta — the woman I knew — Mrs Delario, wife of a Spanish statesman, a lawyer, a scholar in her own right and my Teacher, was gone. Or apparently gone. In her place stood a woman, the same and yet different. She seemed taller, more beautiful in a vibrant way. Her hair, normally brushed back and caught in a coil at the nape of her neck, was now strewn around her shoulders in lustrous auburn waves. She still wore the skirt and blouse I had seen her in, but the face, the face was that of a woman no more than thirty-five or thirty-six. Carlotta as I knew her, was extremely well preserved but looked at least sixty.

The room was clear, unclouded and clean. No fumes of exotic incense or perfumes. The only fragrance which subtly filled the room was from the petals of roses which floated in the clear water of the half-filled crystal bowl. What I was seeing was unbelievable. Was this some kind of yogic feat, I wondered. The renewal process known only to my Teacher?

But Carlotta was now walking with strong, firm strides to the table where the objects of initiation lay. She motioned me to come and stand beside her and as I did so, I saw the strange artefacts lying there. They were old, treasured and very rarely used. Carlotta turned her back to the group for a minute and stood facing the altar-like table, head lowered as if in prayer and thought. Then she turned around slowly and her face was solemn. She looked me full in the face and from the table picked up a narrow parchment with writing on it in black, faded ink.

'These are the first words of initiation — between Teacher and pupil, Ipsita. They have come down to us from a very ancient source. From a temple manuscript of Alexandria, lost and later retrieved. Read it well. It will help you understand what this is all about. And Ipsita, read the words with a great deal of respect.'

I took the paper and looked at the laboriously formed words in a slanting long hand. Who had written this so long ago? Obviously it had been translated into English from some old language of the desert. They were beautiful, deep with worlds of hidden meaning and power.

'Do I say these lines now?' I asked.

'When I ask you to,' Carlotta replied. 'Now,' and she turned to everybody, 'Once more I will place before you the weapons of the Goddess. Understand their meaning and their worth.' With that she held up a magnificent, black cape which had lain neatly folded on a cushion at the foot of the table. She threw it around her slim shoulders. It reached to her knees. It fastened at her throat with a diamond clasp. The lustrous velvet fell into soft, sinuous folds and seemed to swirl around her form with a peculiar life of its own.

'Now, listen well,' she told us, 'I, Carlotta Delario, your guide and Teacher, take upon myself the power of the Goddess for a given length of time, so that I may instil into you the wisdom which you will need on this journey of life. First, look upon me and know that this garment which I wrap around me is the Cape of Athena. In this, our ceremony, no object is without meaning. Nothing is without life or spirit.'

Somehow, as she spoke, her language was becoming more and more archaic — as if from far away. But her face was luminous. That is the only way I can describe it, even though so many years have passed in between. The eyes glowed with a fire I had never seen before, in her or in anybody else. Carlotta had found the secret of Shangri-la, if ever there was one. And there was. Of that I was becoming increasingly sure. Today, I know.

She now turned round to face me and laying her right hand upon my left shoulder, asked me to kneel before her. I did so.

'Ipsita,' she said, 'one day, mayhap, you shall wear this very cape. Mayhap not. But know what the Cape of Athena teaches you. She who was the Goddess of Wisdom. She who was named Minerva in ancient Rome, and presided over strategy in wartime and the domestic arts in peacetime. In the name of Athena I give you the strength and the wit to fight when you are called upon to do so, and the mildness to be at peace when war is over. This cape symbolises the armour you must wear. Surround and protect yourself with the inscrutability of midnight. Know the worth of dignity and the need to stand aloof from the petty distractions of the world.'

She then turned to the wooden altar and picked up what looked like a very long shining knife with a silver handle. The blade was without a point but curved at the end. The edges were not sharp. It was an Athame — a Wicca wand of healing. She laid the blade on my shoulder now and blessed me in the name of Artemis.

'I woulds't that you, like the Goddess Artemis, known also as Diana, remain ever free of spirit and complete in yourself. Like that Celestial Archer, may your goals be concentrated and may you be merciless with this weapon to those who offend the Goddess and Her will. Forget not her who was also known as Actaeon and Arathusa and who allowed not women to be violated of their honour.'

The sound of Carlotta's voice was coming to me from another dimension. I was surrounded by walls of light and banks of many coloured, glowing clouds stretched before me. But make no mistake. My rational mind was alive and kicking. I knew in some far recess of my mind that this was real. This was genuine. There was no hanky-panky, no hocus-pocus here. I had been given nothing to eat and drink, so there could be no mind-altering drug working its insidious way through my blood. And I was not fasting either. I had had my usual lunch at home that afternoon. So this was no hallucination on an empty stomach. There were no fragrant fumes to drug the awareness. There was only a doorway stepping back into a forgotten past and drawing from me feelings and thoughts of a sublimity I had not thought myself capable of.

Carlotta then held up a large silver bowl filled with water and then laid it on the table near where I knelt. 'Look into the Bowl of Aphrodite, my daughter, and reflect. Pray that you may understand the true qualities of Her who was known as Venus. For she inspired the creative arts and also knew the power of love. But She bowed to none and held her own in all joinings of mind, body and soul. So be it with you. Surrender to none your true worth, for know that you are the Chosen One of Aphrodite, Goddess of Love and Beauty. And may the water you gaze into today, hold and preserve the beauty that the Goddess is pleased to gift you. Water shall ever be a friend to you — when you wish to renew the outer self. Plunge into high crested ocean waves or the placid cool of turquoise pools and this image you gaze upon in this bowl of silver water, shall be yours.'

Carlotta now placed in my hand a tall, blue taper in a silver holder and, in the dim room, in the hushed silence, the shadows which flickered on the bare walls were not just the shadows of ourselves, as we sat around — but they were the shapes and forms from the world of Elementals and spirits, who had been invoked through the power of this mistress of high magic. They were there to witness this transition, as I stepped into a surrealistic world which held the real truth and meaning of life.

'Now, Ipsita, look at this lamp and know that the Goddess of the Crossroads, Hecate of the Dark Moon, Queen of Night, the One with the brilliant eyes, guides you on the Way. She is the One who looks straight ahead. So must you. She is unheeding of those who pour venom on her name. Thus must you be. She takes for companions, common curs, and dogs. They will always love you too. When you come upon the crossroads in your life, call upon Hecate and she will cast her lamp upon your path.'

I had been kneeling for more than an hour now, but I felt no discomfort — only a wild but restrained joy and strength, coursed through my limbs. I felt at one with the forces which had entered the room and now pervaded it. I could feel them, yea, even see them. They and I were one. And I was triumphant.

For some time now, my eyes had been drawn to a small crystal skull, delicately carved which rested at the centre of the table on a square of silver cloth. It was not obtrusive but it caught the eye and held it. Carlotta now raised it from its resting place and held it out to me.

'Touch this piece of rock quartz and bow your head to whichever power you worship, for this is the gift from the Goddess Kali — who has always been worshipped as a Mother Goddess in your great country. She will help you to overcome fear, the deadliest adversary, in your journey through this life. So be aware of Her who threatens outworn order and the stagnation of meaningless custom. Learn from her to be fearless and unconcerned about the consequences of the world. Turn away from that which is cloying and clings like dead habit. Stride forward with courage and pride into whatever life brings.'

I bowed my head and touched my forehead to the proferred crystal skull. It sent a tingling cool through the spot where my third eye was and when I looked up I found Carlotta watching me closely. I blinked. My forehead still tingled as if it had been touched with a sliver of silver lightning. Was this the way the Ancients opened the third eye of initiates, I wondered.

Carlotta now stepped forward with a most intriguing object — a large, glowing, translucent ball, the size of a large melon — an orb, perfectly rounded, of extraordinary inner light, the colour of amber. In fact I suddenly realized that the ball before me was carved from a solid and perfect piece of amber. It seemed to absorb the light of the distant stars and to hold it in its polished depths. It shone with the colour of old copper and burnished gold in the dim light. Carlotta held it aloft like the queen of an uncharted universe.

'This, Ipsita is your benediction from the Goddess Isis — she who will mould you into who you will finally be. Isis, you must know was the greatest goddess in Egypt. Remember her as the Goddess of the Serpents. The Goddess of the Tree of Life. The Goddess of the Words of Power. Let it be known to you that Isis was the Lady of Enchantments, who knew how to outwit even the great Sun God Ra. Yet, she was compassionate, a loyal wife and mother. Learn this from Her, O Ipsita. Be like Isis — a woman complete in yourself. Learn the language of enchantment but not deceit. Learn how to play the games life offers. Like Isis be stateswoman, wife and mother. Or if these roles suit you not, take from Life, the part you wish to play but play it with regal demeanour. Even with power at your feet, crush not kindness and compassion, without which power is the tool of fools. Now hold the orb of Isis, look deep into it — and then rise — for you have been blessed by the Goddesses of Wicca.

I took the amber ball and it seemed to pulsate in my open palms. I gazed down at it and the golden brown flecks of old life trapped deep within it, seemed to flicker and flash. Suddenly I knew I had been offered a path very few were allowed to tread — the Way of Wicca. I looked at the orb in my hand and knew this was a path which had been appointed for me by a mysterious and Higher Order, which avenged wrong. I was Luciana. I knew it then. I smiled at Carlotta. I think she must have known it from the moment she met me.

9

# *The Prophecies of Luciana*

Who was Luciana? This mysterious presence whose energy seemed to make itself felt, around me and sometimes in me. No, I am not about to write a colourful ghost story — but what I have to say far surpasses a ghost story in its incredible poignancy and depth. Besides, Luciana was not just a story. Wicca history says that she was real — her beauty, her brilliance, her scholarship and her knowledge about things unknown. Real too, were her enemies, the bitter conspiracies, the torture, the hatred and finally her flight from Austria to Germany. She was glimpsed for a moment entering a castle overlooking the Rhine, near the Lorelei and then the silence of centuries. The world is rid of Luciana or so they said. Those who lusted after her but hated her. Meanwhile the witch trials continued in Europe.

This abuse, mostly of women, — sadistic, gruesome and sexual started in the eleventh century in Europe. But it peaked during the bloody fourteenth, fifteenth, sixteenth and seventeenth centuries. That was the time when men dressed in the garb of the holy and the righteous swooped down upon women they lusted after but hated because they could not have. Women, strong, beautiful or independent minded were called witches so that they could be eliminated. Male bastions, however inadequate and impotent must be protected. Perversion and hypocrisy took shelter behind self-righteous piety and religious zeal. Witches were the consorts of the Devil, these men shouted, even as they probed and prodded the bodies of these wretched women with salacious saliva dripping from their lips.

During these four centuries in Europe alone an estimated eight million women were executed for witchcraft. It was said that they flew through the air on brooms to attend Sabbats and had intercourse with the Devil and his kin. It was also said that if a woman was too beautiful, look no further. It was the Devil's handiwork. If she spoke well, it was a Satanic tongue which prompted her. If she showed a desire to expand her mind — it was with an evil purpose. The Devil wanted her as a tool to taint and destroy the pious and the good.

Luciana unfortunately, was all that sixteenth century Catholicism could not tolerate. Old records presume that she was born around the year 1578 to rather rebellious parents, from whom she may have inherited this particular trait — attractive yet damning in times that were turbulent. Rudolph the Second, in many ways a fanatic, had ascended the throne as Holy Roman Emperor. The place was Austria. Luciana's father Charles Francis Bruckner, of Hapsburg lineage, was allegedly a favourite at court till the time that a strange destiny caused him to fall in love with a Protestant noblewoman of French blood, Marietta Lavance related distantly, on her mother's side, to the Bourbon queen Jeanne d'Albret of Navarre. Marietta was good-looking, head-strong and for a woman of her times, extremely well read. Charles Francis, while on a diplomatic mission to France had become hopelessly infatuated with her. He was obviously not the right match for Marietta, but their wills were strong and Charles brought back his French Protestant bride to the court at Vienna. There, shocked whispers told outrageous tales of how Marietta's wiles had enslaved Charles. The French woman was hated and she, ever proud, did nothing to lessen that hostility. Charles did his best to stand by his bride but he himself was astounded at the venom spewed forth against his wife by court and church alike.

Their lives were somewhat lightened and made happier by the arrival of a comely daughter, whom they named Luciana Genevieve. But even this could not save the ill-starred marriage. As news reached the court of Vienna about clashes between Catholics and Protestant Huguenots in France, all rage seemed to direct itself towards the alien Marietta. Caught in the middle of a cruel religious war that was to ultimately rage for thirty years, the luckless wife of Charles Francis finally wrote to Jeanne d'Albret and said she was returning to France. Charles was melancholy but helpless and agreed to the separation. However, he insisted that Luciana was to stay back with him. And so it was that at the tender age of five Luciana knew the loneliness of existence without her mother in a land that hated her because she was not really one of them.

Desolate at first, Charles recovered sufficiently from the void left by the departure of Marietta to involve himself in other distractions which the women of the Austrian court were more than willing to provide. Marietta had chosen to leave, he told himself. He had a duty to himself and to his kind in his own country. His life must continue at a chosen pace. Maybe, given the circumstances, all had worked out for the best.

But things had not really worked out for the best where Luciana was concerned. She grew up silent and sensitive, spending much time by herself, attended to by nurses and a private tutor. She had a perceptive and innovative mind and sought company in the songs of the winds, the trees and the birds. They were her only friends. At a time when a young woman was being taught embroidery, dancing and the arts of pleasing at court, Luciana was alone with her thoughts and some old books on an ancient craft her mother had left behind for her daughter to read one day.

There were hand-written pages on how to cure ills of mind and body with herbs and flowers. Written in French, a language that Luciana had been taught at the behest of Charles, there were strange lines and rhymes which sounded mysterious and mystical when pronounced. But they had a peculiar efficacy in ridding the mind of fears and in banishing bad dreams. Luciana used to have frightening ones till she was almost thirteen, but one night after saying some words written in one of the books, the dreams ceased to trouble her. There were also instructions on how to make the mind strong and how to keep the body ever youthful. Luciana loved these books. They were the living, breathing presence of a mother who had never really left her.

One evening, while turning the huge globe in her father's study she suddenly chanced upon a mass of blue and violet to the south-east of Europe. THE EASTE was all it was called. She looked hard and long at this unknown area she had heard stories about. Stories of fabulous jewels and spices and wild animals. Luciana took to coming to her father's study whenever he was out and poring over the globe at that misty land mass. There was something there she could see, as if in a dream. Almost as if she could travel there as a mist or a cloud and look down on all that was transpiring — and on that which would transpire — many years hence.

And thus came to be written the prophecies of Luciana in approximately the year 1599, in the city once called Vindobona. They were put down in a very unlikely place. In a small, narrow diary used to write billet doux or amorous jottings. But Luciana had nobody to whom she wanted to write. She merely wished to remember in writing the strange visions which came to her when she looked at that huge orb.

Luciana's diary was destroyed during the ensuing years of witch-hunting in Europe, but about ninety-one quatrains were miraculously hidden and preserved, at first by Charles her father who reportedly gave them for safekeeping to her old nurse Therese. The old woman later passed them on to some good nuns in a convent in the Bavarian Alps. There they remained till they were found a few hundred years later in a small village museum near the abbey of St. Michel d'Aiguille which is set high up on a needle point of lava rock. The pages were sent to our chalet in the Laurentians, I was told, in the early nineteenth century. There were stories that the founder of our society was a descendant of Jeanne d'Albret. I do not know if this was a fact. But I was told that the Foundress had been informed that she was to keep these papers in the utmost secrecy and that they would be deciphered at some point in time by someone in her group. One of the old nuns at the convent, with whom she was in touch had told her this. I do not know from where the old mother superior got this information but I believe she was a woman of great learning, vision and a very compassionate heart.

It was in my third year of study at the chalet that I was given the untouched pages to read and decipher. They were encased in specially treated cellophane-like paper and were yellow and parchment-like with age. The curtains were drawn to shut out the harsh glare of the sun and subdued lamps were lit, and then, in the presence of Carlotta, Margaret brought out the pages with infinite care and spread them out on the table for me to read. I looked at the evenly spaced lines of a slanting, slightly angular handwriting in faded black ink and felt an immeasurable sadness. I do not know how else to describe the feeling. I felt a stab of recognition. Was it the words, I wondered? I touched the cellophane cover of the page nearest me, very lightly with the tip of a finger and withdrew it quickly as it crackled as if in pain. Was this just my imagination? No. There was something more here. I looked carefully at the writing, carefully preserved on those pages for so many hundreds of years. There was a meaning here. A purpose. Suddenly the message behind the quatrains came to me wave after wave.

Some of what Luciana had written was in rhyme — ambiguous at first glance. Twenty-five more years passed before I could bring them before the eyes of the world. By that time I myself was a Teacher. Carlotta had passed on many years ago, having left me the instruction that I could let the world know the secrets at an opportune time.

Some of these prophecies I reproduce here for the reader. This is how I found them. Some were in French, the others in a strange old English. I have translated a few of them into a form which will be more easily understood by the reader. They make reference to a world centuries hence. Different countries are alluded to. It is interesting to note Luciana's obvious interest in the Indian subcontinent. Also of interest is the fact that there are hints regarding the last decade of the twentieth century. 'The last ten bridges which cross the 1990s,' she called it:

> 'The soil and rocks will shake and sway,
> With earth's own energy gone astray,
> Due to man's greed for more,
> In lands where sea meets the shore
> In the ley line of the Azore.'

The ley lines are bands of the earth's magnetic fields which run along similar latitudes and longitudes. They often form strange networks. On a map, one finds that some of the worst earthquakes in the current decade have been along the Azore Islands belt, covering parts of China in the east and California in the west. It is remarkable how the sixteenth century prophecies of Luciana foresaw the earthquake tragedies of this millennium. One notes that the recent, devastating earth upheavals in Turkey in the latter part of 1999 as well as the ones in Greece, occurred within that same 'line of the Azore'.

Another verse reads:

> 'The King will no longer hold domaine,
> In that island west of Saine
> There will be strife 'twixt man and wife
> But we still wish them all a long life.'

This verse refers no doubt to the gradual decline of the British monarchy — which seems to be pointed to as 'that island west of Saine' — the river Seine, in its old English version may have been spelt with an 'a' instead of an 'e'. The 'strife 'twixt man and wife' would indicate the royal divorces. It is chilling when one considers the last line. Did Luciana foresee Diana's tragic end, much before her time? Is that why she saw the necessity to 'wish them all a long life'? When I first brought these quatrains before the world, in print, in the year 1996, I do not think anybody guessed the uncanny implications. Nobody knew that within another two years the luckless princess would meet her end. It would seem that only Luciana, so many centuries ago had been given the vision to see this sad event and had cried out that it might not be so.

There are some startling lines which refer to West and South Asia. I think she saw the Indian subcontinent when she gazed at that globe in her father's study. For this is what another quatrain says:

> 'Beyond deserts and mountains high
> Lie the lands of mysterii
> There one day will women rule
> There one day will ye find the tool
> To combat ills which plague mankind
> The answer lies in its rocks and sea
> Near the rock tower built to Ra.'

It comes to me that this verse indicates India and her neighbours. The deserts and the Himalayan range would have to be crossed if one were looking this way from Europe. Very little was known about these lands in sixteenth century Europe

— thus the 'mysterii'. The prophecy that one day women will rule in these lands is amazing. For the subcontinent has seen so many women political leaders — more so than in the west. There have been strong women like India's Indira Gandhi, Pakistan's Benazir Bhutto, Sri Lanka's Sirimavo Bandaranaike and Chandrika Kumaratunga, Burma's Suu Kyi and Bangladesh's Begum Hasina.

The next few lines of this particular verse can shed hope around the world. Will cures to diseases like cancer and AIDS be found in this part of the world? And what about the place specified? The 'rocks', the 'sea', and the 'rock tower built to Ra', the Egyptian Sun God. It came to me a long time ago, that this line indicates the temple of Konark in Orissa. It was built in the eleventh century and is near the sea. At one time it was supposed to be a centre for healing. Perhaps the ancient builders, in their wisdom chose the site on account of its therapeutic properties. What about the 'tool' mentioned in the prophecy? Could it be a reference to the electromagnetic nature of the building stones? Perhaps the word embraces the quality of sand, sea and air here. During my months of research in the old temple at Konark, about which I shall write later, many fascinating and revealing facts were thrown up. One of these was that at one time, the sea was much nearer the temple than it is now.

Of course, the verse can be looked at differently. We can turn to Egypt and the shrine of Amen-Ra in the Libyan sands. But then, the other prophecies in the same verse do not seem to apply. What about the many women rulers? Also, the temple of Amen-Ra certainly does not stand next to the sea.

Luciana had written some very incisive lines about the political situation in India at about this time. When I first read them about thirty years back, I confess I did not linger over them much. I was more interested in interpreting the prophecies which would seem to apply to the world and its people at that time. But it was a strange fate that was to bring me into the closest contact with Indian politicians from the 1980s onwards. I do not boast here when I say that many an Indian prime minister has sought my advice in statecraft during these years. However, I also state that to none did I divulge the prophecies of Luciana before the instructed time. Sometimes there is a sense of sadness in me when I wonder if, in the final analysis, it is all Fate. Everything charted out for us — the good and the bad. The celebrations and the heartaches. The triumphs and the defeats. If I had revealed any of the verses before 1996, could any of the tragedies have been averted? I think not. Destiny is charted out for us. The prophecies of Luciana prove that. That is the only consolation I have to stave off a feeling of guilt for my long silence.

The following verses refer to a tragic assassination which occurred in India in May 1991. A young political leader fell to a searing explosion set off by a fanatical woman terrorist, a suicide bomber who was assigned this task by some implicated in a deadly and dastardly conspiracy:

> 'The young leader went unsuspecting on
> His friends held back in the throng
> Where were they all when the earth shot fire?
> They merely came to weep at his pyre.'

This verse would seem to indicate the murder of Rajiv Gandhi on the eve of the general elections in 1991. The lines which cry out for attention are of course the subsequent lines which refer to his 'friends'. It is a fact that no Congress leader was at his side as he met his tragic end. A number of them had accompanied him to the meeting ground at Sriperumbudur in Tamil Nadu, but no one seemed to have wanted to go the final few steps with him. They could not even give the excuse that he was surrounded by security men because the Special Protection Group had been withdrawn from him and he was alone when the woman Dhanu, allegedly an LTTE supporter bent over, supposedly to touch his feet after garlanding him but actually pressing the button which caused the earth to shoot fire.

Even more intriguing is the stanza which says:

> 'Though he lies on a bloody land
> His spirit still walks proud and grand
> They felled him with an evil hand
> Who were the three of this murderous band?'

For the love and affection which he had inspired in the people did not end with his assassination. It seemed to increase with redoubled fervour that won the Congress the election and kept them in power till the time that the Janata Dal ousted them at the hustings. The charisma of the Gandhi name and the fact that nobody else seemed to be able to hold the Congress party together forced his widow, Sonia to take the reins in 1998. Thus, there is no doubt that Luciana was right when she saw the spirit of Rajiv walking amongst the Indian people even after his death. Whispers abounded that interested people in the Congress party had been behind the conspiracy that killed him. There were those who were not getting along with him, others who had been sidelined and missed the attention they had enjoyed in his mother, Indira's time. There were those on the verge of retiring from political life because he had brought in fresh, young faces, and he had no use for the older ones. Motives were many but so were the alibis. Thus Luciana's lines open an explosive avenue of thought and speculation. 'Who were the three of this murderous band'? That is what she asked and also implied if we carefully read the previous quatrain, that it was among the people he trusted or who were ostensibly for him. I have my own interpretations regarding the 'three' but if I wish to live to write more, wisdom prevents me from divulging any further.

However, before I write about the prophecies on other subjects and other people, there is one which I feel refers to the assassination of Indira Gandhi in 1984:

> 'The people wept the day she fell
> She was the mother of the land
> But there were those whose hearts did swell
> Had the crown come nearer hand?'

An interesting verse prophesies the solar eclipse which took place in the year 1995 and about a very strange phenomenon which followed:

> 'Strange things occur in ninety-five
> The sun is dark, stone comes alive
> Who is friend and who is foe?
> Those who betray him have to go.'.

The phenomenon occurred in India in the month of September, in the year 1995. There was a solar eclipse that summer and shortly after that, stone really did come alive — or so it seemed not only to the people of India but to those around the world. Stone images of the elephant-headed god, Ganesha, started imbibing milk — in certain cases even water. People went wild with religious fervour, yearning for miracles and just plain curiosity. Thousands upon thousands lined up outside Hindu temples around the world, waiting to offer a few spoonfuls of milk to the god. The press could write of nothing else. Of course the sceptics were there with explanations but they were laughed at because scientific reasoning didn't seem to apply here. For this phenomenon lasted only three days. After that, the spirit withdrew into the stone again.

At the time that Ganesha was taking liquid refreshments, P.V. Narasimha Rao was the prime minister of India and going slightly berserk with the hawala case where he was trying to allege that nearly all his men had accepted bribes from the infamous Jain brothers at some time or the other — hence they must be taken to court. He was paranoid about prospective rivals to the throne. What better way to eliminate the competition than to brand them as corrupt and keep them busy fighting cases at court. The last two lines of this particular quatrain no doubt would apply to that bizarre situation.

In the spring of 1996, I brought before the people of India the prophecies which I thought related to them and their rulers. The previous year I had released a very few to the press -- mainly those dealing with western countries and matters of global and human interest. In February 1996 I decided to illustrate the prophecies through a series of twenty oil paintings which would serve to bring Luciana and her visions closer to the people. At the exhibition there was also a portrait of the seeress herself. The event was entitled 'The Revelations Of Wicca On Indian Politics And Politicians'.

While in Montreal I had won the Arthur Lismer Scholarship for painting which had trained me to be a fairly accomplished artist. In India, I studied Indian painting under Santosh Sengupta, a renowned artist of the Oriental School of Art. Thus what made the exhibition exceptional was not only the extraordinary subject matter but also the competence of depiction. The press appreciated both aspects. The public was interested but I could see that some pictures both attracted and baffled them. They had come expecting a run-of-the-mill art show — but this was something mind boggling. The politicians, of all colours and affiliations could not keep away from the large hall at the Ambassador Hotel in Delhi where it was held. And they came time and time again. Not daring to ask too many questions but poring over the brochure and standing for long minutes before certain pictures, wondering what their place could be in the scheme of things. First and foremost was there a place at all? Who was the winning horse? How long would the current regime last?

The exhibition gave me not only a chance to bring forth the prophecies, it also enabled me to have a close look at the mind of the Indian politician. It was filled with inordinate ambition but limited vision and no compassion. There was an obsessive preoccupation with self.

A strange thing had happened a few days before the show was to go up. I was sitting by myself in my room, going over the proofs for the printing of the brochure, when some lines, in rhyme flashed through my mind and I knew I had to get them down on paper as soon as possible. I had never been much of a writer of verse, but now I knew what I had to write and this was definitely in poetic form. It had something to do with the position of women in our country. Their wretched plight. The portrait of Luciana faced me, propped up on a large easel. The eyes were intense and the face had a shimmering quality — pale yet vibrant. I knew once again, even after all those years, though life at the chalet was far behind me and I was now a wife and mother in Delhi, that my work had only just begun. I took pencil and paper from my desk, put aside the proofs I had been correcting and sat down to write the following verses. I do not know whether I wrote them, whether she did or whether we were one and the same. I suppose only time will tell. I am willing to wait. The lines flowed without a pause:

> 'I am the witch they batter and burn
> I am the girl child killed e'er she's born
> I am the bride burnt for gold
> I am the daughter not married but sold
> I am the one who suffers still
> While our rulers turn the golden mill.'

There was so much to do and so much injustice. A deep, submerged anger told me that a chain of wrongdoing against women had started far back in time. I had seen it. I still felt it. It was a timeless injustice. Women all over the world had suffered — were still suffering. Violated, tortured and killed. Whether it be in the name of witchcraft or statecraft, they were the scapegoats. Yes, I had work to do. And I would do it. I looked in the mirror and the face that smiled back at me was a proud one with a smile which touched the lips but did not reach the eyes.

There were two more paintings I would have to add to my collection. One would illustrate the stanza I had just written. The other would depict a warrior woman — strong and fearless, who had returned to the field of battle with a purpose. She had some scores to settle. Some heads would roll. Of that there was no doubt. I wrote the following lines with an easy pen:

> 'I am She — I rise with the storm
> I was killed — now I am born
> On the winds of revenge
> Blood, lust and greed, I will avenge.'

Times ahead would be interesting.

# II
# The Wheels Turn

*'Believe me: the secret for reaping the greatest fruitfulness from existence and the greatest pleasure is to live dangerously! To found your cities on the slopes of Vesuvius! To send your ships sailing out into uncharted seas!'*
— Friedrich Nietzsche

## Pages From My Diary

Autumn

It has been misty and cold since yesterday. The maples and elms are bare and stark as they stand like sentinels on the hills, and the grounds are soggy and wet with yesterday's fallen leaves. It is that time of year when one lets go and waits for the wheel to turn.

Cindy cajoled old Dupont into bringing in some logs from the shed. We drew the curtains in the great hall and put out the lamps and built a fire in the fireplace. The flames flickered and sent long shadows dancing on the walls. Cindy giggled and said it was spooky but fun. Dupont is building a log house on the grounds for the 'wee animals' as Mrs McComb calls them. The mountainside is full of them, small red foxes, lemmings, ferrets and woodchucks. Jessica says she saw a small brown bear and its mother near the chalet gates one morning. Perhaps they had come for breakfast. I wonder if these animals can be made to coexist in their little cabin when the snow is deep. Come spring and Carlotta says we'll take the roof off the animal shelter and make it into an enclosure for our plants – the ones we are going to talk to. That promises to be interesting.

According to Julia, who is a botanist and writing a paper on plant emotions, the day is not far off when the kind of experiments we are doing will be conducted at major universities. What is off the beaten track today, will be orthodox science tomorrow. I asked her if our experiments can be repeated and get the same results as in a scientific experiment. She said yes. As long as nature repeats herself and has the same seasons, year after year, we will be able to repeat ourselves. Our lab tools are the Elements and our living minds, she said. These are the building blocks of real science.

## The Next Day

Carlotta gave me a rather sad assignment today. She told me to read up on the witch trials in Europe, and why they happened. I went through a lot of books, a lot of history, a lot of names of hunters and the hunted. There was one musty old book in which I found the questions which were put to the poor women while they were being brutally tortured. The questions were written by hand, which made me suspect that once again I had stumbled upon an original document. On a previous page there were instructions on how to 'extract confession from these here consortes of the Devil'.

Between the fourteenth and seventeenth centuries in Europe, there was no escape from a horrible end once a woman had been picked out as a witch. It was only a matter of how cruel the torture would be, how many others would be implicated and how soon she would be allowed to die. It was sexual, sadistic abuse at its most gruesome.

Once the accusation was made, the book said, the witch should be subjected to instruments like the strappado, the boot, the Black Virgin or to thumbscrews. Finally she was to be bound crosswise hand to foot and cast into a body of water. If she sank and drowned, she was innocent. If she floated, the Devil was on her side. She should then be brought out of the water and punished for her 'misdeedes with the Devil'. One could sense the relish in the words that set out the methods of torture. One of the favoured methods was pricking, in which the inquisitors seemed to revel. There was a rush to join in this part of the witch-hunt, where men sought out those places on the witch's body that were 'the Devil's marks' and thus insensitive to pain. It is strange, but from early childhood, I have had a place on my leg where I cannot feel any sensation. I thought of it now and as I did so, I saw before me the faces of three men, hovering, lecherous, contorted with greed, hatred and lust. Even as I looked at the spectres before me, like apparitions or remembered nightmares from an unremembered past, they disappeared and I was again reading from this dusty book.

In their zeal to inflict pain, some inquisitors even used retractable witch-prickers. The needle or the blade slid back into the handle under pressure and the witch's inability to 'feel' was thus 'evidence' of her guilt. If such should be the case, said the book, tie her to the strappado. 'Tie her arms behind her. Hang weights to her feet and with strength hoist her into the air, over a large wheel, which a man of righteousness shall turn, until she cries out and her arms do protest. If she doth confess at this point, put those questions to her which do concern the Devil. If not, hoist her up again'. 'The boot' was an instrument to viciously break the leg. If she still had not given details about her 'union' with the Devil she was to be put inside 'the Black Virgin' which was a hinged, life-size iron form with spikes on the inside. 'Let her be pierced', said the inquisitors, 'and not killed as yet, for she must confess before she yield herself to the forces of Darkness.' Needless to say, many 'confessed' when in the grip of the Black Virgin.

I turned the page which seemed hard and brittle to my hand. There were the questions. I read them. They were the same ones I had chanced upon once, when I had come upon that haunting sketch of Luciana's, drawn probably by the inquisitor himself even as he doomed her to a horrible fate. The words, in a spidery scrawl, crawled venomously down the page.

'How long have you known the Devil?'

'Why and when did you become a witch and what happened on the occasion?'

'Which demon did you take as your lover?'

'What was the oath you rendered him?'

'In what perverse way did you consummate your union with the demon?'

'What are the marks he made on your body?'

'What evil have you and he done to your neighbours?'

'How did you perform your wickednesse?'

'What arts of the Devil have you used to seduce men?'

'With what ointment or evil essence do you rub your body to keep it youthful and supple?'

Once more the shapes of three men stood before me. They seemed to have appeared from thin air or perhaps come in through the open window. They reeked of hatred and I involuntarily started back in my chair. Had I ever inspired such emotions in them? Were they restless energies I had encountered in a past life? They were more than restless. They were bloodthirsty. I did not recollect their faces but I knew I was destined to meet them again. There was unfinished business between us.

## 10

## *Magic in Wood and Stone*

When spring came to the Laurentians that year, we proceeded with our experiments with nature. What Julia had said about our lab tools being the Elements and our living minds had made an impression on me. Though my mindset was that of a sceptic, it made a lot of sense. There was no denying the fact that I was a scholar of science — as the academics taught it. But here I was, my mind being opened up to the avenues which stretched beyond the merely visible. The textbooks were limiting. They made no provisions for the equations of the universe.

The snowdrops and dandelions were the first ones to sprinkle the grass with white and yellow. They were soon followed by the daffodils which raced wildly up the slopes. In our little wooden shed we nurtured saplings of daffodils, tulips and lily of the valley. Every day, we would talk to them and chant to them. On the other side of the house were the young plants which were left to grow without such communication. When, after two weeks, we compared the results, the difference was quite spectacular.

Julia, like a mother hen, pottered around in the shed, bending over her charges and murmuring sweet nothings. One day, I couldn't help laughing. 'Julia, I really feel sorry for the ones on the other side. Why should they be so ignored? Poor things — bereft of all maternal love and care.'

'Oh, I've thought of that. As soon as two weeks are up, I go over to them. Then you should see the way they start growing. I don't have the heart to see them neglected. They feel it, you know. It is a fact that plants release certain chemicals when they communicate with each other — or wish to say something to a human being. Unfortunately, I don't have the proper instruments to work on this phenomena. But it has already been proved by a great botanist from your country.'

'Jagadish Bose?' I asked.

'Yes. He had a great affinity with the Elements. His mind and heart were with them, and they divulged their secrets to him. You see, unless you attune yourself to them, you are blind and deaf to what they are trying to say. The frequency at which they communicate with us is different from the one we are used to.'

'But Julia,' I said, 'apart from using instruments, isn't there any other way to prove that plants respond to us?'

In response, Julia led me to an old elm tree which grew a little way from our herb garden. 'Stand here and put out your hands and gently touch the trunk of this tree with feelings of friendship and peace,' she said. 'Now, feel its bark, its texture — its personality.'

I tried to do as I was instructed.

'Now,' Julia continued, 'press your flattened palms against the rough bark of this great elm and talk to the essence of it, the spirit of it. Ask for a sign of response. Ask for a gift of energy on this cold day.'

I placed my hands firmly on the comforting, brown bark. I

felt as though I were holding an ancient friend's hand. I looked up at its branches and felt a tingle of warmth from somewhere deep within it. Then an incredible thing happened. I experienced a powerful charge passing from the earth beneath me into the tree I was holding and then coming to me through my hands and arms. It was like a powerful current of energy.

I was startled, for I had never experienced anything like this. Till then, a tree was just a tree. Something to admire, sit under, lean against and at the most do a few sketches of. I knew the bark, the leaves, even the roots had their own medicinal properties. They were mentioned in the sacred books of the Vedas and the Celts. They were a part of ancient mythology. But this. This was a strange personal experience.

'I still think I imagined it, Julia,' I said. 'Something passed through my hands.'

'If you think it was your imagination, why don't you repeat it?' Julia suggested.

'Would it work again?' I asked, still disbelieving.

'Try it,' she urged.

I put my palms on the tree again and focussed my mind. I talked to the tree silently, asking for some sign of communication. But at the back of my mind was a doubt that this time it wouldn't happen. Suddenly, ripple after ripple of warmth trickled through my fingers and surged through my arms. I hastily removed my hands from the trunk.

'Yes, Julia,' I said. 'It happened again. But how? How did this tree connect with my thoughts? Or would it have happened anyway?'

'Try it,' was Julia's answer.

'No. I believe you,' I smiled. 'But will it happen with any tree or is it only this one?'

'Any old tree will respond. They are the wise ones. Just like any old rock or megalith will communicate, if you know how to approach them.'

By now I was profoundly intrigued. Trees were understandable — though it had taken me time to understand. But rocks. Stones. Was she taking me for a ride?

Julia must have read my thoughts. 'Here,' she said, picking up a small grey stone lying nearby. 'This has life. Remember, nothing in this universe is dead or inanimate. Everything is pulsating with life but you must know how to tap it. This stone has a life of its own. It is up to you to discover it for yourself. It doesn't matter what people think. But you must be convinced.'

I picked up a small white pebble lying nearby and looked at it. I held it clenched tightly in my palm. Julia was talking but I was looking, looking far up the slopes towards the tops of the misted hills, from where the trees came crowding down, birches and maples and aspens, holding out branches still bare from the passage of winter, to a sky, not yet blue. But there was nothing empty here. Nothing bleak. No, I was looking forward to the changing cycles, charged with an excitement in having participated in the elemental dance of winter. And as I looked at it all an understanding grew within me that had not been there before. A certain knowledge which comforted and made me feel at one with something larger than myself. I opened my palm and looked at the stone lying there and I knew what I must do to let it know that we shared the same life force.

Julia had told me she had work indoors and had left. I remained standing there, near the magical elm which had just shared a secret with me. I had not yet recovered from the excitement of it. Slowly, deliberately, I walked over to a flat rock close to where the slopes rose, behind the house. It was of grey granite, shaped like a table without legs. Jessica, Cindy and I, had often carried our lunch out there when the weather was fine. Now I stood next to that ancient rock and put my little stone on its smooth surface. I looked down at it and it seemed to shine with hidden chips of quartz embedded deep within it. I shut out all else from my mind. The stone gazed back and it wasn't little anymore. It was part of a mountain which was very old. It spoke of deep caverns hung with crystal of many colours. It spoke of darkness and light. Of a million sunrises and sunsets which flushed the dark heart of the earth with a myriad hues. It was a messenger of an ancient knowledge. A part of a whole. A part of me. We were both a part of that One.

Slowly, very slowly, I raised my head and looked at the sun setting over the distant hills. The greyness was diffused with a golden orange glow. I was like some priestess of a forgotten age, before the secret altar of everlasting life. I put my hand over the stone and told it we were as one. We were sisters, from the same earth, moulded by the same waters. I put a finger lightly on it to touch it and it spoke to me by moving. Under the lightest touch from the tip of my finger, it began spinning round and round on the flat rock.

In my elation I watched it dance and twirl under my finger. I watched it answer a thousand questions about the beginning of the world and the mysteries of time. And I knew that nothing was of any importance except what it had to say.

# 11

# *An Encounter with Indira*

In the meantime, my more orthodox academic pursuits were progressing well. I had also shown talent in sketching and painting in oils. While in school, I enjoyed doing portraits and revealing hidden quirks and traits of personality through deft strokes of the brush. From the very early summers of my life, I was an observer of people. I watched their little mannerisms and the way they held their hands. I listened to their words and noted that they often did not match what their eyes said. I looked at the adult world with the knowledge of an old soul and yet a child's curiosity. It was a strange mix – but vastly interesting. As for the people I looked at — most didn't suspect anything amiss at first. Here was an adorable child with wide, dark eyes. I was patted on the head and sat on knees. If only they knew.

The child Ipsita was interested in everything around her. Grown ups with their peculiarities and their petulance. Their wants and their desires. I understood them and yet a part of me – the child who was growing up, was often confused. Old memories stirred through the mists of lives not yet forgotten. But I was a child after all. A child who loved her dolls with their curling hair and toy trains which went round and round on tracks set out on the floor. Only suddenly, the beautiful doll I held in my small arms was crying and I rushed with her to my mother and held her up. My mother was busy at a small desk in her study, going through recipes. I held up the doll with golden hair. My mother looked down at me and smiled:

'What is it, Ipsita? Why don't you comb her hair? I'm busy now.' I looked troubled. I trusted my mother.

'Ma, they're after her. Save her.' I said.

'Who's after her, dear? Put her back into her bed. Let her sleep now.' I took the doll and stood it up in my arms so its eyes were open wide.

'She can't sleep, Ma. She has to fight. Otherwise, they'll kill her.'

My mother frowned slightly. 'Ipsita, who told you things like that? Has somebody been scaring you? Good people are not killed. They are protected by God. And he loves small children. You and your doll are looked after by him. Remember that.'

'Good people are killed, Ma.' I said with certainty. 'The bad ones kill the good people. God doesn't care.'

My mother looked both angry and worried by now. She left her recipes and gathered me up.

'Who said so, Ipsita? Tell me.'

'I don't know Ma. I just know. And there are many more things I just know.'

There were many things I knew, and some things I gathered and gleaned from the adults I watched. Indira Gandhi was one who once made an impression on me. There was no doubt about that. Her fine features, her dedication to her father, her driving ambition and her treatment of those she considered incompetent.

It was many, many summers ago. I remember my parents saying there was to be a dinner at the then high commissioner's in Ottawa. Pandit Nehru and his daughter were the visiting dignitaries and the chief guests. My parents were to attend and flew in from Montreal. They didn't like leaving me behind with friends when both were required to be out of town, so they took me along with them. I enjoyed the trip, the hotel rooms and the sightseeing when my parents were free. My father would take me to the best restaurants and watch with paternal pride as I insisted on talking to the waitress in French and order my own food. People at neighbouring tables would nod indulgently and smile. My mother would look somewhat embarrassed. I have always enjoyed showing off — albeit in a subtle manner.

Anyway, we were there in Ottawa and staying at the Frontenac. My parents were to go to the evening's reception and children were not invited. I was to be in our suite and read story books. But the high commissioner at the time was a kindly man and a friend of my father's. He had planned that towards the fag end of the party, a member of his staff would pick me up from the hotel, bring me to his place and I would have some dinner there. Things went smoothly. I was called for, as the saying goes and arrived at the Indian High Commission accompanied by a kindly, middle-aged Canadian woman – the high commissioner's personal assistant. It was winter and cold outside. She stooped and pulled the fur hood closer over my head and said we'd go in by the main door which was closer. I remember it was snowing. We walked up the steps and stepped into the large foyer leading into the reception room. There I witnessed a scene which was to make quite an impact on me. A few guests were standing around the foyer. The looks on their faces were embarrassed and abashed. Panditji stood near the door to the reception room, his daughter at his side. He was silent and looked with reproving at a certain, junior Indian official, who stood with a lady's fur coat on his arm. The lady, whom I guessed was his daughter Indira, was anything but silent.

'Who told you to bring my coat down now?' she snapped at him.

'I just thought, Madam,' he stuttered, 'I thought you were leaving.'

'Well, think less in future.' She was dripping ice. 'When I wish to leave, I'll call you. I'll tell you, "I wish to leave now. Bring me my coat from upstairs." Do you follow?'

'Yes, Madam,' said the red-faced official.

'People like you have no sense. Make sure about VIP departures before you come rushing down, embarrassing everyone. Don't you know protocol?' she demanded. The man looked miserable.

Then with a smile Indira turned to the guests huddled round and smiled. 'Why are we standing here. Let's go in. Actually I had just come out to see some of the paintings the high commission has acquired from Sotheby's. I don't know why you people followed me.'

There were little apologetic laughs and smiles from the guests as they drifted back into the larger room. Panditji and Indira surveyed the paintings with their host beside them. I remained standing where I had been deposited by my guide and usher who had taken my coat and had told me to wait. The high commissioner suddenly saw me and swooped upon me, introducing me to the Indian prime minister and his daughter as my father's daughter and my grandfather's granddaughter. I folded my hands in a namaste and tried not to stare. Indira bent down, looked me in the face and said, 'That's a very fetching velvet skirt you've got on. Brown is one of my favourite colours.' Then she turned to the high commissioner and spoke about my great-aunt, Kamini Sen, Nisith Sen's sister, who had been a noted Bengali poetess.

'When I was in Shantiniketan, they used to talk about Kamini Sen. She was a woman with determination despite the tragedies in her personal life. So this child is her grand niece? Well, she has her eyes.' Everybody surveyed me. I stood there and wondered how soon I would be taken to my parents.

Panditji sensed my discomfort and patted my cheek. 'Well Ipsita, do you want to be a writer, a lawyer, a politician or a diplomat? Your family has them all."

'I just want to be prime minister,' I said and smiled like an angel. Indira looked a trifle put out. Panditji threw his head back and bursting into loud laughter, turned to the high commissioner. 'Must tell Nisithjee when I see him that his granddaughter wants my chair,' he said.

I remembered that meeting long afterwards. I came to the conclusion that in India people were judged by their antecedents. One day, would I be known in my country just because of my grandfather, or my father? I became confirmed in my assessment that Indians gave a lot of credence to blood and background. But they would have to accept me or hate me for myself. Of that I would make sure.

Something else made an impression on my young mind that day, which I think I carried forward. I wondered if one had to be more than slightly haughty with subordinates – no matter who they were. Women especially, I decided had to be imperious – or they would be sidelined. In fact, it would seem the more brusque one was with inferiors, the more one was taken seriously.

There was something else. Unless one wished to merge into the family aura, an Indian woman had to be a bit of a maverick. Otherwise one would always be known as somebody's granddaughter, daughter or wife. One had to go off the beaten track. One had to be a rebel.

I believed Indira was a rebel in her own way. I think I was a rebel when I chose Wicca.

Some years later, when the President, Sarvepalli Radhakrishnan, visited Montreal to deliver a series of talks on comparative religion, I had the chance to talk to him alone one afternoon over tea and samosas. I did not ask him questions on religion, for somehow it seemed to me that that would be considered inappropriate and presumptuous in one so young. So I asked him about something else which I took out of the closet of my mind every now and then and pondered over. It involved human relations and how to interact with people. As I have said, Indira's behaviour towards the junior official had made an impression. Was this how those in power behaved, and how subordinates were made to function in India? My own experience till then had been vastly different. My grandmother, Shovana rarely raised her voice with the servants. And she was a lady of breeding. Her husband Nisith, hollered at his clients, but then, he was a criminal lawyer. My father, ever the gentleman, was firm but never used harsh words with his subordinates. My mother, on the other hand, often spoiled the staff and servants with kindness and consideration. They always came to her in need. So what was Indian society all about? For some reason Indira had started me thinking. What was the key to successful interaction?

I knew Dr. Radhakrishnan was a remarkable man with an amazing fund of knowledge about the human being and the country into which he had been born. I somehow felt drawn to put my queries to him. I told him about the incident at the high commissioner's and about how it had been bothering me.

'Dr. Radhakrishnan, do people in our country work best when they are shouted at or spoken to with sarcasm?' I asked.

He smiled that famous smile of his. Serene, indulgent and amused. 'Yes, I think three hundred years of servitude have taken their toll. The Indian mind wants and needs love, compassion and understanding but has been weakened by fear. Hence it reacts the most quickly to harshness for that is what it fears. You see, our people have had to put up with so many masters, that even now we understand only the language of compulsion.'

'But what about those in authority today? Shouldn't they try to bridge the gap between the ruler and the ruled? After all, we are a democracy,' I said awkwardly, not knowing how else to phrase my question.

'Well, I think it's like this, Ipsita,' Radhakrishnan said gravely. 'Those in authority, in India, think nothing about commanding — in whichever way it suits them. They feel that that is what is expected of them. Anything else would be construed as weakness. Perhaps also, one is afraid to rule with understanding and compassion because one lacks that confidence in oneself.'

Today, many summer later, when I think about what Sarvepalli Radhakrishnan said that day in Montreal, I find it still applies. The slave still kowtows — and the master accepts his grovelling without a blush because he feels it is his due. This is true on all fronts. Political, bureaucratic, corporate, even domestic. We have not found ourselves as yet.

## Pages From My Diary

Springtime

I have been thinking long and deeply about what could have made that stone move — and move it did, that day while I was on the hills with Julia. Is it really true that nothing is inanimate? That everything has a certain consciousness? What an upheaval that could cause in orthodox science — and yet it is true that metaphysics and science are born of the same mother.

When I came back to the chalet that evening, I started reading on rocks, monuments of stone, relics of wood and on old palaces and places of worship which are known to have an 'atmosphere'. Perhaps the key word is that. 'Atmosphere'. Why do certain old stone buildings have a charged atmosphere? Is it because of the memories trapped within their bricks? There are also reports of strange happenings in these places. According to the Egyptians and the Celts, stone and wood have thoughts and a certain kind of comprehension. It is true that stone plays an important part in many world religions. Hindus pray to the Shiva linga, Muslims worship the Ka'aba in Mecca. The Ten Commandments were engraved on stone. Till today, Stonehenge is an unsolved puzzle regarding the ancient mystery rites of the Druids. In Egyptian temples of old, crystals were used to heal. All over the world, one hears of statues which shed tears.

I have been particularly struck by the lines in an old book which say, 'The equation between objects of stone and wood and the individual seems to be made through touch.' Is that why I succeeded in communicating with both the elm tree and the stone — because my touch and my thoughts were in harmony with theirs?

It seems that wood was the precursor of stone for the Druids' worship. Wood separated from a parent tree still retains energy. Old Wiccans used healing wands made from the branches of special trees. I instinctively feel that man has not really understood the inner nature of stone. I believe that it has a rise and ebb of energy. But the energy is always there. It is never lost.

I intend to go on working with stone and try to find out its mysteries. I believe the first steps towards understanding the nature of stone were taken by the early chemists, Priestly and Lavoisier. The first experiments were made with the magical cinnabar (red mercuric sulphide) and haematite (red iron oxide). Later, Sir Humphrey Davy discovered that metals could only be released from their compounds by electricity. These experiments showed for the first time, the mysterious electrical nature of matter.

A few scientists have experimented with the complex family of quartzite, volcanic lava and sandstone, which make up the earth's bones. It seems that rocks of this kind are actually massive structures of silicon and oxygen. This is the basis for the living stone. It is significant that silicon and oxygen, in other words, silicon dioxide is seen in its purest form in quartz or in rock crystal — both stones have an esoteric tradition. Silicon, aluminum and oxygen make up three-fourths of the whole inorganic world. Carbon is the basis, but that shows a striking similarity with silicon. What then is the dividing line between organic and inorganic in the world of stone?

All this implies that the magical quartz is really a very special stone. It possesses an energy vortex that is released through pressure.

It is true that ancient seers and healers used to meditate holding mystical power objects made of stone. Esoteric rituals are performed within stone circles. Ancient stone megaliths were touched by people seeking healing of body and mind. Perhaps the pressure of touch conveyed the stone's piezoelectrical charge or it may have been something else. I must find out. This is a whole new world which seems to be opening up.

## A Few Weeks Later

Today, I was given a wonderful gift by Carlotta. She met me after morning study and told me to follow her upstairs. I was surprised to see that she was going towards the room of a thousand crystals. She unlocked the door, and asked me to go in after her. I had not been there after the initiation. Once more I felt the magic of it, the beauty of it. It was daytime and the clear sunlight streamed in through the area of glass ceiling. I asked Carlotta why this room was called the room of a thousand crystals and she replied that it was here that we kept our entire crystal collection. I half expected to see a sideboard or a cabinet with cutglass vases and fruit bowls. I think Carlotta must have realized what was going through my mind because she glanced at me and took a key from a small silk pouch she always carried. She fitted the key in a small side door and threw it open. Motioning me to follow her, she clicked on a switch, flooding the room with light, and stepped inside. I was dumbfounded.

There were no windows but stone shelves were fitted into the walls, from ceiling to floor. Each one held crystals of all shapes and sizes. Not cutglass decorations, but rock quartz in its natural formation. There were also carefully carved and polished crystal objects, round and oval, large and small. There were some jewel-like pieces, with myriad facets which glittered with a thousand lights in the lamplight. There were small statues and images of lustrous clarity, which glowed as if the light was within them. This was the room of a thousand crystals. Now I knew why.

Carlotta watched my reaction without saying anything for a while. Then she spoke. 'Over the years, these crystals have come to the chalet from Italy, Belgium, Egypt, Tibet, and Burma. Some are from closer home. We have our theories about the properties of crystal and hence this large collection. Each one has something to say and some specific work. Mind you, as in real life, so here, no two crystal formations are alike. Each one has his or her own personality. They can receive our thoughts and transmit their own.'

'Would this be like some special and unique transmission room, Carlotta?' I asked. 'Can messages be sent afar? Can we tap thoughts which have come from far away — from other spheres perhaps? Other dimensions?'

Carlotta looked at me for a moment. 'Work on, Ipsita,' was all she said. 'You will be told much. It is true, much of what you suppose. The questions have come to you. The answers will be given — by the crystals and by your own mind. I will only guide you in coming to the right conclusions.'

With that she went to a corner shelf of stone and reaching up took down a small clear crystal object which had been glowing with a light of its own. Pink and violet and blue. She brought it over to me and held it out, a beautifully carved and polished skull of the purest rock quartz.

'Here, hold this in your hand and feel its cool smoothness,' she advised.

I was startled. 'A skull, Carlotta? Why a skull?'

'Have you ever heard of the famous crystal skull discovered by Mitchell-Hedges in the course of an archaeological dig way back in the 1920s? It was found in the city of Lubaantan, in the jungles of Belize. Lubaantan means "the city of Fallen Stones". It is an ancient site full of ruined temples and palaces built by the Mayans.' Carlotta spoke slowly, thoughtfully, as if she wished me to understand and consider. I waited for her to continue. 'You must know that the Mayans flourished from around 300 BC. Their civilisation grew for about a thousand years. It was a strange and wonderful culture. There were powerful dynasties, stories of fabulous wealth and at the same time stories of great spiritual knowledge. Their priests and priestesses performed secret, esoteric rituals and communicated with other worlds. Then suddenly, something happened. The cities were abandoned. The people disappeared. The great palaces and temples were taken over by the jungles.'

'What could have caused this sudden exodus?' I asked.

'Nobody seems to know. The books say that there was no evidence of famine or flood, epidemic or war. It was amazing. What had happened to this culture which had reached such a pinnacle of esoteric, scientific and artistic growth? Only the ruins remained — and a few mysterious objects like the dazzling crystal skull found in a temple interior in this lost city.'

'Tell me, Carlotta,' I asked, 'from where do you think the Mayans acquired this fabulous knowledge?'

'That is a mystery,' she replied. 'For that matter, nobody really knows where they originally came from. But to return to the question of the crystal skull, I hear you are experimenting with crystal. Do so. You will learn much.' Then she paused for a minute and held up the small skull in her hand to the lamplight. It glowed as if lit by candles from within. Strange waves of light seemed to emerge from the core. Carlotta turned to me and held out the skull.

'Take it,' she commanded. 'And use it well. It is yours from today. Respect it and learn from it. Through the years, it will have much to teach you.'

I was taken aback. 'For me? To keep? How should I work with it?' I realised I was stuttering.

Carlotta smiled a rare smile and held out the skull. 'Take it,' she said. And putting it into my hands she turned, motioning me to leave the room, switched off the lamp and closed the door behind her. We stood in the outer room. The crystal skull was held tightly in my hands. I looked at it now.

'Is this a miniature of the skull found in the lost city of Lubantaan?' I asked.

'Yes,' she replied. 'But it is different in that it has no detachable jaw, like the original one. But this is a powerful object, with a life of its own. Treat it with great care.' With that, she locked the door to the room of the thousand crystals behind her and walked away. And thus started my research into the mystery of the crystal skulls of the Ancients.

**12**

# *The Crystal Skulls*

It astounds me today when I read about the scientific research being carried out with crystals. The recent and fashionable New Age Movement has also decided to embrace crystals to its bosom. But I believe that, long ago, a few women in the Laurentians knew much more about the magic and science of crystals than do the most specialised instruments today. After that day in the room of the thousand crystals, I started reading whatever I could on the subject — old research documents, current findings, encyclopaedias. It fascinated me. The skull of Lubantaan and the miniature one I had been given — both held me captive. I discovered that the Mayan priests believed that the original crystal skull was over a million years old. There was a theory that the priests of old knew how to make it talk — but how, no book could tell.

I also came across an old Red Indian legend according to which there are thirteen ancient crystal skulls in the world. They are the size of human skulls with movable jaws. The legend held that these skulls are the storehouses of vital information regarding the origin, purpose and destiny of mankind. They may also be able to answer some of the greatest mysteries of life and the universe. According to the Ancients, all thirteen skulls will one day be rediscovered and brought together for their collective wisdom. In fact an old Cherokee legend says that there are twelve planets in the cosmos inhabited by human beings and that there is one skull for each of these planets. The thirteenth skull is vital to each of them. Why, the legend does not say.

It is true that in the course of time, more crystal skulls have come to light. After the skull at Lubaantan, the second one to be discovered is housed in a glass case on the first floor of the British Museum's Museum of Mankind in London. Experts have labelled it an 'Aztec Sculpture. C.A.D. 1300-1500.' The quartz is slightly cloudy, and it is rumoured that the skull often moves about by itself in its glass case. The origins of this skull are as mysterious as the Mitchell-Hedges' one. The museum records show that the skull was bought from Tiffany's in New York in 1898. How they acquired it is still an enigma, but in his book, *Precious Stones Of Mexico*, George Kunz, mineralogist and occasional Smithsonian adviser, says, 'Little is known of its history and nothing of its origin. It was brought from Mexico by a Spanish officer, some time before the French occupation of Mexico (which began between 1862 and 1864), and was sold to an English collector, at whose death it passed into the hands of E.Boban of Paris, and then became the property of Tiffany and Co.'

Another smaller crystal skull was found with a well-to-do Mexican family. It is now in the possession of the youngest daughter, Norma Redo, an interior decorator by profession. The skull sits on a base of gold, dwarfed by a huge, heavily carved golden and crystal reliquary cross that emerges from the top of its head. According to its owner, the skull has been in the family since the 1840s, from the time that the government took over the properties of the Church. She believes it is Aztec and was precious to the Mexican people but that later on, when the Spanish arrived and wanted to show the supremacy of the Christian religon, the cross was added to the skull in order to transform it.

Norma Redo also claims that a crystal skull is kept in secret by the Vatican in Rome. She feels her own crystal has healing powers. She considers herself a normal, rational person, scientific in her approach to things, but maintains that since she has had the crystal, she has started to feel different, better in both body and mind. She says she has been told that the skull in her possession will eventually come together with the other crystal skulls scattered through the world to bring knowledge to humanity. To her, the skull is a symbol — 'Symbols are very powerful, more powerful than words. They connect us with deep levels of truth that cannot be reached with words. They are a sign that we can access the realms of spirit. They can connect us with a higher awareness of our purpose, help us to be more spiritual. It is not just the fact that the crystal is shaped like a skull that makes it important, that makes us think of death and spirits. It is also the crystal.'

It is a fact that in many ancient cultures, crystal was considered a stone from heaven. The Eskimos called it 'light stones', the Australian aborigines 'wild stones'. They believed that the throne of their god Baiame was made of crystal and that he would drop pieces of this sacred stone down to earth. To the Greeks, crystal was 'holy ice'. It was the gods weeping at the follies of mankind. This was their gift to man so that with it, he could heal himself.

Two more life-size crystal skulls have been found, one in the jungles of Peru amongst the Campa people, and the other with a family in Argentina who prefer to remain anonymous for fear of being robbed of their prized possession.

The seventh skull to come to light belongs to woman called JoAnn Parks in Houston, Texas, who claims she was given it by a Tibetan healer by the name of Norbu Chen who ran the Chakpori Ling Healing Foundation in the city. He himself used to work with this particular skull and performed many amazing cures with its help. JoAnn recalls that the monks in the Chakpori Ling organisation held the skull in great reverence and would chant and talk to it in Tibetan. It was used by them to direct energy into the bodies of those who came to be healed. Even though the quality of the quartz is not as pure as in the Mitchell-Hedges' one, the skull contains as much power as the others. The face is partly cloudy and partly clear, and the jaw bone is not separate. It is supposed that the quartz which crafted this skull was formed under conditions of great geological instability. According to JoAnn, the skull has named itself 'Max' and meets and sits with people all over the country. He has been able to carry on the work he was meant to do. Heal.

An eighth skull lies at the Smithsonian Institution in Washington, D.C. It was received in a box in the mail, accompanied by a note stating that it was an Aztec skull supposed to have been in the collection of the Mexican President, Porfirio Diaz. It was purchased by the sender in 1960, in Mexico City. He was offering it to the Smithsonian without any consideration. However, he wished to remain anonymous.

The Smithsonian were happy to keep this mysterious gift — even though many who saw it said it was cursed. The story went that you should never look it in the eye. It is, till date, the world's largest, and perhaps ugliest, crystal skull. It is ten inches high and eight and a quarter inches wide, and weighs a hefty thirty-one pounds. The quartz is cloudy and one of the most curious features about it is that despite its tremendous weight, it is completely hollow. The features are crudely represented, and some who have examined it think it looks almost Neanderthal. Attempts to track down the donor led the Smithsonian to his lawyer, who informed the institute that he could not divulge the name of his client, but revealed that he had committed suicide soon after sending them the skull. Apparently, from the time he had come into possession of the skull, he had been dogged by tragedy. His wife had died, his son had had a tragic accident that left him brain dead, and he himself had gone bankrupt. Finally, he decided to kill himself. The point was, how far had the crystal skull been responsible for these mishaps?

The Smithsonian decided to believe that the tragedies had occurred independently of the skull. However, the Mesoamerican specialist at the institute did notice something rather strange. Though she insisted that she did not believe that the skull was cursed, it was peculiar the way it had started attracting other skulls. She had had people who knew nothing about this one, calling and bringing in skulls from other places. A small four-inch skull was brought in from Altadena, California, by Larry Hughs, an antique dealer who said the person he had bought it from seven years earlier had found it somewhere in the 1880s or '90s. The skull had ancient hieroglyphics carved across the top. It was identified as being in the Xochicalco style of Mesoamerica. If authentic it could be dated about AD 800. Researcher Joshua Shapiro believes he saw such a skull in 1989 which belonged to an old Mexican who claimed to have found it during a field trip to some old Mayan ruins in the Yucatan. The odd thing was that after this skull came into his possession, every hope and desire he had ever had came to be fulfilled in strange ways. Each skull seems to have different properties or work to carry out. This then is the ninth one.

The tenth may be the near life-size crystal skull in the Trocadero Museum in Paris. It is of very clear quartz and has stylised features. The curator believes the skull to be of Aztec origin, from the fourteenth or fifteenth century. It could have been an ornament on a sceptre carried by an Aztec priest. And an eleventh skull was discovered hidden deep in the earth in an old tomb in Guerrero state in Mexico, by an Italian, Nick Nicerino. This skull has a yellow tinge to it, but is of clear quartz and is slightly angular, with slanting eyes. It is known as the Sha Na Ra, a name given to it psychically by its owner.

Nicerino believes that all these crystal skulls contain hidden knowledge, which we could dig into if we knew how. He often scries or gazes into the depths of the one that he possesses. He sees forms, strange objects and shapes. He feels that the skulls have recorded memories, and the information that is given him is not about the future but about the skull's own past.

I myself have come to believe that the skulls are like very superior computers. There is no doubt in my mind that quartz can trap thought waves, emotions — and as such entire happenings in time. I have worked long hours with the crystal skull Carlotta gave me and I am convinced that this is the twelfth one. I think I have discovered a way in which to tap its secret knowledge. The thirteenth skull has not yet been found.

13

# A Strange Prophecy

But what of love? What of passion and flirtations and fancies?

After all, I was a young woman by now, in the chronological passage of time and years. I had a winsome face, a comely figure, a rich father and high connections. This is the scenario which makes a young man's fancies turn to thoughts of love.

Young ladies whom I met at parties and at class, talked of boys and men and how wonderful they were. My friend Edda had decided to drop out of college and get married. My neighbour, Elaine was going out with a tall, lanky, blond boy in his twenties. They went to the movies, like a well-worn ritual, every Saturday. She said that when he was beside her, sitting there in the dark, she felt a savage hunger within her. I advised her to munch on popcorn. I just hoped that she would spare him his honour. I truly feared for him. The fair sex can be quite predatory.

But I jest. The truth was that I viewed my friends with superior detachment because, till then, I had felt none of the cravings for romantic bonding — physical or emotional, with anybody. I was secure in the knowledge that I was attractive to the opposite sex. I enjoyed and revelled in the admiring looks and compliments that I received. Attempted overtures at friendship, phone calls, visits to the house, I encouraged — only to nip them in the bud soon after. I knew I could have any of them anytime I wanted. But I really did not want anyone.

I think this was just another way in which I was enjoying the power that I knew was growing within me. I could feel it stir, as one day I would feel my child move within me and know that she was mine. A being of my being, of my blood and flesh. Carrying my strength and mercurial insight. A daughter whom I had willed to come.

During the first two years of discipline at the chalet, life had been slightly monastic. Carlotta had made it clear that she expected no 'excess' in anything, from the initiates. 'No excess' meant no drinks, drugs, smoking or sexual intimacy — even when we were away from the confines of the chalet. Furthermore, there was to be no hectic socialising. No close friendships with anybody — male or female. It was a regimen that suited me very well.

In the winter of my second year, Carlotta called the whole group over to her house on the river one evening and introduced us to five members who had come over from Europe. Marsha was from England, Barbara from Ireland, Janine and Louise from France and Sophia from Italy. The French girls were students at the Sorbonne in Paris. Barbara was a spry sixty and a housewife. Sophia was in show business, married and very glamorous. Marsha was a senior partner in a law firm in London.

The five women had come to participate in the ceremony of the winter solstice. The ceremony of silver, as it was called, was held every year in front of a glowing log fire in the great hall in the chalet. Here, as the circle gathered round the long table, Carlotta would don her regal black cape and preside over the makeshift altar, on which were arrayed the most arresting and exquisite objects of silver. A bowl with fullblown red roses, a chalice of wine, a silver vial containing the oil of gardenias, and a silver tray on which were laid out small pieces of paper, twice folded. In each piece of paper were two or three lines in the nature of an oracle, written by the Priestess of the Solstice herself, predicting the way destiny's dice would roll in the coming year. And right in the centre of the altar was a large and effulgent crystal bowl, sparkling and glittering and filled to the brim with clear water. The bowl of water had been left out in the sun the whole day to absorb its myriad rays and now charged with them, it was placed before us, so that we could dip our hands in its sparkling purity and imbibe its energy before settling ourselves for the ceremony.

In front of the bowl was a small, smoothly polished quartz ball, the size of a tennis ball. The silver ceremony was an old pagan ritual held by the Wiccans to welcome the winter season, with its silver frost and ice — for there was much beauty in this time of year. It was also a time to invoke the spirit of the fire, for its warmth and light would be needed in the months to come. It was a time to gather by its amber glow and be comfortable, to have a feeling of wellbeing and thus to be at peace with one another and with the Elements. It was a time to bring out the aging wine from the cellar and mull it with cinnamon and nutmeg over the fire and to pass it round in small silver cups, so that all could drink of it and be cheered. And nuts would be cracked and small round cakes made of honey and raisins would be eaten.

It was an evening I relished and absorbed in every pore. The sensuous beauty of it was overwhelming. I realised that my real love affair was with the seduction of the Elements and the mysteries of the dark. To me, the darkness was not ugly. It stood for the enigmas of a half remembered past. The mysteries of untapped knowledge. The power of the Goddess Hecate, the Dark One, of the Crossroads. It stood for skies with stars unending and dimensions beyond our own arrogance. I could never love a human being in the same way, or feel the intoxication which wrapped itself around me when I looked up at midnight galaxies or surrendered myself to the swirling, frothing, tempestuous ocean waves.

At the end of the ceremony, when the invocation to the sun and the fire had been said, and the chants of power completed, the Priestess told us that since this was a time of good cheer and light-heartedness, we must now look into the coming months to see what they would bring. This was an aspect of the ceremony we all looked forward to, like children. We eagerly crowded near and watched with fascination as Carlotta took the folded pieces of paper on the tray and spread them out, helter-skelter, on the space in front of the altar. Then she lifted the crystal ball and told us to come before her, one at a time. As each of us, Teacher and student alike, approached, she took the ball in her left hand and held it over the papers in turn, until it seemed to be drawn to a particular paper. She let the crystal rest on it while she opened a small, silver casket, with many signs and hieroglyphs on it from which she picked out an exquisitely made miniature silver charm which she put into your outstretched palm. This was a symbol, an oracle regarding the coming year. We were then touched on the shoulder by the athame and the paper on which the crystal rested was given to us. In this way, each of us received our symbol of silver and a written oracle.

I must mention that this was the only time in my knowledge, that any form of divination was practised. Otherwise, we were repeatedly told to keep away from all forms of fortune telling. It was thought to be a pastime for the gross, worldly glutton, the weak and the foolish. 'The powers you will acquire with this form of discipline, will be considerable,' Karen would say in her practical, matter-of-fact way. 'For heaven's sake, don't let anyone beguile you into telling their futures. People are greedy little maniacs when it comes to knowing about themselves and what's to happen tomorrow. Steer clear of them. You are scholars of a very high order. Not gypsy fortune-tellers.'

Anyhow, on this day, our little papers held messages that had an uncanny way of fulfilling themselves. And the message in some way seemed to fit in with the silver symbol we had received — each one different from the other. I remember that year, Carlotta gave me a little silver guitar. I wondered why, since I didn't play any music — and it was highly unlikely that I would — mainly because that was one talent I did not claim to have. My little paper read:

> 'During summer and after spring
> Will come a bard, who plays the strings,
> His handsome smile will win your heart,
> But alack, alas, all must part.'

I read my oracle and smiled widely. Cindy looked at me curiously but couldn't ask what I had got. Each individual was to keep her paper to herself. This was a secret prophecy which only the year would unfold. But there are some things in life which cannot be explained away by rationality. At heart, I was still a sceptic. To me this part of the silver ceremony was a pleasing bit of fun. How could I possibly be smitten by some bard? A poet? A singer? It couldn't be. I was too hard a nut to crack.

But that was the summer I was to meet a man, a singer, who left a profound impression on me. Elvis Presley. Just for that summer, only for that summer, I was captivated by him, his songs, his personality, his sadness and his smile.

**14**

# *A First Love?*

In August that year, Elvis was at Graceland, his home in Memphis, preparing to go to Hollywood in a few weeks' time to start filming *Loving You*. I had heard that his first movie *Love Me Tender* had been a big hit. But the fortunes of Elvis Presley did not concern me much. I was occupied with other things.

I was in the midst of my summer holidays in Montreal. Lazing, watching TV, hanging around with friends, sniffing the fragrance of lilacs which drifted in from the garden when the sun was hot and listening to the whir of the neighbour's lawn mower. I was doing some serious reading for a change. I was deep in the study of comic books. 'Little Lulu' and 'Uncle Scrooge' were current favourites. Summer afternoons were for swinging in a hammock and viewing the world through half-closed eyes. Orange ices were for ten cents at the corner drugstore. I slurped my share and sent down for more. I couldn't think of a better way to spend one's life. In the middle of this idyllic existence, Jean S. phoned one morning from out of the blue.

'Hi, Ipsita. My goodness, you sound drugged. Were you dozing?'

'No, doing the rhumba, with a few cartwheels thrown in. What do you want, at this unearthly hour?' It should be obvious that Jean and I both considered ourselves great wits.

'Well, drop the dope and listen. I'm going down to Tennessee to an old plantation, for a shoot. I have to leave tomorrow,' she said.

'So what do you want? A fond farewell? Goodbye dear Jean. You shall be sorely missed. Now, let me get back to the big bucks of Uncle Scrooge, you good-for-nothing breaker of the peace. By the way, what are you playing? Don't say Scarlett O'Hara.'

Jean giggled. 'Very funnee. No, I'm more the Melanie type. I get my man. You'd make a good Scarlett. You're vicious and mean. But listen, jokes aside. I want you to come down with me for the weekend. We'll leave tomorrow. Come back Tuesday morning — latest.'

'No,' I yelled. 'I will not be your odd job girl. I will not help you with your pin curls. I will not prompt you when you forget your lines — as you're sure to do.'

'Shut up, will you. You've just woken up my dog. He's got sensitive ears. Nobody's asking you to do anything for me. I want to drive down to Memphis on Sunday morning. Elvis is there. I have some things to discuss with him before he flies down to Los Angeles next week. I just thought, you being at that vulnerable time of life — might be interested.' She delivered her speech with the right emphasis and pauses. Then she waited for my reaction. I could almost hear her choking on her smugness.

'Well, Jean, you may be a big star in your part of the world. Your friends may be singing sensations. But I have my place in the sun too. What makes you think I'd jump at this chance to meet Elvis Aaron Presley?' I said as sarcastically as I could.

'Gosh, you know his middle name too. Just imagine. That's more than I knew. Maybe you should meet old Aaron then. Not a bad bloke, I'm told.'

'No,' I yawned, 'maybe another time, another place. The living's too good here, at the moment. Can't drag myself away.'

By now Jean's patience was wearing thin. 'Listen, you lazy potato,' she nearly screamed, 'time and tide wait for no one. Gather ye rosebuds and all that. Don't you want to meet the dreamboat?'

I thought about it. 'I've heard a lot about him. That's true. It would be fun meeting him. That's true too. But what I don't get, is your angle. Why are you so keen that I go?'

'Well, if you must know ... my secretary just eloped. I'm in a mess. I have to go tomorrow but I can't find a paper or a pin. Then my housekeeper suddenly decided to go on leave over the weekend. So I'll have to take Octavius with me ....' Jean trailed off sheepishly.

'Who's Octavius?' I asked.

'Octavius is my dog. A small terrier. My mother refuses to baby-sit him because he bullies her. Growls when she switches off the TV. And she says she's not going to keep it going all night and day, just so he can watch the soaps.' Jean paused to get her breath, or maybe for effect. But I could tell she was in a jam. With a TV hookie for a dog, who wouldn't be?

'Well, Jean, I'd love to help my dear, but I don't see how. I couldn't possibly sit with it all day watching TV in Tennessee. And I have my own dog here or I'd have asked Octavius to stay over. But you know the two would fight. Specially since Octavius seems to have such sensitive nerves.'

'No, no, Ipsita. You wouldn't have to do a thing. Just be there for us. Loll and laze as much as you want. The studio's giving me a lovely bungalow. Meals on the house. Just don't desert Octavius. Please. I'll owe you one.'

I yawned again. This was getting better all the time.

'So, we drive down to the Presley estate, do we? I suppose they'd expect us to lunch there?'

Jean was so relieved, it was touching. 'Well, I hadn't thought of it, Ipsita. But I'll call him and tell him to keep a bite for us.'

'Yes. That should do. But no American fast food, please. A good, hot meal after a long drive will be just fine. It is a long drive, isn't it?'

'Well, about thirty miles. But I'll have my limousine. You won't be uncomfortable. Anyway, I'll call Elvis right now. He'll be thrilled you're coming down. He has a thing about India. Fascinated by it. Wait till I tell him you're so pretty.'

'Well, I leave all that to you. If it amuses you.'

I wondered for a moment why Jean wasn't interested in Elvis herself, if he was such a dreamboat. But, I rationalised, she was older than him and besides she was engaged to be married to a prominent British actor. So, why not check out Memphis, Octavius and the Dreamboat for myself. Besides I had completed my years of rigid discipline and concentrated study at the chalet. Now the training was about to take a different route. I would be told what it was, after the summer.

Graceland was a sprawling, green estate with undulating lawns and big trees. An old, southern type mansion stood in the centre. On the wrought iron gates in front, were musical notes and if I remember right, the figure of the owner. Fans swarmed around the gates, day and night, hoping and waiting for a glimpse of the man who had in a few short years become a living legend — Elvis Presley. The boy who had revolutionized rock and roll, in fact the whole music industry, with a rhythm and a beat which seemed to incorporate the hypnotic sound of African drums.

Tales abounded about his extravagant lifestyle, his uninhibited tastes, his power over women. Girls swooned over him and kissed the ground on which he walked. Anything he touched became sacrosanct. His records were selling in the millions. The cash registers were ringing. He had become an industry, the likes of which America had never seen before. His agent Colonel Tom

Parker kept a close guard on him. So did his secretaries, and his hangers-on or his 'buddies', as he chose to term them. He was a golden goose to beat all others.

This was the scene as I knew of it — or rather had been told of it, mainly by the magazines and by Jean. My reaction was curiosity and the desire to observe a human phenomenon who had given rise to such mass hysteria in women of all ages. Most men disliked him. One couldn't blame them. They nicknamed him 'Elvis the Pelvis', because of his gyrations on stage. Was the magic in the man? Or was it something in the music? I wondered.

It was about one o'clock and time for lunch when we arrived at Graceland, the home he had named after the mother he adored. I had heard his parents Vernon and Grace lived with him here. The security man at the gate had got his instructions already and opened the massive gates for us. Fans peered in curiously to see who we were and why we were being allowed to drive in — and up the curving driveway, to the house, which couldn't really be seen from the gates. Jean, never one to resist the limelight, waved at a few girls. They glared back at her but a few screamed, 'Touch him for me and when you come back, touch me.' Such was the nature of the adulation the man had inspired.

Elvis was waiting at the entrance on the large porch, when we alighted from our car. I had to admit that he wore his charisma lightly. There was nothing vain or conceited here. Dressed in a light, silvery grey silk suit, and a white shirt, open at the collar, he looked relaxed and happy.

'Hiya', he called out, 'how was the drive?'

'Good,' Jean replied. 'You look all dressed up. Anything up? Or is it all for us?'

He laughed. 'Well, sure it's for you, Jeannie. But actually a bit of rehearsing was going on. Some new numbers with the boys. The studio's sent over their chaps to take pictures. But it can all wait now that you and your friend are here.' He strode over to where we stood near the car and reached out to shake our hands. I think it was in the eyes. I have studied many a famous and celebrated human being, and I would say that usually, the eyes have it. And next, it's the set of the mouth. As Elvis stood before us, his auburn hair tumbling over his forehead, he tilted his head down and glanced up with hazel eyes, through lashes that were long for a man. And then he smiled tentatively, almost hesitantly, as if he didn't know how it would be received. But there was no mistaking the self-assured set of the shoulders, the sensuality of the lower, slightly petulant lip, the restless seduction in the feet, unwilling or unable to stand long in one place or one position. Here was an exceptional person, who had by accident, not by design, found that chink in the female armour, which thrives on mothering and at the same time taming. But this was more than a sexual phenomenon. His was a force which was asexual, perhaps androgynous. Of course in his preferences, Elvis was known to be completely straight. I stood there, taking the man in. There was no doubt about it. His energy was other dimensional. His entire being spoke of life on another plane.

Introductions over, he led us to the swimming pool at the side of the house. 'I asked them to set out some pink fizz here ... in case you're hot. How about lemonade? Or would you like champagne, Ipsita?'

'Lemonade's fine,' I replied. 'But don't mind me. Have champagne by all means.'

'Naw. I'm not much of a drinker. My particular vice is pretty girls,' and he winked and smiled.

'Oh, just smell those magnolia flowers. You live here like a southern gentleman, Elvis,' Jean drooled.

'Yeah. Life's good. Can't complain. My mom loves the magnolias too. Actually, I never thought I'd ever be able to buy a house like this.' He suddenly turned to me. 'We weren't that well off at one time, you know.' The smile had left his lips. His face looked almost wistful. 'But my Momma has always been there for me. Dad too, it's true. But she believed in me.'

Jean broke in with, 'Elvis, that reminds me. Do me a favour. I won't be returning to Los Angeles for another fortnight. My

Mom's in Montreal and I want to stay with her awhile. So take this copy of my new contract back with you when you go, will you? Don't want to send it by post. Be a doll and hand it over to Mr. S. With my thanks and regards.'

'Okay Jeannie. At your service. I don't know why. I don't like Hollywood much. Maybe it's because I don't sleep well there. Spooky place.'

'Sensitive, sensitive,' Jean teased.

'By the way, you know, I keep having this dream of something from my very young days.'

'What dream?' I asked.

'Well, it's something like this. I was healin' this young boy.' He looked at me and said, 'You do know don't you, that at one time, I did some healin' work?'

'No, I didn't know,' I said, surprised. 'Tell me about it.'

'Well, there was this youngster, had a really bad injury of the spine. Had fallen off his pony when he was about five years old. Lived next door from me. Now, I don't know why, but every mornin' when I passed his house, he'd call out to me, sittin' there in his wheel chair. And one day, he just said, "Elvis, touch my back." And I did, Ipsita. I did. I just felt I could help him. And the next day, when I'm walking by he said, "Elvis, guess what? I can move my legs, ever so little. Touch the back of my neck." Well, it took a whole month, but that little tike who hadn't walked for five years started walkin' again. And I was real happy for him.'

I just looked at Elvis and many things started falling into place. 'This is amazing,' I said, 'but not many people are aware of this gift you have.'

'Hardly any. I guess they'd think I was pulling a fast one for publicity or something — or maybe to whitewash my image.' He gazed into his glass of lemonade.

'No,' I said, and I felt the conviction sweeping through me. 'You're not that sort of person. One can know.'

He smiled a quiet smile. 'People are funny that way, Ipsita. They'd rather believe the worst of a person. They don't like anyone to have it too good. You know, most people think I'm selling sex. They say my attitude and my movements are indecent. They seem to think that the only commodity that is saleable and earns money is sex. But I know for a fact, that's not so. People want healin', not sex.'

'Maybe you're healing through your music and your songs,' I said.

He looked at me as if I'd just said something he had been trying to say for a long while but hadn't found the right language.

'Why do you say so, Ipsita? Do you really feel my music can heal?'

Jean suddenly jumped up from her reverie. 'Hey, don't you feed anybody around here? I smell something cooking and it ain't dog food.'

As if on cue one of his buddies came out on the lawn to say that lunch was served. We went into the large cool house. There in the living room area were his music boys, strumming and beating time on some instruments. His mother, Grace, sat on a corner sofa, near a window and watched them. She was a woman who could not have been more than fifty but looked older and there were tired lines around her eyes. Something in her seemed to be there just for her son. The TV was on even though nobody was watching it. Elvis's agent was screaming shooting dates to somebody on the phone. Grace smiled when we came in, got up, shook our hands, and led us by our arms into the dining room. Elvis put an arm around her and said, 'What are you feeding my friends for grub, Ma?' She laughed and looking at us said, 'I hope your friends like southern cooking, Elvis. I made them fried chicken!'

Jean and I both said we loved it. We couldn't wait to get to it. Grace looked delighted.

When it was time for us to leave that afternoon, Elvis suddenly took me aside and said, 'Ipsita, would it be okay with you if I phoned you sometime?'

'Yes, of course. I'll look forward to it.'

'You know of things others don't talk of. I don't know. Can't explain it. Just know I've got to see you again.' Then the boyish grin was back. The troubled look was gone. 'By the way, you've got a lovely face. Did you know that?'

'Oh yes,' I replied and turned to find the others.

He phoned the next morning and asked us over for lunch again. Jean wanted to know why. He said it was because he had a free day and we could swim and drink pink lemonade. He'd sing for us too.

'Spare us,' teased Jean. 'And what are you going to sing?'

'Tell Ipsita I've got some new lyrics here I'm experimenting with. Tell her I'm going to sing them for her.'

'And what may they be? *I wanna be your teddy bear?*'

'No. It's a new song. She'll understand when she hears it.'

We did drive down again. I was not infatuated with Elvis. Not really. Was he? Perhaps. In a way. I would say he was intrigued. We were both possessors of an alien energy which didn't have a name. I knew that his phenomenal attraction was misunderstood by people. They couldn't find the right word for it because they didn't know what it was. So they termed it 'sex appeal'. But that is a term overused and trite. But I knew that his time with this special energy was short. It would leave him about the time that his mother passed on. From that time onwards he would return to the mundane world dimension and life would be a struggle like it is for most people. The magic would have gone. I think what happened in years to come, sadly, proved me true.

We stayed on the whole day, chatting, listening to him sing and swimming in that lovely pool. In the evening he offered us a barbecue in the garden behind the house. The gardenias were in bloom — or maybe it was the honeysuckle. Their scent came wafting over in the dark as we settled into our chairs and the lights came on in the big house. Jean had gone in to make a few phone calls, when Elvis suddenly said, 'Will you ever be comin' to Los Angeles?'

'Not that I know of. At least not in the near future,' I replied.

'One day, I'll go to India,' he said, more to himself than to me.

I was startled. 'Any particular reason?' I asked.

'Well, for one thing, I guess you'd be there — I hope. Then I've read some parts of the Vedas you know. Of course, I always keep the Bible by my bedside. I also keep some spiritual books from India. They comfort me. Sometimes I feel everything around me is unreal, and I've just come here to experience great highs and great lows. I don't know what I'll do when the highs stop and the bad times come.'

'Why should they come?' I asked. 'Look to the happiness and fun you have — now. Live in it. Let everything just be. I know that helps me when I'm down.'

In the light from the house I could see his face dimly. He smiled and put out a hand and held mine briefly, 'But then, not everybody is like you, you know,' he said.

That summer there were a number of phone calls and some meetings. Was he my first love? Jean would often tease me. No, because I was not really meant for love in the way the common world understands it. Men who stand too close to Elementals get burnt by the fire or swept away by the tides of their own desire. Of course, Elvis was special too. I recognized that. And I basked in his magic for a while, before I set out like the desert winds, moulding and shaping all in my path.

In later years, I lost touch with Elvis, being bent upon the courses I was destined to follow. But once or twice he did send word, saying that a certain emptiness had come upon him with the death of his mother, while he was serving in the army. Later, he married a young girl, Priscilla and the emptiness seemed to lessen for awhile. The birth of a daughter, Lisa-Marie, brought further hope and cheer. But his career was never the same as before. The things which had brought him joy previously, seemed without interest. He seemed to be forever searching for something he had lost — but he did not know what it was. Finally, the decline intensified when he became a victim of drugs — uppers and downers, to pep himself up and to tranquilize himself later.

At last, the body collapsed one night. That tormented spirit must have found what it had been searching for, for so long. He died in the month of August — the month we had met, many years before. On the day he died, I suddenly came across the little silver guitar Carlotta had given me along with the oracle. They had been tucked away for ages in the back pocket of an old purse. I had all but forgotten about them. As I unfolded the paper to read the lines once more, I noticed that by a strange quirk, the first three lines had been smudged and almost erased by the damp and the passage of days. Only the last line was as clear as when Carlotta must have first written it.

'But alack, alas, all must part,' it said.

I did not agree with Carlotta. I did not believe in partings. I raised my chin defiantly and a sudden whiff of gardenias drifted by. A neighbour's radio was playing an Elvis song — as a tribute to the singer who had passed on. Strange, it was that song again. After all these years. The one he had sung for me that afternoon at Graceland.

> 'You look like an angel,
> You talk like an angel,
> You walk like an angel,
> But I got wise ... you're the devil in disguise ...'

I tossed my head back and laughed. Elvis couldn't have been more correct. I was glad he had cared for me for what I was.

## 15

# *Raising the Power*

With the coming of autumn I would have finished three years of learning at the chalet. This had been a time like being children at school. A carefully monitored regime. Discipline. Concentrated study. Experimenting with ancient theories. And of course obedience not only to the Teachers — but to a way of life. It was absorption in the written word and in thought. The mind was now like a finely tuned instrument which could be detached from all else.

I had heard that now was the time we were let loose — so to speak. The bonds of imposed discipline were cut. We were allowed to do what we wanted, and no questions asked. I think this was one of the subtlest psychological tests ever devised. After three years of living by the rule, the sudden freedom brought with it a danger of going to the other extreme and instability. Also, by this time new powers had been acquired, new arts had been learned. It was very easy to lose one's head and tumble into the pits of excess. I think the initiate who had truly profited from her learning, sailed on smooth waters and maintained an inner discipline. The less fortunate foundered.

The initial training had been difficult because we were seekers on a special path, and yet were expected to lead our normal, daily existence at home and work. I now realize that the strongest metal is tempered in this way. This unique double life was led by not only the students but by all of us in the Circle. We were wives and mothers, daughters and sisters. We were carrying out our functions in society. We were with the world — and yet not really of it. A particular group of women with intelligence and intuition far above the normal, who had appointed ourselves the guardians of ancient knowledge and secrets, which might or might not be, one day, brought forth into the world. There was no certainty that the world would ever be privy to this knowledge, because the members of our Circle were not altruists, humanitarians or social workers. We were scholars and seekers and not great respecters of the world. What we were doing and finding out, was for our own sakes — not for anybody else.

It was interesting to watch, almost like a disinterested spectator how the body and mind had evolved. After months of discipline in breathing and chanting, the lungs had grown stronger. Walking in the fresh air and climbing the steep slopes had made the feet agile and the mind alert. We had been told to make our meals frugal even while at home. And this had resulted in a well-toned system. There was no restriction in the type of foods we ate, but excess in anything was forbidden. Meals were taken on time. Sleep too, was measured. We were told to be in bed by ten o'clock and rise by six — winter, spring or summer. While carrying out our work 'in the world', as we liked to call it, we realised we were reaping the benefits of the training we were receiving at the chalet. Our attention was more acute. Our minds were clearer. Our bodies, fit and alert, were like those of young panthers, at times restful and listening, and yet ready to spring at a moment's notice.

I thought of Wicca as a martial art — involving mind as well as body. We believed that the mind and spirit lent full cooperation to a body which was fully awake and without sluggishness. It had to be kept healthy and fit. Elderly members had regular medical checks with orthodox doctors — but the surprising part was that they came away with advice to carry on as they were. The Wiccan regime had done well for their systems. All of us, young and not so young, participated in a physical drill routine in the mornings out on the chalet grounds. When we were in the city, we did the exercises on our own. They combined yogic as well as more strenuous routines. The body was taught how to retain energy. The postures toned up the endocrinal glands. Correct breathing techniques were taught and practised. The muscles were trained to listen and respond. Physical stamina was a part of physical strength. Ultimately, physical wellbeing aided mental confidence. And maybe the other way round too.

Cindy nearly fell by the wayside. Towards the end of September, Carlotta called us to her room and gave us what we had affectionately come to term one of her 'sermons'.

'You have mostly done well. I shall call you individually from next week and discuss your life's work with you. Of course I shall only advise. You must make your choices. Jessica, of course has told me that she wishes to carry on the family tradition and go into business. I think that is commendable. With her abilities she will be an asset to her family and to those she comes in contact with. Ipsita, I have wondered about you. Your talents are versatile but your nature is volatile. On completing your higher studies, you could delve into the world of art. However, you have been given a rare insight into men's minds. That ability may bring you into close touch with the common man. It is up to you to decide what you will do with this talent. When you return to your country, you shall know.

'Cindy, you have been restless of late. You have broken some of our rules. You may wonder how I know. Suffice to say, that I do. You shall have to be careful — for your own sake.'

Jessica and I looked at each other and at Cindy, who was staring at the rug and had turned a furious red. Carlotta said no more on the matter but went on, 'Before you enter the next year, remember the purpose for which you are here. You have been chosen because we believe that it is possible to evolve and train a superhuman. Women are more attuned to the higher levels of mental development which includes intuition and vision. You have each chosen the paths on which to walk in order to reach the common goal — Jessica, through the Kabbala, Cindy through Tao, and Ipsita through Wicca. Now as your time comes to enter the world — remember that you are expected to partake of everything that life has to offer. You will not shun or avoid any experience, which comes your way. This has been a mere beginning. Life is the real school. Observation will be one of your chief aims. Participation another. You will assess. Then you will choose. That which you choose as worthy of acceptance will be stored in your minds. The discarded material will be treated as waste. You will be aware of what it was — but will have no further use for it.

'The atmosphere and lessons you have imbibed here have conditioned you to quicker reflexes — both mental and physical, heightened perception, increased objectivity, greater resilience, but decreased emotional reactions — or should I call it sentimentality? I feel you can do without that. You will have compassion — and I believe that is essential. But people will comment on your inability to experience and display the "softer side" as it is called.'

Cindy suddenly broke down and cried. 'I can't go on, Carlotta, I can't.'

Carlotta turned to look at her, and her eyes were stern but strangely enough, kind too.

'Cindy — you should have talked to your Teachers before this. Why did you keep silent?'

'I didn't want to leave, Carlotta. I was afraid you'd throw me out. I just went out with him a couple of times. I didn't think we'd get so involved,' Cindy stifled a sob.

Carlotta watched her, letting her cry on a bit. Then she said very softly, 'Cindy, what do you wish to do now? Tell me in truth and without fear. Like all of us, you too have your future in the world outside. You too will marry, settle down, have children. It is something to be desired. Something I would want for you. But by indulging in this petty distraction at this point of your development, you have harmed yourself immeasurably. You have further deliberately concealed this relationship, knowing it was against our rules. You have given evidence of weakness, Cindy. Deception and weakness cannot be tolerated.'

'Carlotta, I want to come back to the Path,' Cindy said weakly.

'Then you must give up this boy you have chosen to fall in love with,' Carlotta replied. 'Give him up completely.'

There was a fresh burst of tears from Cindy — 'But Carlotta, he's not interfering with my work. I promise you he's not. He'll wait for me, till I finish my years here. I really do want to complete my learning here. Please permit it.'

'No,' was all Carlotta said. 'Make your choice. Perhaps this is a test for you to see how well you can overcome yourself. Now you may all leave. I shall call you individually next week.' She walked to the window overlooking the hills and stood with her back to us. We left.

## Pages From My Diary

### The Coming of Winter

Today was a day for learning and the night was for an extraordinary experience which I cannot stop thinking about, as I lie here gazing up at the stars. Eight of us have come on a field trip to the Grand Canyon in Arizona — and the Earth Spirit is close. For the last two days we have been experimenting with ley lines — the energy tracks which crisscross the earth. Here where the rocks and waters meet, the earth power often surfaces and is almost tangible. We have been following a trail through the south canyon which descends to the Colorado River. We have come across caves and the prehistoric Pueblo ruins and the perennial springs called Vaseys Paradise.

Tonight, when dusk fell, we huddled round a small fire and looked up at the towering walls of rocks around us, cut and carved by the Elements over millions of years into strange and forbidding shapes. The river glittered under the moon and unknown sounds could be heard. Maybe it was the wind blowing through the crevasses and crannies in the rock. Our guide, a native American, did not have trouble descending but I am sure the trek up will be laborious.

After he had retired into his tent for the night, eight of us sat around the fire we had built on a slab of rock and tried to feel the presence of the Earth Goddess — Gaia. We had seen the mist rising from the earth and knew that she was near. From the beginning of creation, consciousness has pervaded the land. The Ancients said it was the life force of Gaia. They searched for ways in which they could attune themselves to her presence, and so they visited places of earth power. This ritual became a part of the Earth Mysteries — a recognition of the depths of awareness which can occur at these places where contact with the living earth can be made and where we can be in awe of Gaia.

Gaia is complex, powerful and wise and we are constantly getting proof of this. The awareness of her presence was alive in paganism and formed a part of the Old Religion. As we sat in a circle in that gigantic gorge, carved by wind and water, beginning at least five million years ago, I realised that nothing was really important. I knew then that time was of no consequence. The passing years are like the specks of sand which are strewn around the bottom of a canyon. We should measure lifetimes by events and experiences, not years. And these towering pinnacles of shale and limestone and sandstone which loomed up against the dark skies could tell many a tale of strange happenings if we would only pause to listen.

I wonder if what I record tonight will ever fall into other hands. What will they think at that distant date — when I myself do not know what to make of it on this night. As I was saying, our guide had retired for the night, and Jessica and Cindy and I were sitting huddled round in front of our tents, talking about the day. The Teachers still sat by the fire, away from the brush which grows at the base of the canyon. Suddenly, Karen called out to us, 'Girls, the forces are near. We shall raise the cone of power. Ipsita bring your athame and charge it.'

Perhaps I should mention that I carry my athame or power wand with me, wherever I go. It was given to me by Carlotta when I completed my three years of study at the chalet and I treasure it. It is a living entity. Well, Cindy, Jessica and I scrambled up and arrived at where the others were — Carlotta, Karen, Julia and Jean. Somehow the entire scene seemed surrealistic and pristine. Carlotta told us to stand around in a circle, raise our arms, look at the skies and breathe the chant to the ancient Egyptian goddess, Isis. I write it here in the knowledge that at some time in the future, someone who needs the power and protection of the goddess will say it and feel the power descend and envelop her:

'Tua Anset
Tebu a neter Anset
A Anset....'

There is more, but I hesitate to put down those lines of potent power. It is enough if Isis is invoked through these three simple lines that I have revealed.

As we chanted the invocation to Isis, ancient goddess of Egypt, wife of Osiris, mother of Horus, enchantress and stateswoman, queen of Wicca, I saw the fire in front of us, flicker and tremble. And suddenly a strong breeze rose from somewhere near the canyon's rim, miles above, and swooped down upon us, swirling around, scooping up sand from the base and whirling it into strange shapes. Our voices echoed through the dark spaces and the rocky walls seemed to part to allow the magical words to pass and race through the chasms and gorges of red stone. The dark skies, studded with stars till a moment ago, suddenly cracked open and lightning sped across. There was a roar and then a shriek as the wind became a gale and tore round the corridors of rock. The fire was slapped out. We flattened ourselves against the canyon wall behind us, fascinated by this strange manifestation of the Elements. The Power had been raised. Of that there was no doubt.

Then, as suddenly as it had arisen, the wind fell and slipped into a dark cave. The sky, once more, hung dotted with specks of light. Only, of the fire which had been extinguished, remained a bed of blown ashes and charred wood. Carlotta and the group now stood round in a circle once again. Without the firelight, a dim white moonglow surrounded us and reflected against the red canyon walls.

'Tua Anset

'Tebu a neter Anset ...' we chanted. 'You are Isis. All hail to Isis' ... and we recited the words of power. Very gradually a blue light, pale and shimmering, seemed to emerge like a slim jet of water from the ground in our midst. It rose slowly and grew like a spewing fountain as we raised our voices together. In that ancient landscape, we seemed to be the guardians and keepers of an alien mystery.

One by one, we entered that stream of blue light and bathed in it — heads flung back, arms held up, eyes closed. When my turn came, I stepped into the circle awash with the pale blue, and at once felt the warmth and tremendous energy spiralling round my body — strengthening and renewing. I could feel my thoughts infused with crystal clarity as wave after wave of knowledge and awareness swept over me. My body had never felt more energetic yet rested. My mind never more alert. I remembered to take my athame into the magical arena and watched the metal glow with a life and charge of its own.

Then we stepped away and held out our arms parallel to the ground, palms facing down and said the last lines of the Isis chant. The fountain of light trembled for an instant and slowly started subsiding into the earth from where it had risen. Soon all was as it had been before and we retired to our tents.

In later years, I have often thought about what I saw and experienced that extraordinary night in Arizona. I have tried to explain the phenomenon to myself and have attempted various 'rational' theories. But to no avail. However, I have come to believe one point, and that is that in many inexplicable happenings the world of magic may throw up, there is sometimes a meeting ground with orthodox science. But there are limits. Certain boundaries beyond which this meeting ground does not extend — and that is the 'X' land. The land of the unknown, where we stumble upon mysteries unsolved, and not to be captured by petty mental frames.

Where this strange light phenomenon was concerned, I have talked to both contemporary physicists and mystics. They agreed that the physical universe and the spiritual universe both share a lot in common and have parallel principles. In the book, *The Looking Glass Universe and Synchronicity: the Bridge between Matter and Mind*, the author, F. David Peat maintains that the latest scientific discoveries suggest that matter is not mere matter. 'The whole notion of the material has been extended into regions of indefinite intangibility.' And underlying both the material and mental worlds are 'patterns of information' — as he calls it. There is an essential unity in all nature.

Wicca's work has been to tap these patterns of information. What I saw and felt that night at the canyon was a display of this. The discovery that on the subatomic level all things are composed of energy and radiation reinforces what Wicca has always said — there is nothing which is dead. Nothing inanimate. Earth, stone, plants, water, wood, the moon and stars and we ourselves — all give forth light and life. We emit x-rays, ultraviolet, infrared, and radar. So does the earth.

Finally, physicists are supporting a concept of the universe that the Ancients have always held. According to Peats — 'The universe springs from a creative source ... out of which the orders of consciousness and the material world unfold. The heart of this movement and hierarchy of levels is meaning.' Consciousness in all its forms — human, animal, plant, stone and earth lies at the heart of the universe. Consciousness lies at the heart of magic. And I believe that this is what makes Wicca work. Our consciousness can bring about phenomena in the physical world. In other words, two conscious entities from two different worlds, can unite to produce magic.

Formerly it was assumed that scientists were merely observers of the universe who watched and reported. Physics does not agree with that. We can all be active participants. On that night, I think Carlotta and the six of us were just that. Active participants in raising earth power. The new physics has disproved Descartes' conception that dominated scientific thinking from the seventeenth century — that mind and matter are separate. We now know that is not so. There is no discontinuity between mind and matter, just as there is no separation between the human mind and nature. Wicca has always believed that the mind can be projected out into the universe and can make nature do her will. After all the word witchcraft in one of its connotations refers to the use of extra natural forces to bend the world to one's will. The noun 'witch' may have been taken from the old Teutonic word 'wik' meaning, to bend. There is no doubt that the Wiccan is one who has the power to bend things as she wants them to be.

The Elements themselves can be made to do our bidding and we know how to align ourselves with their tremendous power.

Elemental Wiccan Magic For Those
Who Thirst For Power

My experience with human beings has shown me that everybody — and I mean everybody, thirsts for power above all else. I never believed in unselfish, altruistic motives and now more than ever, I see I was right. People will lie, grovel, aye, even kill for power. Their desire to enslave their fellow animals is all consuming. Thus, to encourage that side of their natures which has any existence or meaning for them, I reveal a few rituals which have come down from a forgotten pagan past. If any exist, who would be detached from the power and pelf of the world — my advice is, ignore these pages. If any exist who are tired of the froth and fever of transient physical pleasures — I again exhort you, ignore these lines. These are not for you. But for those, who like me, glory in bringing the base world to its knees, who revel in its glitter and glamour, who laugh into its eyes and tease it till it does your will — then read on.

Be aware that the four Elements are the potent tools of Wiccan power. Use them with knowledge, daring, but caution. Remember, that powerful tools must be mastered, or else they can turn against the very one who holds them. They are living entities who must be acquainted with your strength and ruthlessness. In today's world, more so than in any other age, we are in need of power. Power of body, mind and spirit. But not mere abstract power. No, we want power over people, over circumstances, over situations. We want the world and its gifts at our feet. We wish to command. We demand obedience. And why should we not get our way? We deserve it. We are not ashamed to say this with pride. We are better than our peers.

So draw round and form a circle of three or seven or twelve. You may also work your magic by yourself if you so desire and if your will is strong. Draw down the moon on some starlit night. Raise the power and drench yourself in it and let the high tides wash over you. Then listen well. Here is a ritual by which the High Priestess takes the power of the Goddess unto herself — and for a while becomes She, Herself.

The rite is performed on the first night of the full moon, at midnight, which you must know is the 'witching hour'. The Wiccan evokes the Goddess unto herself and calls upon Her, who is the triple-goddess — the Moon Goddess, with the three faces, waxing, full and waning. On this night, She who is Diana, Artemis, Astarte, Aphrodite is pleased to help her daughters. Chant her words, meditate upon Her. If you are in a grove, dance and sing. Let Her be invoked. And feel the power descend and know that for a while, human and divine will become one. Ask what you will at such a time. But take care in what you ask for. Remember, the reins of power are hard to hold if the mind and heart are too full of greed. But I leave you to your fate.

## Raising the Cone of Power

The Cone of Power is invisible intangible — but it is formed by a group of seven or twelve Wiccans, in a circle. Arms held high, faces upturned, movements clockwise, voices in unison chant an invocation to the Goddess. Some English witches have claimed that during World War II they helped to stop a German invasion of Britain by raising a Cone of Power against Hitler. And many years before that, their sister-witches helped defeat the Spanish Armada using the same methods.

## A Potent Rock Ritual to Attract the World's Gifts to Yourself

Seat yourself in solitude at a round wooden table. Take a sheet of yellow or white paper and write on it in black ink, a list of all the things you would have of this world. Think of things you passionately desire and objects and situations you genuinely feel will bring you joy and happiness. Then, rise from the table, fold the paper into half and put it away in a secret place for three hours. Go about your work and return to your table with the paper after the three hours are completed. Maintain solitude. Now open up the list you had made in which are written the objects of your desire. Read them with care and contemplate on whether this is really what you want and require. Would you rather make a wish for another? Would you help someone heal in body, mind or heart? Would you help to lessen another's pain or distress? Would you invoke worldly riches onto another? No, I thought not. It is for yourself that you have come seeking. But no need to look uneasy. Come then, let the dark side in you unfold. No need to feel guilty. Rejoice in yourself.

Now, take a very small piece of paper and smear it with the oil of red roses. On it, recopy in black ink the objects your heart desires. Fold the paper into half and then once more. Once this is done, take the paper to a place where rocks are strewn about, preferably in the countryside, in your garden or in a park, when all is quiet. Find a rock small enough to move but large enough to hide the paper. Sit on the ground beside the rock. Check for snakes, scorpions and such like first. Hold the paper in the hand you write with and visualise for a few minutes what it is you have asked for. It is not too late yet. Do you want to change your wishes? Perhaps help another? No? Then proceed. Place the paper on the top of the rock and cover it with your hand. Feel the strength and energy of the earth projecting itself through the rock. Say these words quietly but firmly:

> 'I want power for myself
> Power is my goal
> The world's riches and its pelf,
> Cover my body and soul.'

Repeat the verse thrice. Then quietly lift a side of the rock and slide the paper under it. Leave the Earth Spirit to do the rest.

Be aware that two kinds of energy are used in earth magic. The first is earth power which includes everything which is born of the earth and is of the earth — specially potent are large, spreading trees, trees with gnarled roots and knotted branches. Rocks are strong with earth energy, so are certain plants with yellow and red patterned leaves. Deep and dark caves are full of the magic of the earth.

But to be truly effective, earth power must be wedded to yours. Your inner power. That energy which springs from your body and mind and suffuses you in moments of great joy and ecstasy. When you are able to combine this energy with earth energy — the magic begins. Remember, power is usually released through the body through the projective hand. This is the hand used for writing. The other hand draws in energy from the earth and the other Elements. If you wish to refrain from giving of yourself to others, in help, blessing or healing — do not lay your projective hand on them. I am sure, from what I see of you, that you will be eager to hoard all the power for yourself. So be it. May you grow in earthly glory.

## Tools of Magic

### The Inner Eye

Visualization of what you desire is an important part of every Wiccan ritual. Through the creation of images in your mind, you give your hopes and wishes a powerful thrust towards fulfilment. Your inner power gives the Elements direction. The inner eye must see, before what you will, comes to be. That is an ancient, unwritten law of Wicca.

Practising visualization is not difficult. Close your eyes and see yourself in the mirror of your mind. Picture others who interact with you. Visualize yourself obtaining your heart's desire. See yourself in your mind's eye, triumphant and in control of what you most want. Be aware that the inner eye is a powerful tool of magic. It steers your inner energy towards the goal — whatever you have chosen that to be. That is between yourself and your conscience — if you have one.

### Empowering Yourself and Your Equipment

Be aware that the Elements are the four creative energies of the universe. Earth, air, fire and water. This concept has come down to us from ancient Greece. A worker of Wicca works in close alliance with them and they help her to bend nature to do her will. She becomes attuned to them. She becomes as one with them. When a Wiccan is working with the Elements, charging or energizing oneself and one's tools becomes very important. The power must be drawn in from without, absorbed and then projected into a tool. It may be an athame, an amber or quartz object (which is already partly infused with its own energy), or a bowl of clear water.

To draw in the energy from the elemental powers, put out the hand with which you do not write, and hold it palm outwards towards the elemental source from which you intend to draw your strength. In time, the entire body learns to absorb energy from the outer universe, every pore alive and alert. Put out the projective hand or the hand with which you write, and hold the object you wish to charge. Grasp it firmly and with your inner eye see the power flowing into you, mingling with your own energies and then swirling out to meet and suffuse the object in your hand with power. Combined with your personal power, the elemental energy becomes fully potent, bestowing on the instrument an electrifying strength.

Your Magical Words

In chanting or reciting magical verses or words of power, it does not matter if your pronunciation of certain words falls short of perfect. What is in your heart is what matters. And I know what is in your heart, do I not? Say the words with assurance and confidence. You may whisper them and they will be just as effective. The elemental powers will accept them. Keep your concentration focussed and your intent strong. You will obtain whatever you desire. Just be cautious that what you most desire does not destroy you. Be aware that you are not playing with the toys of children. You are using the most powerful instruments in the universe. The Elements. Do not trifle with them.

The following chant is very potent. Say the words under an open sky as twilight descends. If the skies are stormy so much the better.

> 'I invoke the Spirit of the Earth,
> Of caves and chasms deep,
> I call upon the winds that sweep
> Through the lightening's path.
> I climb the high volcano's rim
> And invoke the fire that glows therein.
> I call upon the swirling coil
> Of waves that dash upon the soil.
> Come to me from your world without end
> Come to me as lover and friend.'

# III
# Revenge

*'Of all that has been written, I love only that which has been written in blood. Write with blood, and you will soon learn that blood is spirit'.*
— Friedrich Nietzsche

# 16

# *Daggers and Uncles*

I chose to be born in India because there was work to do here. My work. Scores to settle. Otherwise, in all truthfulness, I must confess that in the beginning this country and I did not share a close and perfect understanding. When we returned from Canada, I was not a young woman longing to find her roots — in spite of having ancestors who had sacrificed everything for the sake of the motherland. My bloodline showed men and women who stood staunchly behind Indian tradition, values, khadi and the nation's freedom. My mother's father, Nisith Chandra Sen had become a legend in his time by fighting the sensational Binoy, Badal, Dinesh case against the British Government, at a time when most Indians were too scared to oppose the rulers. He risked his life by sheltering hunted terrorists in his large house on Beltola Street in Calcutta. The house was frequented by his friends, Subhas Chandra Bose, Motilal Nehru, and Chittaranjan Das. Mahatma Gandhi would make it a point to see Nisith when in Calcutta, and once told him that the freedom fighters of Bengal had got their fire and inspiration from him. It was true that Nisith Chandra, with his piercing eyes and unsmiling set mouth, was not a man to be trifled with. It was said that even a British judge would hastily give a decision in Nisith's favour when faced with that unrelenting stare.

My grandfather wanted freedom for the land that he loved. He hated what three hundred years of slavery had done to its people. He believed that the British had broken the backbone of the Indian psyche. He said this with bitterness, because he hated any kind of weakness in a man or woman. An Indian, he said, would not hesitate to serve an English master but rebel before an Indian superior. And he despised the Indian fascination for a white skin. Anyone with a fair complexion was worth serving, marrying, and fostering, a girl unfortunate enough to be born with a dark complexion regarded as a miserable liability. Thus the British rulers were doubly held in awe by their subjects. Their skins were white and they knew how to treat Indians like doormats — to be walked on and over.

Nisith's own father, Chandi Charan Sen, had been a magistrate and a writer who had settled in Hooghly. He had infuriated the British by writing two fiery, historical novels — *Raja Nando Kumar* and *Jhansir Rani* — the stories of two great patriots who had fought against the British. He had fired the Bengali imagination and raised an unexpected patriotic fervour amongst the common man and intelligentsia alike. The British, fearing the worst, promptly banned the two books and started a systematic persecution of Chandi Charan — to the extent of burning down his house. He was forced to come over to Calcutta for the safety of his family.

This was the rebel blood that ran in me. And rebel I was — though mine was to be a different fight.

Back in India, we chose to live in Calcutta. I was now a graduate with a degree in English but I had retained my interest in painting. Though I had completed an exhaustive course in Western art in Montreal, I felt I should become acquainted with the intricacies and rich heritage of Indian painting and started studying the works of painters of the old Bengal school under the tutelage of Santosh Sengupta of the Oriental School of Art. My natural patience and discipline helped me in drawing the careful lines required in Indian painting. Each grain of the bark of a tree, the leaves painstakingly painted one by one, the minutely worked embroidery on a garment, each stone on the ground, each twig on a bush, each gem on an ornament.

My teacher, Santosh Sengupta, was a man of talent caught in a milieu that had no place for a creative man, if he had no money to prop him up. One could see that the travails of making a living from art were telling on him. He was a short, slight man with shoulders stooped from long hours of labouring over his paintings, and a perpetually harassed expression. In his fifties, he had a demanding wife and three young children. While stooping over his work or guiding me in mine, he would confide in me about how he was trying to reconcile his artistic life with the practical necessities of home and hearth. The Oriental Society had allowed him to take on private students and though this brought in the extra rupee, his lean and emaciated face showed his exasperation with those 'girls who were learning art just for the fashion' as he put it, or as an added qualification in the marriage market. 'Nobody loves art anymore, Ipsita,' he would lament.

He confided that his wife was a talented artist herself and quite a bit younger than him. However, marriage and the struggle of raising three children on an artist's salary, had taken their toll on her and she greeted him each evening with demands for more money and an acerbic tongue. In desperation, Santosh Babu had consulted an astrologer who had told him that both he and his wife needed to wear moonstones. He had promised that Mrs. Sengupta would be transformed into a mild and compliant wife. From his next month's salary Santosh

Babu bought two relatively cheap gems and had them framed in silver — one for himself and one for her. The result, he told me, was startling. As I bent over my work to hide my merriment, he said that she had suddenly stopped complaining. 'I have experimented with the efficacy of the stone by scolding her on some pretext or the other and she remains absolutely docile and quiet,' he marvelled. As a result he had asked her to wear his moonstone also. 'A double dose is better than one,' he told me with satisfaction.

He generally depicted scenes of rural Bengal — women with red bordered saris placing brass thalis heaped with flowers and fruits before a stone Shiva-linga, women with saris hitched up around shapely knees, bending down to plant the green saplings of rice in paddy fields flooded with water. Women serving their menfolk their midday meals of rice and freshly caught river fish. The village scenes of a Bengal I had never known came alive for me through these portrayals which I carefully studied. Santosh Babu also initiated me into the mystical beauty of works by the Bengal masters like the Ukils, Nando Lal Bose, Rabindranath Tagore, and others. I was fascinated.

My teacher also suggested that I start painting studies of the Hindu goddesses. Durga of the ten arms, white and chaste Saraswati, Kali of the fierce aspect and the terrible red tongue. For some time I lost myself in my art. I forgot the unpleasantness of contemporary Bengali society and the hypocrisy it had surrounded itself with.

In the course of my work with Santosh Babu, I realized that genuinely good and simple people had no place in the society in which we lived. Talent was not sought after.

I lost touch with Santosh Babu after I completed my training in Indian painting and moved on to other spheres, until one morning many years later when the doorbell rang and there he was, looking as harassed as ever, perhaps a few years more haggard and bewildered.

'I hear you are having a painting exhibition in Delhi soon, Ipsita. I am very proud of you. One day you shall be another Lady Ranu Mukherjee. A great artist and patroness of art.'

I was aghast and amused. I really did not aspire to become another Ranu Mukherjee, who ruled the art world with an iron hand, her position as wife of industrialist Sir Biren Mukherjee, and the title that had been bestowed upon her late father-in-law, R.N. Mukherjee. The Academy of Fine Art was her masterpiece in Calcutta, and her mansion in the city contained some of the finest antiques and art treasures. Well into her seventies, she stood at the pinnacle of what was referred to as 'Ingo-Bongo' society. Half English and half Bengali. The finest hangover from the British Raj.

I asked Santosh Sengupta to come in and he quickly made to take off his dusty, hard leather sandals at the threshold of the living room.

'Would you like some tea or lemonade?' I asked. 'Tea, please,' he said as he sank into a chair. Without further small talk, he took out a rolled up canvas from his cloth bag and proceeded to unfurl it on the living room carpet. It was a beautiful work in tempera. A rural setting with village folk at sunset, coming home from the fields. I gasped in admiration and he looked up, pleased.

'It is for you and your parents. For your house,' he said. 'Go and tell your father and mother I have brought them this painting.'

As I hesitated he said, 'Go. You like it. Don't you?'

'Of course,' I replied hastily. 'I'll see if they are free.'

When I told them about the visit and the purpose while Santosh Babu waited in the living room, more than a little nervous, my father was puzzled. 'Why has he taken all this trouble?' he wondered. 'I haven't commissioned any painting.' But my parents liked Santosh Sengupta and the three of us sat around the painting in the living room, admiring it. A few minutes later my father took him into the study and soon after Santosh Babu left, looking relieved if a trifle embarrassed. My father had just bought the painting at a handsome price.

There was another visit a few months later, and another painting. And then another. The next two paintings looked as though they had been done in something of a hurry, and perhaps the price was a little less handsome each time, but after the third painting the visits stopped.

I admired and respected Santosh Sengupta not only for his talent, but because even though he wasn't aware of it, he was constantly fighting the system, trying to make a living in the only way he knew how — through his art. And because even when he was painting his delectable rural, Bengali society, he was laughing at it. One day, I asked him why the women were doing all the hard work — not the men. He looked at me over his round, plastic-framed spectacles and said very seriously, 'Ipsita, you've been abroad too long. In Bengal — I don't know about other states — women have to serve. They are born to be servants. That's how I paint them. First the men eat their meals. The women serve them. Then they eat — last. You see them in front of the Shiva-linga? What do you think they are praying for?'

'Success, prosperity?' I asked.

'Husbands. Husbands. Someone who will take them off their parents' hands. Girls are a burden in our society, Ipsita.' Then he suddenly seemed to realize I was my parent's only child and a girl. 'Of course, you are different. You are like a princess. Like a foreigner. This applies to our Bengali girls, especially those whose parents don't have money.' And he shook his head and sighed, remembering his own daughter of twelve. He sighed again and absent-mindedly dipped his watercolour brush into his cup of tea and carried on painting the hapless women of Bengal.

Seemingly innocuous, insignificant people. But these were the ones along with the rich and famous whom I encountered who made all the difference in fanning that anger which was already there within me, brought to this life from some place, some time, far away.

I realized in ways which were strange yet revealing, that the cards were stacked against women. I was indignant when we learnt that certain male kin from my father's side of the family had designs on his property, since he had no male heir. It came to my father's ears that at a family gathering at which he had not been present, the discussion had come up that in the absence of a son, a Hindu's property could be claimed by his nephews — his brothers' sons.

My father was concerned and consulted a lawyer who assured him that such a case could not arise after the passing of the recently introduced Hindu Court Bill which prevented daughters being deprived of their fathers' property. Still, to ensure my future security, my parents made a will stating that I was their only and natural heir and that nobody else had a right over what was mine.

I hated the thought of my parents making a will because it implied that one day I would be on my own on this planet. And if I was capable of love, they were the only ones I did love. Wills also confirm the worst in human nature. It makes one realize that without legal documents and safeguards, people are vile, greedy and corrupt. There is something very sad in this realization.

This incident, which occurred soon after our return to India, opened my eyes to the dominance of the male species and the neglect of girls in Indian society. I noticed that elderly male relatives, even dependents, were treated with more consideration than widows. Their dependence on their male relatives brought out the subservient in them, and the most vile in their kin who supported them and made sure they were ever aware of it. It was strange that in a land that had worshipped the deity in the form of goddess, for so many centuries, there was really no respect for women. How many daughters, I wondered, had been left out in the cold due to the injustice by a society which pampered its sons?

The awareness grew in me that here, in India, one would have to bare one's fangs in order to defeat society's exploitation of women and obsession with its men. I had been trained and prepared for a bitter fight, and now I had come to the battleground. I realized that. I asked myself wryly whether I had become a lover of the west. I was never one to spare myself in my acute analysis of people and situations. But such was not the case. Perhaps it was the position my parents held in society, or my own self-confidence, but I had never been in awe of anyone. Of course, I gave age, position and wisdom the respect that was due, but I would never suffer an insult lightly, be it from a westerner or an Indian. Once, at a concert of Indian classical music in Montreal, a Canadian had commented that it was a pity that the west took no interest in Indian culture. For instance, he proclaimed, a Canadian artist would not be able to name a single Indian artist. This stung me. 'But Mr. S.,' I shot back, 'that is strange. But then artists in the west are not really artists, they are merely artisans.' The Canadian turned away, red in the face.

In India, I discovered awe. People were in awe of bosses, mothers-in-law, national leaders, film stars and football players. They grovelled before superiors and expected their servants and subordinates to grovel before them. I disliked what I found here. No wonder the British had had such a field day here. In Bengal, the idealism and inner fire I had read so much about as a child and heard about from my parents, had obviously been extinguished.

In the beginning I would complain to my father that I wanted to return to Montreal. I found nothing to interest me or hold me here.

'What you are searching for is Shangri-la, Ipsita,' he replied. 'Perfection does not exist anywhere — here or in the west. Learn to understand your countrymen. Be patient. The west has its own shortcomings.'

He himself was a man of amazing patience and tolerance. He got no gratitude and very little affection from his family, for whom he had sacrificed a great deal. Even though he was the least boastful of men, and never flaunted his position, Debabrata Chakraverti's success was a sore point with his brothers. His brilliance had enabled him to make a mark in London at the Imperial College and later at Glasgow where he received scholarships to study under the finest professors in aeronautics. At the time of our return to India, he was considered one of the pioneers in the field. His brothers envied the respect in which he was held, the dazzling marriage he had made, and the fortune they were convinced he had amassed while abroad. Above all, they disliked him for refusing to get embroiled in family politics, never giving them a chance to get back at him.

My parents had a sense of duty, family feeling and forbearance. I did not. I was a cynic in most matters. I was convinced that most of the people we now found ourselves related to, wanted something out of us, and had no desire to make friends. Still, mostly because I did not wish to embarrass my parents, I tried to put on a sociable and friendly face. But, thinking back on it now, I realized I made it unpleasant for myself and caused the other party extreme discomfiture. I realized it was not only the fact that I was my parent's daughter that they resented, it was also my looks. In fact, I had taken my appearance rather matter of factly. But I had forgotten that it would disturb others. Through the years, I had developed a strange kind of allure. That is the only way I can describe it. When both self-discipline and the Wiccan and Elemental powers are mastered, acquiring and maintaining a goodly measure of what the world terms good looks and beauty, is not difficult. The net result of this was that my social circle fell into two categories. Those who hated me, and those who were enslaved, and followed me around like hapless urchins. I scorned the first set and was kind to the second — for as long as it suited me. Because after a while an excess of devotion is a burden.

I loved only my parents. Apart from them, I knew no family, and I did not need one. Cousins, aunts, uncles and the whole paraphernalia. I had it in me to be complete in myself.

For about eight months we lived at Monoharpukur Road in Calcutta, in the spacious house which my father had once helped his parents to build. It was now inhabited by his brothers and their families and by his aged aunt Sushila. The same aunt who had been widowed as a child and had known only the life meted out to her by callous social norms. Her skin was dark and leathery and her fine head of hair, cropped short long ago had turned white. She was hard of hearing and lived in fear of displeasing her two younger nephews who now ran the house in my parents' absence. Long ago she had doted on my mother and now clung to her with her frail, bony arms. She wept and kept looking over her shoulder when she told my father of how his brothers' wives were rude to her and did not buy her fruit which they said was too expensive, on the days of her fast.

Seeing her condition made me even less well disposed towards my relatives, and I was glad when we moved to a separate residence on Palm Avenue. It was a spacious, two-storeyed, yellow stucco house, with green wooden shutters and a garden at the back. The house had been built by my maternal grandfather, Nisith Sen, many years back for the purpose of renting out. Next door was his huge, marble floored house, 14 Palm Avenue.

My grandfather had lost his elder son to tuberculosis at an early age. His only other surviving son, Ranjit, had been pampered and spoiled by the family as the only male heir. Nisith Sen loved his three daughters but after all, they were to be married off and would lead their lives elsewhere. Ranjit was good-looking, fond of the good things of life and enjoyed having a rich father. He was happy when his sisters got married and left home, and never welcomed their visits during holidays and family gatherings. He was never sure what gift of money or jewellery his parents would make to them. In time, he chose a wife who shared his love for luxury and leisure.

This life of indulgence had made Ranjit wayward and weak-charactered. Nisith and Shovana were aware of this and were disappointed in their son, but never knew the levels to which he could stoop.

I had last seen him when I was little more than a child, but

I knew him for what he was, from the moment I laid eyes on him. His forced avuncular smile seemed sinister, his eyes watchful and guarded. Suddenly, his face would become distorted with hate and malice. I shook my head. Was I being fanciful? No, he was laughing at something, showing a row of white teeth. Then suddenly he stopped and looked at me with narrowed eyes. Gone was the pretence, the fond uncle act.

'What's the matter? Why are you staring? You have a rude habit of looking at one strangely,' he said. He seemed uneasy. I apologised and turned away but in that moment, I recognised him. I knew I had seen his likeness before. The same hatred. The same malicious smile. He couldn't fool me. I knew that in this life he and I would fight a bitter battle. Luciana would be avenged. Suddenly I knew why I had been born in a land where women fought and struggled for survival. This was the country which could best provide the arena for the fight till the last. Even now, the methods were different but the rules and reasons for roasting women were the same.

When my parents returned to Calcutta, Ranjit Sen made his moves cleverly, playing the fond brother, inviting us home for lunch and to the prestigious Calcutta Club on New Year's Eve. He would smile and chuck me under the chin and say I was exactly what he would like his own daughters to be. He would often tell me stories of his childhood and youth, in which he was always the good guy, sacrificing all for the family. He said he would have gone to England to study law had it not been for his old parents whom he had to look after. Besides, he had to feed the family fires. Considering the fact that Nisith Sen was a rich man, this was laughable.

It was he who wanted us to rent the house next door. He wasn't getting a good tenant, he told my parents. Next, he told my father that he wanted to restart some business ideas and projects which he had had to give up due to personal reasons. He wanted my father to be a partner and help finance a recording company. This was certainly not something towards which my father had any inclination. But he liked this fun-loving man who showed such devotion to his sister and niece, and so he agreed.

As the days progressed, my father learnt that Ranjit had always had a penchant for earning big money quickly — and losing it due to bad management and extravagant spending. He had gone into various abortive schemes in the past with a series of feckless cronies. These forays had always cost him or rather Nisith, dearly. In his trusting brother-in-law Ranjit had found another Nisith who was willing to give him a chance.

I was surprised that he was always short of money. He certainly lived well, drank very well, and ate well. He reminded me of an ageing and spoiled playboy, who was getting disgruntled because he was losing his charms and power over people. He had a passion for boasting, and often talked about how girls fell like nine-pins around him when he was younger. He could never tolerate anyone better, richer or more intelligent. He would invite me to play checkers with him, a game for which he had a great fondness. He liked to emerge the winner by a series of quick moves. With me he generally lost. He would then claim that I was very much like him, but I could see the irritation behind the avuncular exterior.

His business ventures had generally been glamour oriented. He had once tried to produce a Bengali film which had flopped badly. But he had enjoyed the ambience of the whole thing especially the fact that pretty young actresses were at his doorstep, pleading for roles. That was a key point in his character, which I saw at once. He had a vampirish need to feed his ego. I felt that this is what would bring us to the arena one day. We would have to have a struggle to resolve something bitter and vicious.

Slowly, Ranjit started an insidious campaign against us amongst my father's younger brothers, at the same time trying to turn my parents against them. In the meantime, the demand for favours continued. One day, he would want us to make some major renovation in the house we had rented from him, the next, he would tell us some expensive fittings were required.

Eventually, even my father's patience began to run out. By this time, he had bought a plot of land in Ballygunj, and we planned to build our own house there. An architect was appointed. This did not fit in at all with Ranjit's scheme of things. A good source of income was about to be stopped. In his frustration, he started indulging in his favourite pastime. He used to keep an air rifle with which he would sit in his huge verandah the entire morning till lunchtime, facing the trees and the lawn. There was a tall cotton tree in front, and Ranjit would aim at the pods and burst them when they were in season. Otherwise, the birds which sat on the tree were the targets. He laughed when they dropped to the ground or else flew away in fear, in a frantic flutter of wings. He had another occupation about which he once boasted when he had had enough to drink. He kept an expensive pair of binoculars with which he watched people in the neighbouring houses when they had guests. He had rented out the ground floor of his house to an executive of a multinational company. He would watch him and his family through his binoculars at various times through the day. He said he got to know everything about them in this way. I once caught him directing his binoculars towards us, when my parents and I were sitting in the garden having tea. His behaviour confirmed what I had always suspected, that there was something vicious and psychotic about him.

At just about the time that we were thinking of moving, Ranjit suffered a severe heart attack. He was panic stricken and pleaded with my father to be there for his family if something should happen to him. My father promised. I wanted to carry on with our plans and move. Ranjit had cousins, other sisters and their husbands. Let them take care of him, I told my father. But my father could not bring himself to turn his back on his brother-in-law, in spite of all that he had done. 'Ipsita, when a man is down — no matter how much you may dislike him, try to help him. Ranjit is a weak man, and dishonest. I know what he is. But now he is also a sick man. We have to stand by him.'

And my father did stand by him, helping in every possible way. He let no problems financial, domestic or business worry him. For the next few months things went on as they were and my father did not mention moving. Our land in Ballygunj lay unattended, waiting for the surveying to begin. Ranjit rested in bed, till he was well enough to sit out in the verandah again every morning with his air gun.

In the meantime, the stresses of family and work had been too much for my father. He fell ill with a massive heart attack in October. My mother had been keeping bad health herself. Now, she was devastated with worry. My uncle would look out of the window of his room, from which you could lean out and almost touch the shutters of our house, and enquire offhandedly about my father. In the course of my father's illness, he visited us only a couple of times, telling us that the doctors had advised him to take care of himself. I had expected no support from him and I got none.

In the midst of all this, he suggested that instead of building a new house now, why didn't we buy the house in which we were already living which we had taken on rent from him. My father, helpless in bed, asked him how much he expected. My uncle quoted a figure way above the market price. 'This is your best alternative,' he said. 'You'll never be able to build a house. Not now.'

The months went by and my father somehow pulled himself together but the attack had taken a serious toll and he never fully recovered his strength. He worried incessantly about my mother and myself should we be left alone. 'Of course, I cannot believe that Ranjit will turn away completely,' he said, more to himself than to us. 'Nobody can be that callous.'

The following February, my father wanted to return to work. He was a director in a major company based in Calcutta and had allowed Ranjit to look after the recording company that he had helped him to start. During Ranjit's illness my father had tried to keep things going for him, but Ranjit, in his usual fashion, had got things into a mess which my father had a tough time sorting out.

Within a month of joining office, my father had a second massive heart attack from which he never recovered. I knew that in his last days he was a desperately worried man. I tried to put a brave face on it and tell him all was well, but I could never fool him. I had not loved or respected many people in this world. In fact, most I had despised. With my father's leaving, there remained only one reason for love and softer feelings. My mother. Otherwise, everything else within me was arid, dry and stony. Without emotion, feeling or compassion. Storybook witches, as in Hansel and Gretel are made of such stuff. I was worse.

Hardly had a few months of mourning passed when my mother underwent major surgery and had to stay in hospital for several weeks. The Bangladesh war had started, and every evening was blackout time. Ranjit took this opportunity to start his games in earnest. He asked me how I intended to manage the house and our financial affairs with all the turmoil that was going on. He informed me that he would have to change the house lease to my name, and did I mind if he did not give me any rent receipts for a few months. After all, it was all in the family. He also said the house needed repairs, and he would be sending some workmen over to fix the roof. He knew I was alone in the house, but what could he do? He couldn't let the property fall apart. Then he asked me if I was interested in buying the place. I said no. In that case, he said, he would be sending prospective buyers over at various times of the day. After all, he couldn't suffer a financial loss, since I was unwilling to buy. I kept silent. I knew I would have to play his game out.

I spent the days with my mother in the nursing home and returned home in the evening to a dark, dark house through streets deserted and blacked out. As darkness enveloped the city, unsavoury shadows moved about on the roads and lurked in corners. Anti-socials were abroad but I took my chances, almost daring life to do what it could to break me. My strength was a strange, savage sort of strength. I was a sinuous feline. A silent, watchful jaguar who walked with tightly coiled tread, ready to spring if required. I trusted no one. I knew that in the world in which I now found myself, I had to destroy or be destroyed. I was ready to fight for myself and whatever I held dear. I needed no help.

People knew I was all alone in the large house. Our servants refused to live in, and would go home as dusk fell to be with their families. My bedroom was on the first floor. Downstairs were the living and dining rooms, the study and a small library. My bedroom doors opened onto a long, glassed in verandah. As one came up the stairs, it was the first door to the left. Beyond that was a second bedroom and a small breakfast room. From it, a door led onto an open terrace. On the third or fourth day, I came home as usual and let myself in, fumbling with the lock in the blackness. I lit a candle and made myself some dinner and ate it quietly behind shut windows and drawn curtains in the bedroom. There were strange noises and knocks about but I ignored them. Then I went to the kitchen, candle in hand and searched for a long knife with a sharp blade. Back in my bedroom, I kept it on my bedside table and undressing quickly in the dark, I lay down between the covers and closed my eyes. I knew if required, I would use the knife. The Laurentians were very far away but the season of the witch had begun.

It was a Friday evening and I was late in getting home from the nursing home. Our driver had deserted us after my father's demise and I now moved around in cabs, which were difficult to find on the streets during blackouts. As I reached the front door, I heard a rustling sound from some bushes nearby. It could be a bandicoot, I told myself. There were many which ran around in the dark. But my instincts said someone was watching. I clicked on my small pocket torch, fitted my key into the front door latch, opened the door quietly and stepping into the pitch black house, shut the door behind me. My torch guided me up the stairs. On reaching the landing, I turned around and cast its narrow stream of light downwards. There were no sounds from within. But a distinct knock sounded on the door. Then it was repeated. I knew something was not quite right. I went into my room and opened the drawer where I kept my knife. I felt its cold, wooden handle and picked it up. Its steel blade shimmered in the torch light. Then I returned to the stairs and started making my way down, carefully, one step at a time, feeling them with my bare feet. I had clicked off the torch.

As I came to the last step, the knock sounded again accompanied by a rattling of the brass door handle. I stood silently at the other side of the door, listening. There was a narrow, wooden-shuttered window at one corner of the entrance hall, and I cautiously moved to it and peered out through the slats so that I would not be seen. There was some light from the skies and I could make out two shadows, standing huddled outside the door — shapes without distinct form, wrapped probably in shawls. But they were men. Surreptitious and waiting.

Was this what Wicca had trained me for? 'The school of life,' Carlotta had once called the experiences which awaited me. I could have gone upstairs again and tried phoning the police but in those days of war and blackouts, I knew by the time any policeman arrived a lot would have transpired. This was a present danger. I could not wait for future, possible help.

I slowly undid the window latch and pushed the shutters open. They opened with a creak. The dark forms started. I knew surprise was my weapon. In the dark silence I gave a shout of laughter and suddenly shone the torch full on them. They instinctively raised their arms to cover their faces. In that moment I noticed that even though they apparently carried no weapons, the one in front had something like a bottle in his hand. Some yellowish liquid within, shone in the light from my torch. He quickly hid it under his shawl. I wondered if these were just a couple of drunks, on a pilfering spree. But I knew instinctively that this was not so. I went on talking loudly as it seemed to unnerve them. Then suddenly I brandished the knife and casually ran it down the side of the window, scraping off the paint with its sharp edge. They had moved towards the window now and I was aware that it had no grill or bars. The window ledge was almost within their reach. One of them inched closer, but the other one pulled him back.

The first man appeared infuriated by my brandishing the knife. In the torch light I had had a glimpse of a long, lean face, half covered with a muffler. The other man was in the shadows now. I had not been able to see his face because of his raised arms.

'So, who are you?' I asked loudly. My voice was a challenge in the sinister ambience.

'Come to the door,' the first man said through his scarf.

'Really? Without knowing who you are?' I sneered. Something in his voice had sounded strangely familiar. 'Why don't you come closer and take what you deserve,' I added softly. 'I know how to use this thing, you know,' and I twisted the blade of the knife in the air.

With a sweep of his arm, one of the men took the bottle from under his shawl and flung the liquid in my direction. It splashed against the shutters and made a fizzing sound. A few drops splattered on my hands and I knew what it was. Raw acid. Then they ran, taking the empty bottle with them. I knew their gait and their forms as they fled, the shawls no longer wrapping them. My torch still switched on, lay on the window ledge, lighting their guilty retreat. One was a new employee from my uncle's staff. The other? No, not Ranjit. But one of his very close kin. I do not name him — not out of charity but because his deed failed, and Wiccan justice overtook him in the end, in a strange way.

I shut the window. Then I washed my hands and sprayed the room with the perfume of roses to disperse the acrid smell and went to bed. They would not return, I was sure of that. I felt good. I had won.

Some years after I returned to India, I agreed to teach English at South Point High School and found it extremely rewarding.

At that time, South Point was one of the biggest schools in Asia and one of the best co-educational institutions in the country. The students were keen and intelligent, and I discovered a talent for teaching I hadn't known I had. I found I knew how to discipline young minds and bring out the best in them. And the youngsters responded by giving me the kind of affection I hadn't known before — in India.

At this time, I was also teaching art at the American International School, and they paid me extraordinarily well. My uncle was extremely curious about my earnings. I knew that I would soon shift from this house of ill vibrations to another one, far away from where he and his family lived. His pressure tactics had failed. He had stooped to every device under the sun, from calling me foul names from his part of the street, to sending me legal letters alleging I was not paying his rent (he had stopped giving me receipts). He sent common labourers over to thieve and steal on the pretext of working on the grounds. Finally, the acid attack. I had watched him and bided my time.

Now, I had found a lovely apartment for my mother and myself on Hindustan Road. We were to shift the next day. For the last time I stood on the terrace of this cursed house on Palm Avenue and looked towards Ranjit's garden where cotton pods lay burst open on the ground. I did not look closer. I looked up at the skies which were darkening after sunset. All seemed to be clear. No clouds. But I wanted a sign. Was I to be avenged for the trouble he had caused? For the wrong he had done? For the darkness within him? I closed my eyes for a minute and the Power was there. A stiff breeze started up out of nowhere and swirled in a spiral round and round. It seemed to be coming from the cotton tree from where the birds had once sung their songs. Suddenly the spiral was cold, even though the day had been warm. It seemed to take form and shape — an identity. I looked into its centre and there was darkness in its midst. Dry leaves, sere and brown, were being whipped around. It was an unforgiving, serpentine coil of wind, which had merely come to remind one that the evil in a man's heart often lives on. It does not die. Year after year, through the centuries it lives off innocence and goodness. Unless something happens to chastise it and plunge the dagger of revenge into its blackened soul. Some of my tasks were being completed. The Elements would take care of this man. It was bound to be.

When you fall once, I say it is God's carelessness. When you fall twice, you should have been more careful. When it happens again, you belong to neither darkness nor light.

17

# *The Witching Hour of Marriage*

There is a season for everything. For many summers I had not seriously considered matrimony. At the chalet, nobody was against marriage but I was much struck by what Karen had once said about the tentacles of habit. One of her friends was in the process of getting a divorce and Karen while a wife and mother herself, and a successful one, was empathizing with those who chose freedom. After a certain session discussing the philosophy of Nietzsche in relation to the inner psyche of man, she jokingly said, 'I agree with Nietzsche about what the free spirit needs. It abhors habits and rules. Everything which goes on and on.'

'But can marriage become stifling then?' I asked her.

'I suppose it can, to certain natures. Such a nature, even if it marries, needs space. You know, don't you, that Nietzsche compared marriage to a spider's web. Finally, the threads become traps. That is why, after a time, the spider stuck in the middle, painfully tears apart the mesh enclosing him, even though it will suffer from the wounds — because it must tear these threads off itself, away from its body, away from its soul. It must learn to hate where it used to love and vice versa.'

At any rate, I had hesitated in sharing my life and giving of myself to a man who would henceforth be entitled to call himself my husband. My mother who felt her health was failing her, was eager to see me settle down. She would gently chide me when I laughed at the young men she now and then suggested as prospective partners. I told her they would be miserable with me. They wouldn't know how to cope. I found the whole game quite entertaining and teased a few suitors, till I sensed that my mother wasn't really happy with my irresponsible conduct.

Time passed, till finally my sense of adventure and curiosity took over. I decided to try out the married circumstance and looked around for a man who would hold my interest. There were many who responded with alacrity to my new quest.

Mothers of young men in India are generally on the hunt for daughters without siblings and well-to-do fathers, and I fitted the bill perfectly. Many did not know about my dark leanings. A few did. But material considerations generally outweighed fear about a daughter-in-law in a black cape.

I found I had no patience with these greedy, obese women and their simpering sons. I remember a certain young suitor, a journalist in whom I took some interest for a while. He gave me a very good insight into the psyche of the Indian male. 'Ipsita, when you think of marriage, remember to show the man that he's superior to you. Our men do not like intelligent women — at least not more intelligent than them.'

I experimented with playing dumb for a while but it soon bored and then disgusted me. In those days I used to write for a certain English daily. My suitor, I was aware, resented my success and felt I was encroaching on his domain. Nonetheless, he wished to marry me.

He had a distant aunt who had married an Italian count of sorts. He was enormously impressed with the pair. One day, he invited me to a party at his house where the aunt and the count were the guests of honour, and the outcome was hilarious. The aunt, a pretentious woman but not lacking in intelligence, took a great fancy to me. So did her blue-blooded husband. They invited me for dinner to their place the very next evening, along with their nephew. My suitor, or should I say fiance, was enraged. 'We will not go,' he screamed shrilly. 'She has never invited me before. She only wants to curry favour with you because of your connections. The snobs. The upstarts. The climbers.'

I had little desire to accept the invitation, but the incident brought matters to a head. It showed up the man's pettiness, his insecurities. I regretted having invested time and energy on him and started showing favours elsewhere. He turned vindictive, which gave me an excuse to call the whole thing off. When we parted, I pretended to be sorry. Afterwards, I raised a glass of champagne to myself in the mirror.

'Ipsita, there's only one of you. Remember that. Watch your step.'

I was too valuable to waste.

There were a few more suitors and admirers with whom I played along from time to time. I can honestly say they were no more than an afternoon's — or maybe an evening's diversion. When I did get married, it was for reasons that were weightier.

Besides the procreation of a better race (which can be done anyway without marriage, but is more convenient within), I believe that marriage should be a new and worthwhile experience for a woman. It is like adding fresh territory to an existing map and is definitely worthy of exploration. When I finally decided to marry, I saw it as unsurveyed territory and was considerably interested in launching forth on this safari. However, I do believe that every woman must carefully study the partner before undertaking the trek. An unsuitable mate makes for a miserable journey and that is not to be tolerated. Of course, I admit that in matters of matrimony, destiny plays more than a hefty part, but Wiccan women have never left everything in the hands of fate. If the cards of destiny deal you out a man not worthy of you, either tame him or leave him. The choice is surely yours. A solitary existence is better than one with a bothersome man. In such a case, it is more wholesome and interesting being on your own.

There are many varieties of men, but in most, and I really do not include them all — the driving factor is the same. Ego. In the course of my career, I have observed the species from quite a close range and I have been astounded at times by their bloated self-esteem. Such types do not require wives. They want foot-warmers. Wiccan women do not oblige. Then there are the sorts amply prevalent in India, who never grew out of mama's arms. Tease them a little, kiss their soft cheeks and leave them. You don't have time to play nursemaid for a lifetime. Of course, there are also the genuinely obnoxious, the slimy, the manipulative. If you are unfortunate enough to be in the clutches of one, don't despair. There is only one way to deal with him. Feign affection, love, infatuation, call it what you will, and then — just when he's secure and snug in the rug — whoosh, pull it out from under his feet. Find another man under his very nose. Disappear from his ken. Shatter him. Then laugh at him.

The secret, of course, is never to lose yourself in a maze of emotions. Never surrender yourself totally. To husband or lover. I think there lies the key to dealing with a man. Innumerable women, young and old, known and unknown, have come to me through my years of Wiccan counselling on how to make the best of relationships with the opposite sex. On how to turn up trumps. On how to make the creeps get what they deserve when they play foul. My advice has always run on the same track. Don't invest so much of yourself in any relationship that you run dry. Keep vast reservoirs of goodies — tangible and intangible — for yourself. You never know when you'll need them. And one big secret is this. A man finds a woman with aces up her sleeve, irresistible — whether this be another man, a successful career, or most tantalising of all, self-sufficiency. That's how I play Circe — with legal luminaries and erudite editors and self-centred stateswomen.

I met Joyanta Roy at a friend's house in Calcutta. I believe he had expressed a desire to meet me. He was young, shy but with a ready sense of humour and a sharp wit. What endeared him to me the most, was that he seemed thoroughly smitten by me. He wanted to take me out to dinner, lunch, plays and theatres even though he could afford none very well at the time. He was a young officer in the great Indian Railways, South Eastern, to be exact, and I realized he had made of himself whatever he was, the very hard way. I was told he had grown up in Orissa. He talked mostly about his work which seemed to be an obsession. I listened to stories about his first postings as a probationer at Bilaspur, a small scenic place — that is, when the tigers didn't saunter out of the jungles to sun themselves on the railway platforms. He had also been at Chakradharpur and Asansol. Once he had been captured by tribals when there was a dispute over some land between them and the railway authorities. He had been locked up for a whole day while they decided what to do with him. He had spent his time looking up at the ceiling and thinking.

'What did you think about?' I asked him.

'Well, it was a little mud and brick room with a thatched roof. The floor was caked mud and nice and cool. Not unpleasant at all. The tribals were all sitting outside with bows and arrows and refused to speak to me. They were the silent, angry sort. So I sat back on a chair they had provided and spent the first hour counting how many times we inhale in an hour — under normal circumstances. Then for the next part of the day,

I decided that taking all things into consideration, the tribals really did have more claim on the land than the railways. It was their pride and their requirement. Then I slept for some time. They brought me lunch on a huge dried leaf. Some rice and lentils and water in a cup. Some volatile young chaps were talking amongst themselves about burning down the hut but they were quietened by the elders. I quickly finished the rice because I didn't want to burn on an empty stomach.' I laughed at that. Eventually, he was released. The land dispute was settled with tribal interests in mind — largely due to Joyanta's intervention.

Something about this young man intrigued me. He was not like the others I had met. There was something sincere but detached about him. He reminded me of dark, forest soil after the rains — soft on the surface but with an unyielding quality if you prodded a little. I knew he was connected with the earth. It seemed he wanted my attentions but would understand if I turned away. He told me about himself in bits and pieces — but said that strangely enough he remembered very little about his childhood. He looked almost sad when he said this. He seemed excessively grateful to his parents and his brothers for just being there. He had three of them, two elder and one younger. He said he admired them and they had always been very good to him. When I asked him why they shouldn't be good to him, he said nothing. I had a bad feeling about his family. I gathered that one reason he talked so much about work was because his home life had been unhappy.

I knew I was developing an interest in Joyanta. My Wiccan antennae were up but I also did a bit of down-to-earth research on the man. My sources worked quickly but in the strictest confidence. What I discovered was interesting. He was the love child of a certain erstwhile raja of Orissa. His mother had been a favourite singer in the harem but due to the jealousy of the raja's legal wife, he had not been able to marry her. When they had had a son, the wife threw a tantrum and forced her husband to give the child into a foster home when he was barely two months old.

The home was found in Cuttack, with not very well-to-do parents, who already had two sons of their own. But for a hefty monthly consideration and other favours from the raja, they agreed to bring up the child. The child was to take their surname. Joyanta was not given much affection by his new family. He was there merely to run chores and hang around. For many years they did not even consider sending him to school while his elder 'brothers' were given a good education, thanks to the handsome allowance which was sent over on the first of every month. Finally, at the insistence of a kind family friend, young Joyanta was sent to a small local school when he was about ten years of age.

His education was haphazard. Nobody cared to see whether he was attending school or not. If there was work to be done around the house, he stayed home. But due to his native intelligence and a burning desire to succeed in life, he managed to graduate from school and entered Ravenshaw College in Cuttack. There, he did extremely well, obtaining his Bachelors degree in physics and a Masters degree in statistics. After a short time as a research scholar and lecturer in Vani Vihar in Utkal University, he decided to try his luck in the Public Service Commission Exams for the Indian Administrative and Allied Services. Joyanta did very well for the Indian Railway Traffic Service. There followed a hectic time of training at the Academy in Dehra Dun. He had really made it against all odds.

But circumstances had not taught him to lighten up or have fun like other young men. He had few friends, and spent most of his time studying or reading or taking long walks by himself on the hill roads. When I met Joyanta he had been working hard at his career for eight years and was posted as the Area Superintendent Officer in Bokaro — an area troubled with labour unions, constant strikes and tribal head-hunters. He handled the working classes very well. They had an empathy with him which made him an excellent go-between for the administration and the workers.

I married Joyanta on a rainy, thunder-filled August evening. I knew the Elements would be present and they were.

I wore my mother's wedding saree — an exquisite red Benares silk embroidered with gold. I wore the jewellery that had been handed down to her from her mother and her mother before her. It was a traditional Brahmo wedding. The acharya or preacher was there and Joyanta and I exchanged rings and our vows. But because Joyanta was a staunch Hindu, we also had a short Hindu ceremony in front of the ritual fire and walked seven times around it. As the last circle was completed, the lightning streaked across the skies and somewhere thunder rolled like the drums from a distant kingdom. I knew all was well. Before marriage, Joyanta had courted me, a trifle uneasily I thought, with a few dinners at expensive restaurants in Calcutta and with much aplomb took me shopping for a diamond ring from Satramdas, the jewellers on Park Street, after I had said 'yes'. I later heard he had had to take an official loan to buy that ring. His own earnings and savings were all religiously taken over by the family. His foster parents had had another son, a few years after Joyanta was taken in. It seemed that the man I intended to marry was the one who was expected to earn and look after everybody's needs within the family. On the other hand, I found that if he needed anything, from clothes to food — the cheapest was bought for him. It was something like a story out of Dickens. When I married Joyanta he did not have a single suit. He had one pair of rough shoes and a few faded cotton shirts which he wore everywhere — to the office, to board meetings and to the few social dos he was forced to attend. I guess as a grown man he should have had the initiative to look after himself — but the fact was that long ago, he had stopped bothering about himself. He had been ambitious as a child, but somewhere along the road, he had come to the conclusion that there was nothing else to look forward to. He was of average height and medium build, slightly wiry, and had an innate physical stamina which had been strengthened by walking for long stretches in railway yards during inspections. He had acquired quite a tan from spending long hours outdoors in the hot sun of Bihar. He smoked and drank innumerable cups of tea when he was hungry. When he came home at night, there would be a plate laid out on the table, with some cold rice, lentils, and vegetables. If he were lucky his parents might have ordered his peon to boil him an egg. The rest of the family would have eaten their dinner and retired for the night. Joyanta had learnt never to expect much from anybody. Every night he would lock himself up in his room and read. That was his only luxury. Buying books from the Wheeler's book stalls, from the little money he was spared for his own expenses. His brothers and their wives were in Delhi — very much a part of the social circuit. His younger brother was an IPS officer, also in Delhi. He was fond of a good life and had acquired expensive tastes and girl friends. Every month he wrote to Joyanta to send him money.

I must confess Joyanta didn't tell me all this. When I revealed to him the information about his true parentage he was startled but not surprised. He said that an old family friend, a doctor who attended on his family, had often taken him aside as a child and made as if to tell him something but never had. Joyanta had never thought more about it. But now by hindsight, things started fitting in. The family's callousness towards him. The gifts which would come from the royal household when he was very young. The large baskets of mangoes and jackfruit which used to be sent from the raja's gardens to the Roy household. A car which would be on attendance. They had never been able to afford one of their own then. I found out more for myself, and from others outside the family as time progressed. His family remained silent. When we decided to marry, his brothers wrote to him saying that they expected him to continue doing his duties by them even after he got married.

※

So that was Joyanta's life when I met him. But there was a lighter, mischievous side to him. I discovered that though he had a great sense of humour, it didn't earn him too many friends because his punch lines were often too close to the truth. His peers didn't like him for his bluntness. His bosses, I discovered didn't know how to handle him because he didn't kow-tow to them and his colleagues avoided him because he didn't play the games they were into. In fact like an absent-minded professor or a blundering puppy, he often upset the counters when they were all set for their kill. The only point, which intrigued me and maddened others, was did he do it deliberately or was he just being himself. His colleagues fumed but they couldn't do anything about it. Life to him was just a road one wandered down. The underdogs adored him. The peons, the poor, bullied staff on railway platforms, the faceless, the nameless, the ones without a future in the great Indian Railways. He was a people's man. I knew that he and I would make a great team. He had heart. I did not. He was completely unselfish. The word did not exist for me. He adored me. I admired his good taste. I knew I had found a man with an inner endurance, grit and a sense of humour. An unselfish man with grit is a good combination.

I knew Joyanta Roy was not a slick dandy like the ones I had dated in Calcutta society but he would be able to give me whatever my little black heart desired. He'd make a success of himself. That was important to me, there was no denying that. I have always believed that a woman, especially a witch, should have money, a mansion and a Mercedes. In time, he would be eligible for a big, sprawling bungalow. I would travel in luxury in a saloon from the days of the British Raj. I have always enjoyed travelling. I did not expect him to be ever rolling in money — but I had enough of my own. And I knew life with him would never be dull.

My assessment was not wrong. Joyanta climbed the ladder of success. Not only as a successful bureaucrat but as a much sought-after advisor and officer on special duty to various ministers in the Government of India. He is respected for his work and his honesty. I know he is bitter about the past. But he believes whatever has been, has been for the best. He believes in a Power and as a devout Hindu he calls it by the many names of the Hindu pantheon. I do not believe in ritualism but I respect his faith. In the beginning he was intrigued by Wicca. Now he is amazed by its power. I do not worry about his ever straying to extra-marital affairs, because I know that after the taste of champagne everything else is yesterday's soda.

The railways is a very inbred organization with its own colony life and inhouse functions and gossip. It has all the trimmings of an incestuous joint family. As a new bride, I first went to Bokaro, later to Adra and tasted a new sort of life. I enjoyed being a housewife in a large, British bungalow, with sprawling lawns, shady trees and a big, inefficient staff. Life in the districts has a distinctive flavour for the railway wife. You are expected to be a memsahib. You rise early, have a cup of tea with the husband, then go back to bed while he goes off to bully trains into running on time. The lackeys line up to see the sahib off. You rise at a respectably late hour, stretch, inspect the gardens, tell the mali how to do his job and order a few vegetables picked for lunch. A lawn chair is brought out for you and the dhobi's wife and the cook's wife come scuttling out from the outhouses to relate the gossip from neighbouring bungalows. While all this is going on, one of them gives you a head massage and then you proceed leisurely for a hot bath. The husband comes home for lunch and you exchange notes. Who's being posted where? Who's got a promotion out of turn? Did the boss accept a small gift in return? Railway wives, it is said, know more about running the railways than the men. They have even been known to run parallel offices at home. Subordinate officers are generally more scared of the boss's memsahib than the sahib. If they take orders from her, their promotion comes without a hitch.

After lunch, the husband has a short snooze then departs for another few hours' work before a few drinks at the officers' club. The wife sleeps on till four when she makes up her face and dresses quickly for the women's welfare organization meeting.

There, she can find out when the next D.R.M. Panel is due to come out and assess her husband's chances. Over samosas, pakoras and tea, they discuss how to teach village women the effective grinding and selling of masalas. Then the boss' wife is presented with a bouquet for her kind cooperation and everyone goes home.

All this amused me for about three months. Then I was bored to my teeth. Joyanta took a transfer back to Calcutta. His bosses did not like it. They put it down to the fact that his wife was a snob. Couldn't get along with the railway family. As for my reputation in Wicca, they were curious of course and I am sure discussions and speculation were rife — but to my face everybody was extremely cordial. They merely said I had hexed the Railway Minister into granting my husband's transfer. Come to think of it, maybe I had.

I had always wanted a daughter. A girl with my eyes, my hair, the tilt of my chin, and my wicked, wicked ways. Sons always get reformed by their wives. Daughters are the wily, foxy, irresistible ones. And I had a dream. I had to leave an image of myself behind when I moved on. The world should not have a chance to forget me. Vivé la witch.

She was named Deepta by my mother, who adored her. Deepta for brightness and light. Deepta for the glow of a lamp on a dark evening. That was when she was born. At dinnertime, in the heat of May. In the Wiccan calendar, Beltaine had passed, the time of sun-drenched earth and emeralds on leaves had come. The time when waters splashed cool against the skin and the air was empowered with the sounds of summer. The nights retained the fires of day. And I willed Deepta to carry on the torch of my inner strength. My dignity. My spirit. My standing tall.

It suddenly struck me that I was a mother. A woman who had learnt to fight and conquer, who had slept with a sharp dagger, ready to torment her tormenters, who stared into the face of society and called herself a witch, but was at a bit of a loss when faced with a squealing bit of softness and wet lace. I looked into my daughter's sleepy brown eyes and puckered up face and laughed triumphantly, holding her up, letting the sunlight play on her dark curls. She opened her eyes wide, angry at being woken up and flailed her arms about. I laughed into her face, teasing, provoking her to fight. This was no ordinary child. This was a child of Wicca. A daughter born of my limbs, nurtured by my will. She would be ready to stride the world when the time came. In the meantime, my mother's comforting arms took her and held her close, lulling her back to sleep.

'Really, Ipsita,' she said, 'practise your martial arts by yourself. Not on my granddaughter. The pet.'

I could swear the child smirked. She'd learn fast.

As she grew up my daughter Deepta besides resembling me, showed a talent for many things, quite unexpectedly. When she was of twelve summers or so, she sat down one day at the piano and played with her fingers literally rippling and skipping over the keyboard. She had never had a day's lesson. She could identify and name composers by listening to their music. She was obviously carrying over old knowledge. When a few more winters passed, she wrote poems on nature and flowers, evoking their colours and fragrance. She loves freedom and change, hates being in one place too long. She has grown tall and is slim like a Wiccan, carrying herself with a certain insouciance which is not unpleasant. Her hair curls round her face and gives her a rather impish look at times. I have noticed she is a keen observer of people and even as a very young child, instinctively knew friend from foe. Sometimes she would warn me — me, about certain people! Like me, she adores animals. The squirrels in the garden, come and paw her when she's sprawling on the lawn and our dog Peeg, rolls over and over when he hears her walk up the stairs. She is my daughter — almost all the way, except that she has her father's mathematical astuteness. From last winter, she has been experimenting with a new talent. She is able to sit before the computer and make up complicated diagrams and drawings of advanced jet propelled engines and aircraft. I think I have finally bitten off more than I can chew.

But in all seriousness, something in me — maybe the mother, is concerned. She must develop the toughness of Wicca. I know she has my qualities of quickness and sharpness. She also has distinct psychic gifts. She loves mountain mists and wide open spaces. She displays very little apprehension about the future. She draws in the scents of air and earth and water and she rides high when her friends ask her about her mother who is a witch. They are fascinated and she basks in the fact that her mother is a pioneer of sorts. She is convinced I can do anything. I tell her I am mere dabbler. She, little devil, laughs in my face and says I'm like Mary Poppins. She likes my witchy cooking and the way I roast chicken with parsley and herbs. I know she's fond of a colourful table and so when the weather is right and the cherries and strawberries come down from the hills, I lay out the red berries encrusted with sugar to watch the expression on her face. Like me, she has a sensuous appreciation of beauty, be it in clothes, flowers or food. When my study is lit with lamplight of an evening, she'll bring in a crystal bowl of red and yellow roses, bury her face in them, put them before me and sit down on the carpet next to Peeg. Like any mother I wonder who she's going to marry. Fathers of daughters think their daughters are too good for any young man. She should take up aeronautics — like her grandfather, Joyanta feels. She shouldn't waste her gifts. A husband can come later. Deepta says that at the moment she's Alice in Wonderland. She's having fun. In time she'll find her Lewis Carroll. Joyanta looks as pleased as witch's punch. Have I been able to wipe away the unhappiness of the past from his life? Have I turned out to be a wife and mother in a million? Joyanta and Deepta emphatically say yes. Even Peeg comes and licks my hand. It astounds me. Wiccan wonders will never cease. And I had thought I was the wicked witch.

In my life, have I ever known desolation? Darkness and despair? Yes, I knew unending tides of grief when I lost my mother. I had been devastated when my father left me but then, the circumstances of my life had not allowed me to brood too much. The fight for survival had been too intense. I knew he looked to me to carry on and to protect my mother. In the twilight of her life she had been frail and ailing and carried on just through an indomitable will. I placed myself in the role of both her guardian and child. She was my inspiration and the most ardent advocate of the work I was doing. She understood the harshness I wore in a hostile milieu. She was my link with a world I had left far behind me. If I had a better part, she brought it out. She believed in goodness. When I was with her I could drop my armour and my weapons for a while and bask in her gentleness and her love.

I had married on the condition that after marriage, she would allow Joyanta and myself to look after her. I insisted that we should live under the same roof. In the beginning, she had resisted but I had been unyielding. I wanted her with us. And I must say that was one of the reasons which had drawn me to Joyanta. His capacity to love the mother I adored. He had come from a home where he had been unwanted. I loved to see him banter with her, tell her the office news at the end of the day, listen to her reminiscing about bygone days, tease her at times and then plump out her cushions so she'd be a bit more comfortable. She doted on him like a son. I would look at my family and be filled with pride. Here was my fortress. A world I had chosen and built. Nobody could take it away.

That is why when my mother was suddenly taken grievously ill, I was hurt and confused. I was deeply angry with the Power. Till now, when she had fallen ill, her own reserves and will, medical ministrations and my tenacity in holding onto her had always helped her to recover. But now, it seemed the Power had other plans. I couldn't keep her with me anymore. She left me. And I couldn't see the *raison d'etre* for anything anymore. At some level, I was even angry with her for leaving me.

But I am sure everybody feels like this when he or she loses a loved one.

I didn't shed any tears. People said that was unnatural. But then, I hadn't wept when my father passed on either. I think sorrow has many faces and I didn't want the world to see mine. The world had no right to it.

## Pages From My Diary

It is well to remember that power can be used for weal and woe. For good and evil. For healing and destruction. There is no use denying it. Darkness and light are two sides of the same orb. You can choose the part you wish to work with. You will surely get results. Of that there is no doubt. But you must be strong enough and knowledgeable enough to bear the consequences. For to work woe on another is surely to invite the same on yourself. My motto always has been, trouble not another, until he or she troubles you. And then of course, let the magic of Wicca take its toll. For he who dares to intrude on what is mine, must surely pay a steep price. He who denies the help received from the Forces must suffer. It is a law written by the hand of Hecate. He who is my foe will not remain my foe very long. That is all I have to say. Time and again I have seen the Powers at work. I do not deceive you. If you choose not to believe me, that is up to you. But blame me not if with a shudder of the unknown, the truth is taught.

And for you, gentle reader, who would work mischief on another, here are a few spells that will serve you well. But cast them with care for once spun, there is no unspinning. There is no going back. But I am sure the gentle reader does not wish to retrace his or her innocent way. The darkness is so much sweeter. I have always found it to be so.

### Spell To Daunt The Foe

On the darkest of nights, when the sky hath no moon, take a fistful of clay or earth from where no man or woman doth tread. Put it in a bowl of copper and mould it to be that which opposes you or would do you harm. Wrap a parchment yellow round the figure and with black ink make a spiral round the head or the top of the figure. Wish confusion upon him or her. Let his thoughts be in disarray and his deeds undone. Defeat be the fruit of his ill will to you. Take the clay and hold it in your clenched fist, the left one will do. Think upon your power and direct it to his downfall. Say this in silence.

> 'I take you in my grip of steel
> You who do me ill not weal
> Let Hecate tell us who will reign
> From my life remove the bane
> Your defeat is my gain.'

Say it silently thrice. Then take the clay object you have moulded and bury it deep in a corner of a field or even in your own garden. Victory shall be yours. Let none disturb the figure of clay. I leave this ritual to your conscience. You will know best whether it deserves to be worked. For know this as a truth — he or she who works unjustly against a fellow human, will have the same defeat thrust upon him. Play not with the tools of power for your own whims or lust. I tell you this to warn you.

For reasons which can only be categorized as revenge, witches of old were often able to cause impotence in men who had deceived or angered them. They induced this by means of ligature — the art of tying knots in threads or leather cords to cause male sexual inadequacy or total incapacity by a kind of sympathetic magic.

The witch would perform a ritual that included tying knots in a cord which she would then hide. Impotence would follow and remain thus, until the cord was found by the offending male. If the cord were never found, that was his bad luck.

There have been tales of witches being able to make penises disappear — but fortunately or otherwise I have never had reason to search for proof of the above mentioned. I mention it merely as a matter of interest to those who search for the salacious.

## 18

## *Jyoti Basu and I*

Wicca believes in completeness. Totality. The full circle. No avenue is to be left unexplored, no wine unsipped. A woman of Wicca is eager to experience life in its entirety. I say woman, but there have been men too who have lived and died for the Craft, the Wisdom. In fact, one of the most poignant accounts to come from the age of witch-hunts is a letter, dated 24 July 1628, from an accused male witch, Johannes Junius, Burgomaster at Bamberg, to his daughter Veronica. It gives us an insight into the torture in witch trials: 'Many hundred thousand good-nights, dearly beloved daughter Veronica. Innocent have I come into prison, innocent have I been tortured, innocent must I die. For whoever comes into the witch prison must ... be tortured until he invents something out of his head .... When I was the first time put to the torture,

Dr. Braun, Dr. Kotzendorffer, and two strange doctors were there. Then Dr. Braun asks me, "Kinsman, how come you here?" I answer, "Through falsehood, through misfortune." "Hear you," he retorts, "you are a witch; will you confess it voluntarily? If not, we'll bring in witnesses and the executioner for you." I said, "I am no witch, I have a pure conscience in the matter; if there are a thousand witnesses, I am not anxious" .... And then came also — God in highest heaven have mercy — the executioner, and put the thumbscrews on me, both hands bound together, so that the blood ran out at the nails and everywhere, so that for four weeks I could not use my hands, as you can see from the writing ... Thereafter they first stripped me, bound my hands behind me, and drew me up in the strappado. Then I thought heaven and earth were at an end; eight times did they draw me up and let me fall again, so that I suffered terrible agony ... and so I made my confession ... but it was all a lie. Now follows, dear child, what I confessed in order to escape the great anguish and bitter torture, which it was impossible for me longer to bear .... Then I had to tell what people I had seen at the Sabbat. I said that I had not recognized them. "You old rascal, I must set the executioner at you. Say — was not the Chancellor there?" So I said yes. "Who besides?" I had not recognized anybody. So he said: "Take one street after another; begin at the market, go out on one street and back on the next." I had to name several persons there .... And thus continually they asked me on all the streets, though I could not and would not say more. So they gave me to the executioner, told him to strip me, shave me all over, and put me to the torture. Then I had to tell what crimes I had committed. I said nothing .... "Draw the rascal up!" So I said I was to kill my children, but I had killed a horse instead. It did not help. I had also taken a sacred wafer and desecrated it. When I had said this, they left me in peace ... Dear child, keep this letter secret else I shall be tortured most piteously and the jailers will be beheaded ... Good night, for your father Johannes Junius will never see you more.'

1692. It was a bleak and bitter winter in Salem, Massachusetts. A rigid and emotionally suppressed community of Puritans lived a dark and dismal life there. One day, a group of young girls got together for a bout of fortune telling. Their lives were monotonous and unbearable. Soon after they suffered from hysterical convulsions and began accusing their neighbours of witchcraft. Of the accused, one hundred were imprisoned. Nineteen were hanged and one was pressed to death. Why did it transpire? How did this group of girls, ranging between the ages of nine and nineteen, convince practically the whole population that respectable farmers, tradespeople and matrons were conspiring with Satan? As people hanged and bodies went limp, the crowd clapped and jeered. What caused seemingly decent people to act thus? Clergy and magistrates and pillars of the community.

Perhaps the fault lay in the hearts and minds of the Puritans, in their conception, or rather misconception of what their religion expected of them and their consequent frustrations and repressions which gave vent to this inhuman bout of cruelty. Among those hanged was Sarah Good, the mother of a four and a half year old child. Sarah was one of the first three people to be accused of witchcraft by the people of Salem. Perhaps because she was poor and defenceless, or perhaps, as happens today, because she did not have influential friends. She was born in 1653, the daughter of a well-to-do inkeeper who committed suicide in 1672. The innkeeper left his large estate to his widow who remarried. Sarah's stepfather succeeded in disinheriting her and her six brothers and sisters. Her luck worsened when she married an indentured servant who died soon after, leaving her with a baby daughter, Dorcas, and huge debts. She managed to get a small share of her father's estate but it was seized back by the court to pay her late husband's debts. By 1692 she was driven to begging for food to support herself and her daughter.

It was this hapless woman who was accused of witchcraft and of working ill against her neighbours. In one of the most barbaric and meaningless witch-hunts in history, both mother and daughter were accused of being in league with the devil and thrown into jail. Sarah was hanged on the nineteenth of July 1692. Dorcas, not yet five, went insane, after being confined to the dungeons for eight months.

It was 1988, and I was living in Calcutta. Times had changed — or had they? I still read in the papers about women being branded as witches in Indian villages and even in cities and towns. About how the word was used as an excuse to harass and torture innocent widows and wives and daughters-in-law and those who stood up for their dignity as women. But it wasn't going to be like that anymore. I would make sure of that. A deep, molten anger like seething lava, surged upwards in me. I knew that the time for work had come. In 1692 in Salem, my daughter and I might have hanged by the neck till we ceased to breathe. Now, I held the dice. I knew they would roll for me.

May was a swelteringly hot month in Calcutta that year. West Bengal was ruled by the Marxists who believed in neither God nor the Devil. The chief minister was Jyoti Basu, an unsmiling, rigid, ambitious old man who headed a cold, ruthless team like a Nazi chief. He was a comrade who delivered speeches to the poor at election time about his party's belief in plain living and high thinking, in between frequent trips abroad. His son Chandan was an industrialist who had amassed considerable wealth.

In the meantime, West Bengal plodded on with its daily drudgery of crowded streets and homeless vagrants. Beggars slept on sidewalks amidst tatters and grime. Filth poured out of sewers and water from drains. Children dropped without a trace into open manholes during the rainy season and tenements collapsed because nobody bothered to repair them and Calcutta Corporation wouldn't budge unless incentives were more concrete than leaning buildings. In the villages, tubewells were scarce, and of the few that existed, most gave only a trickle of water. Women trudged miles over dusty tracks to ponds and drying pools, to bring back water to their homes in pots and earthen vessels. When the crops failed there was really no way to survive. Many farmers and their families took recourse to suicide.

In the midst of all this, another ugliness reared its head. Witch-hunting. It started in the rural areas of Bankura and Purulia and spread to the north to Malda and Raigunj. It had already started stalking the neighbouring states of Orissa and Bihar and Uttar Pradesh. The victims were usually widows, old and infirm, or young girls without fathers or brothers, with some landed property in their name and interested relatives. Male kin would insidiously start rumours that a certain woman was practising black magic. They talked glibly of unholy rituals and evil eyes. If anybody fell ill, if somebody's child took to bed with a fever — it was the witch. The woman, alone and defenceless, was held responsible. She would be dragged out of her hut or hovel, stripped and beaten, stoned and paraded around the village and if she still breathed, she was driven out. If she had ceased to exist, her male kin with approval from all, took over her property. This was the condition of many a woman in West Bengal villages in the eighties.

In the towns and cities, if a young girl repulsed the attentions of a neighbourhood ruffian or goon with political connections, she was harassed, often molested, then called a woman of easy virtue. In the villages, it was easier to say she was a witch and force her to leave house and neighbourhood. It was more devious, sly.

After a few months, the matter came up in the Bengal Legislative Assembly. By then, several women had died. The chief minister briefly perused the numbers and nonchalantly made a statement in the House that such was the case. He quoted figures but there was no condemnation or shame. Much less a possible solution. The usual sop that 'appropriate legal action would be taken against those associated with the killings' was given. Then silence. What was specially disturbing was the way the statement was phrased: 'Mr. Jyoti Basu, in a written statement informed the West Bengal Assembly on Tuesday that seventeen women were killed in the state in 1987 on the suspicion of being witches. Three other women were killed during the first two months of this year on the same suspicion.' It sounded like an accusation from the Middle Ages. It was almost as though there was a valid ground for the killings — 'on the suspicion of being witches'. It was exactly what the inquisitors had once said about innocent women before condemning them to horrible torture and death. Were we going back to those times, thanks to our modern day leaders?

The statement appeared in a major English daily in Calcutta. I read it and knew the time had come to bring the battle out into the open. To speak out against the injustice of centuries, the infamy heaped on Wicca, the cruelty to which defenceless women had been subjected. I spoke to the press, and I spoke as one who knew. I spoke as a witch. I let them have my credentials, and gave them the relevant facts — but only some.

'Calcutta witch blasts Jyoti Basu' screamed the morning headlines.

'Witch defends her craft.'

'The Serpent rears its head.'

'The witch who dared to tell.'

The press and the public were mesmerised by me. I was articulate, educated, and had the right family background. My husband was a highly placed bureaucrat. And yet I said I was a witch. Journalists clamoured for interviews and men and women from all over the country began contacting me. I revelled in my triumphs. But it was not only about Wicca as warrior that I spoke. I told them about the powers of this ancient craft — the healing, the balance, the wisdom it could provide. Even journalists who were working under Marxist duress or had vested interests had to admit, albeit unwillingly that, 'there is no doubt that she and her craft have fired the imagination of thousands.'

It was not necessary for me to claim that I was a witch. I could have just as easily told people that I had belonged to a society that studied the old civilizations and cultures and the ways of ancient man, that I was an anthropologist. I knew the ways of nature and I understood the workings of men's minds. I could have said I was an environmentalist or a psychologist. But I chose to take the rough road. The way of the warrior and the healer. For it was at that moment that I realized that Wicca, at one time called 'the craft of the wise' and which had been used as an excuse to kill millions of women, including Joan of Arc, the Maid of Orleans, would be the weapon which I would use to help the wretched women of Bengal in India in the twentieth century. And I would do so by coming forward and saying boldly, 'Look, I am a witch. You have taken to stoning, and beating and burning women because you say they are witches. If you are strong, brave men with conviction — do the same to me. I am here.'

I knew that this was the only way to deal with the adversary. Don't mistake me. The adversary wasn't just the chief minister of West Bengal and his regime. It went deeper than that. It was the very society in which we lived. It consisted of the men in the villages who tortured and brutalized women for the sake of greed and control. It comprised the hypocrisy in an urban milieu which would not let a woman be free socially or economically, which still battered its brides for dowry and killed its infant girls in the womb. And I knew they hated me for it, that they would have gladly killed me if they had had the courage or the opportunity. But that opportunity never came their way.

And that is how some of the hapless women of Bengal found refuge and shelter, and someone to fight for them. I spoke not only to the English but also the vernacular press. Not only was this good copy. This was something women in thousands wanted to know and read about, because it gave them confidence that even if they were branded as witches, there was hope that somebody was willing to speak up for them.

19

# *The Witch-hunt Continues*

started my work with Wicca in earnest. Concrete, solid, work that involved healing of the mind and body. People began streaming in with all manner of ailments. Troubled spirits and restless lives torn apart by pain and suffering. I would be there for them thrice a week, from morning till evening — seeing them individually, listening to their problems, counselling them when required and administering the ancient therapy of Wicca.

This did not entail anything to ingest, no pills or potions. It required that they sit before me for a while talking about their difficulty and then I would position them in front of the healing quartzes and crystals of differing shapes, hues and sizes. There they would sit in all quietness, communicating with the Elemental life force which I had already proved was trapped within these rocks of varying qualities. Natural sounds emanating from storms, waterfalls, rain and ocean waves were played on tape while they relaxed and absorbed the energies. Sometimes the sound was of chimes, or bells of varying pitches and tones. They were taught to listen and if necessary to emulate certain deep-throated humming sounds themselves.

The therapy room was like my room of a thousand crystals in the Laurentians. It was true, there were not half as many crystals here, but it worked. People talked of feeling better. Healing started taking place. I will not say that this was miracle healing and that the lame man threw away his crutches and walked away. No, this was healing of a holistic sort. Where the body, mind and spirit, were calmed and then fed with energy of a strange and inexplicable kind. Was it my presence and my healing aura? Maybe. But I do not make any claims. Was it the secrets of the ancient Wiccans at play through the crystals and sounds of the Elements? Perhaps. It is a fact that the crystals worked more effectively when the natural sounds were present. Sometimes, I turned off the tapes and let the sounds from outdoors come and play around. I was living right next to the Dhakuria Lakes in Gol Park, Calcutta, and my therapy room included a little balcony which looked onto tall, yellow flowering trees and the lakes, quiet except for the occasional splash of the oars of boatsmen from the nearby rowing club. There was also the rustling sound of leaves, the breezes, the waters as they rippled and, if the session was after five in the evening, the calls of the birds as they prepared to nest. These were the aids I took from nature, and my patients healed.

Of course there were those who fought and struggled against themselves and the forces. Those who tried to tell me that they were still sick. But I realized soon enough that the real reason was that they did not want to give up therapy. They wanted an assurance from me that I would not send them away if they said they were better. This was something I had made into a ground rule. Neither Wicca nor I were to be used as a crutch. I tried to impress upon those who came to me for help, that the strength and the magic lay all around them. The key to unlock doors was within them. I was merely their guide for an hour. Sometimes to help them in focussing or in calming themselves, I would gift them natural quartz pieces or power objects. I told them that these were not to be looked upon as talismans. These were merely aids along the way to finding the power that lay within each and everyone of us.

And this was the truth. Wicca never sought to control anyone. It merely showed the way to the magic.

I believe that rock quartz does have marvellous properties — but why does it not work for everybody? The answer lies in the human factor. How well can you use it? How effectively can you tap it? How quiet are you on the inside? That piece of crystal is a channel which tries to put you in touch with the Elemental powers. What are these powers? How do you recognize them? You know them, sometimes through the senses and often times you know and yet cannot explain how you know. They are the sudden, swirling winds which rise on a clear night, play around you and leave you with unnamed thoughts and inspiration. They come as the rays of the moon which dapple your bed even though the sky is dark. They come in different forms and many shapes. And you recognize them. They congregate in that one glistening, white pebble which suddenly crosses your path as you walk down an ordinary courtyard on your way to work. They swoop down in a whiff of evocative fragrance which only you remember as you cross the road. They are the inexplicable messengers from that Mystery which haunts our lives and sustains us. Beyond the veils of stars, and swirling galaxies and endless light years — so far, so terribly far and yet right beside us, a touch away.

I held individual therapy sessions for five years — five long years. And I feel that I did my bit for humankind. I served it well. Normally, Wicca is reclusive, self-sufficient and does not seek to publicize its knowledge. It does not need the shackles of society. Neither does it work with missionary zeal, seeking followers and converts. I felt I had to speak out because there were old wrongs to be rectified, injustices to be set right. But let it be known that I did not court neither did I encourage people to follow in the way of Wicca. I have always believed that each should walk his or her own path. And I do not take Wicca to be a mere man-made religion. It is a discipline and, more than that, a way of life. But in spite of my discouraging attitude, scores of people wrote in to me, and to the papers, wanting to know more and more about this enigmatic study from the past. They came to therapy, for ailments small and major. I served them. I had a success rate of ninety per cent. Orthodox treatment and most conventional practitioners did not like Wicca for this. Most significant was the fact that this was a therapy which was completely non-invasive. There were no risks or side effects. Wicca was not a dark and sinister practice, it was above board and publicly practised for anybody to check and experience. I proved it to the country. I also brought back the ancient science of quartz therapy to India. Wicca showed the way, once the path had been cleared.

I say after the path had been cleared, because there was a lot of clearing to do. A sweeping away of the cobwebs of prejudice and the more dangerous vermin of vested interests.

Among those who came to interview me was S.N.M. Abdi of the *Illustrated Weekly*. He was a sceptic about the occult and the esoteric. He came expecting to find a fad, a gimmick – at best a sort of godwoman. But he was taken aback by the poetry and knowledge and power of this most ancient craft. He met some of the people who had come to me for help and were willing to talk about their experiences. One of them was Dilip Deb, a former international water polo player who had represented India against Russia and Sri Lanka in 1962 and 1966 respectively. He talked to Abdi about how he had gained from Wicca therapy in his business affairs, where he had been taking wrong decisions. He told the *Weekly*, 'At the very first meeting, she instructed me to get rid of my lawyer'. Within ten days, he said, he had recovered around forty per cent of his outstanding bills. Somewhat to my embarrassment, he went on to claim that

I was divine, that I could work miracles and even had the looks of a goddess!

There was also the story of Swapna Sinha, a middle-aged housewife from Dhanbad, whose husband worked for Coal India. Four years earlier, Swapna had fallen from the first floor of the building where they lived and suffered serious spinal injuries that left her paralysed from the waist down. Every form of medical treatment was tried, the best neurologists consulted, but she remained almost bedridden. Then she came to me and Wicca — as a last resort.

Abdi met Swapna after she had completed only four sessions with me. She told him, 'Now I can walk with a little support. Previously, I experienced a burning sensation in the soles of my feet. Now this has disappeared.' Her family said they were determined to continue with Wicca.

Swapna's case, like many others that came to me, proved beyond doubt the efficacy and power that I had inherent in me and which had been emphasised by my special training in a very ancient art. Otherwise, I cannot claim that I was a particularly compassionate person with a calling to heal. I did not particularly like the human race. But I had triumphed in proving myself. Once again I was who I was. The supremely powerful and beloved witch.

The people were with me. Of that there was no doubt. But other forces started to operate. Not the least were certain political lobbies which considered me to be a threat. I had attacked the Marxist chief minister, that was bad enough. But they now felt that I could become a potential crowd puller who had the capacity to influence people against them and their misdeeds. Many women, victims of panchayat and police atrocities had already given me gruesome and verified versions of what they had suffered. The politicians were afraid that the people of Bengal, especially the women, were becoming influenced by someone not under their control. Somebody who was a nonconformist and hence posed a threat. I knew that male ego and chauvinism were also at play. There was envy — and rage — that their power wouldn't hold here, that a woman was laughing at them.

One evening, a certain man claiming to represent the Bengali paper *Aaj Kal*, knocked at my door. He had brought along a photographer and said that he would be grateful for a few moments of my time as he was a student of the esoteric and was writing an article on the subject. I knew that he was out for mischief. Something told me to slam the door on his face but I had to be sure. I asked him what he wanted to know and watched with amusement as he gave me a false name. As he stood before me with an oily, false smile pasted on his face, some memory stirred within me and for a second I felt sick in some deeper recess of my mind. Some instinct told me that this was the second man. One of the evil faces which had condemned me, or rather Luciana to a horrible fate. In this life he was a petty man. He looked like a political stooge. A dark, sinister face and slightly hooded eyes. The lips were thin and showed a potential for cruelty and greed. But he kept on smiling. I hid my contempt easily, for I had been well trained by my discipline to mask my true feelings. This was a time when I would have to play a game. Give him a long rope to see what transpired. Was this the man who had committed Luciana to the strappado and ordered her tormentors to keep her there till her limbs tore out of their sockets? I would see.

I asked the man and his friend to come in and invited them to sit down. They did so. The friend with the camera looked uncomfortable. He did not or could not utter a word. The man started asking me about my therapy. Did a lot of people come? How many? What kind of ailments did they suffer from? I told him that that was none of his business. My patients had a right to their privacy. He said he had heard that people were waiting in line for appointments. How much did I charge? 'Two hundred rupees for three sittings,' I told him straightfacedly. And for those who were genuinely unable to pay, I charged nothing.

His expression showed he didn't believe me. I could see the wheels turning in his head as he calculated the astronomical amounts I must be cleaning up. I asked him what sort of article he was planning. He gave me a strange answer, considering he had said he was a journalist. 'You see, I have graduated with psychology from Calcutta University. I am looking to set up a practice of my own here. Why don't you and I conduct sessions together? You have the qualifications from abroad. That counts here. I can help you with the publicity. Are you willing?' Was the man a fool or a maniac, I thought. But he was looking at me with greed in his eyes. 'I am not looking to go into business, Mr. Ghosh,' I said coldly. Somehow his actual name had suddenly appeared in my mind. 'And certainly not with a partner like you. I really have nothing more to say. I thought you wanted to know about Wicca. As such I had asked you to sit down. You may leave now.'

His face grew ugly. 'I have the names of a few people who have come to you for Wicca. I will go to them. I shall ask them if you are genuine or a fraud,' he said threateningly, his voice rising shrilly. I knew the man was obsessed with strange ambitions. But I would have to find a way to get him to leave.

'Can you show me a piece of magic?' he demanded. 'I want to know whether Wicca can perform magic. Show me something.'

I could see he was bordering on hysteria. I knew what to do. There was a certain sleight of hand to calm the mentally violent, but I needed the props. 'I will show you a wonderful piece of magic, Probir Ghosh,' I said. 'But afterwards you must leave.'

He nodded never once taking his eyes off my face. 'Tell me the secret of success,' he suddenly shouted.

My young daughter was in the next room. Hearing a strange man shouting she came in to see what had happened. He turned to her and asked me, 'Is this your daughter?'

'Yes,' I replied curtly. I turned to my daughter and ordered, 'Go and get the magic things.' She understood what I meant.

Quickly, she brought me what I needed. I took the objects and asked the man to come out onto the verandah. There with a swoop of the arm and the athame, I sliced some vegetables that were over-ripe and before his eyes, warm, scarlet blood gushed out from them. Probir Ghosh, the venomous viper from the past, the mischievous irritant from the present — blanched. He tottered backwards, almost losing his balance.

'I want some photographs,' he demanded.

'By all means,' I smiled.

He left soon after. I had silenced him for the moment but I knew I would hear from him again. He hated me. Within a few days he phoned me and once again, he asked to join me in 'treating patients' as he put it. I refused and asked him not to disturb me again. A few days later, he brought out an article in *Aaj Kal*, blaspheming me, and accusing me of things which the inquisitors of the Middle Ages would have found after their own hearts. I read it all and knew that in this life at least the man had overstepped himself. He would suffer.

Some months later, I heard Probir Ghosh was in trouble at his work place. He worked as a petty clerk in some bank, and tried to make money on the side by writing smutty sensational stories. I shook my head, not in pity because that is an emotion I have never felt, but in wonderment. Vivé la Wicca. Long live the Witch. He would never know the success he so desired. He would be consigned to darkness. He should never have tried to tangle with me.

I knew of course that certain politicians had hired him to attack me. He made one or two other half-hearted attempts to bait me. But his spirit was broken by the problems that engulfed him. I dismissed him from my thoughts completely. One need not be vindictive. I put away the conjuring equipment till the time when I thought fit to use it again. To shock and startle for somebody's weal or woe — as the case demanded.

# 20

# *If God Forgets*

Before I proceed with other matters regarding men and magic, I must pause to recount the case of Sushma Kumar, a young woman from Uttar Pradesh, who came to me some time ago for therapy. She was a lovely and intelligent girl from a well-to-do family in Kanpur and had been married just two years earlier into an influential business family in the same town. In the January of the year she came to me, she had given birth to a healthy and lively baby girl. That was when her problems had started. Her appointment with me had been made by her husband. All he would tell my secretary over the phone was that his wife desperately needed my help and that they could come to Calcutta as soon as I could give them a date.

I usually had a long line of people waiting for appointments but in her case, it seemed so urgent that I gave a date the coming week. On the appointed day, Sunil, her husband wanted to meet me before he brought his wife in. She waited in the anteroom. Sunil came into my visiting room and stood there, nervousness and confusion struggling with attempts to appear jaunty and confident. He was young, well-dressed in the current fashion, with a degree in business management from Mumbai. I asked him to be seated.

His English was fairly good. After a quick glance around the room, he began, 'Madam, my wife is possessed by some evil spirit which is turning her mad.'

'Why do you say that?' I asked.

'She was always very nervous. Even before marriage. I think in her parents' house she wasn't given the chance to go out much. She is very unsure of herself.'

'So,' I kept looking at him, 'what do you want me to do?'

'You see, I just wanted to give you a background. She says all kinds of things. Some are nonsense. Talks of ending her life. I want you to make her normal.' Then he seemed to consider. 'Actually, the problem really got worse after the death of the baby.' His voice trailed away as he said this, and I could not get any more details out of him.

'Wouldn't it be better if I just had a talk with your wife?' I asked. 'Over the phone, you said she needs immediate attention. Let me find out what the actual problem is. The death would certainly have had an effect on her, but I would like to talk to her alone. Kindly wait outside,' I told him. He seemed reluctant to leave but did not linger.

After a few moments, my secretary brought Sushma into my chamber. She entered and remained standing, looking at a painting behind me on the wall. It was a seascape with mountains in the background. My secretary left and I asked her to sit down, but she seemed not to hear. Dressed neatly in a pale pink, starched muslin saree, with a matching blouse she looked like what she was — the well-turned out young wife and daughter-in-law of an affluent business family from the Hindi speaking heartland of India. Her thick black hair was shiny, slightly oiled and plaited down her back. She wore no make-up and looked younger than her twenty-four years. Only her eyes were kohl-rimmed with a heavy fringe of lashes. Set in her slim face, they gave her a certain lost look. Suddenly she seemed to become aware of where she was. She gave me a frightened look, half startled. I asked her again to sit down, firmly but softly. I knew now that her heart was sorely troubled. But she certainly wasn't possessed by any spirit, evil or otherwise. Her grief lay deep within her.

Nervously wrapping her saree pallav around her slight shoulders, she took a chair. She now seemed to have shifted her gaze from the painting and looked with a fixed stare at some crystal objects on my table. I asked her to lay her hands, palms up, on the table. I took up my athame and laid the cool blade without an edge, on the pulse point at her wrist. She gazed down at it and slowly something within her seemed to quieten. She looked up at me and there was stark despair written in her dark eyes. I took the triangular chunk of rock quartz and positioned it on her left. But I knew the comfort — if any comfort could come at all — would have to come from me and the strength within me. Otherwise she was lost in a terrain from where one did not return.

'Tell me when you came to Calcutta,' I said.

'Yesterday,' she replied tonelessly.

'You were looking at that painting behind me. Do you like it?'

'Was I? Maybe at the mountains in the background. I don't know.'

'Do you paint yourself?' I asked.

'No.' There was silence for a few minutes while she kept staring down at her hands, small, delicate, with well-manicured clean nails.

'Your husband wants you to talk to me. Do you know why?' I asked.

'Yes. He thinks I have gone mad after the death of the child.'

I did not think he had told her about his theories regarding possession. I looked with eyes half closed at the area around her. There seemed to be a grey haze. But something was becoming clearer. A child's form. A very small child, smiling. It had come for a few weeks to this life and had returned to a higher power. At the moment it was perfectly happy. But I was not a medium. I had other investigative work to do. For instance, what was wrong with this young woman? I was sure she would have other children. I knew it. But she was unable to remove a certain darkness around herself. A blackness. Was it guilt? What had she done? No. That was impossible. I looked at her. She was now holding up her right hand towards me. The gold bangles interspersed with a few green glass ones tinkled on her wrists. Suddenly she cried out, 'Do you have the power to help me forget? I want to forget everything in my life that has happened till now. Make my mind like a blank paper.' A 'kora kagaz' she said in Hindi.

I was seeing more. A young woman bending over a cradle. A child crying. A mother's hand reaching out to snuff the life out of her daughter. That hand, soft and fair with the tinkling gold and glass bangles.

I knew now what it was that Sushma wanted to forget. Why the distracted faraway look. The grief. The intolerable guilt and grief. But why had she done what she had done? Only she could tell me. And then, I would have to heal her with unspoken thoughts. Bring defiance and truth to a lacerated heart. In the meantime, I kept on talking to her. Talk she could relate to at the moment.

'Forgetting is not the real answer, is it, Sushma,' I asked. 'Other people were also to blame for what you did.'

She looked up at me with a look of something almost like relief after days of torture. Like taking a gulp of cool, clear water after miles and miles of relentless desert.

'Didi,' she whispered, 'but I did it. Only it is true, they made me go insane. I was myself and yet it wasn't me. I don't know what sort of monster had come into me. But I couldn't have been mad because I knew what was happening. I knew ....' she cried.

'It was some abnormal pressure on you, Sushma,' I said. Suddenly I glanced down at her hand clenched tightly now, on the table. The fingers seemed to be covered in a red haze. I knew how she had done it. But now the floodgates seemed to have opened. She wept at last and talked through her tears.

'From the time that I came as a bride, everybody, my mother-in-law, my sisters-in-law, my husband, all said that I must prove my worth by giving birth to a child — a boy — within two years of marriage. Otherwise, I would be thought to be unlucky for the house. This was the test. My ability to give them an heir. When I became pregnant they all were so happy. My husband said that his father had once told his mother, after the birth of two daughters, his elder sisters, that if there were any more girls he would have to take another wife. Her sister had been lined up for the purpose. Luckily my husband had been born, and so she was saved.' She gasped, as if choking for lack of air.

I finished her story for her. I could see it quite clearly. 'But you had a daughter. They must have made life miserable for you. Your husband must have made his disappointment quite clear.' She hung her head. 'They looked at me with such pity and contempt. My mother-in-law talked within my hearing of other proposals they should have taken for my husband.'

'So, one night when the baby was crying too much, and you were ragged with fatigue and frustration, you lost yourself for a few minutes, Sushma. Is that what happened?'

She broke into sobs. 'I want to forget. Just forget. How can I go on otherwise?'

'But you will go on. We all have to. As long as we are destined to. Here, keep your hand in mine and gaze into that crystal pyramid.' Meekly, she did as I said and the grey clouds around her hands grew less.

The picture was in my mind now. Painful and excruciating. I could see Sushma, hair dishevelled, eyes red with tears and lack of sleep. Distraught with fear about her future and the child's. Reaching out to quieten the child and then the index finger is stuffed in, deep into the baby's throat until the crying stops.

She was speaking quietly now as if from a distance, 'Afterwards, I phoned the police. But they turned away from what I told them. They wouldn't arrest me. Said I was mad. My in-laws are influential people, they didn't want any noise about it. The doctor said no enquiry was needed. Babies often suffocate in the cot by turning over and becoming helpless to breathe. Everybody said I was sick in the head. They sent me home to my parents for some time. Put me on tranquillizers. But I killed her. That's the truth.'

The crystal was flickering in the light. That was a promising sign. A sign of life. New life.

'But Sunil, your husband brought you back didn't he, Sushma?'

'Yes, after two months. He told his mother the madness was less. But I was never mad. For some point in time I had become cruel, heartless, a murderess. That's all there is to it,' she said matter-of-factly, without any emotion now.

I held her hand and let strong thoughts flow from my hand into hers. The broken battered spirit was banished into oblivion. She had to be renewed with courage and yes, defiance.

'You will have another child, Sushma,' I said.

She bowed her head. 'I am afraid. What if it is another girl?'

'You must let her return to you. You must make it up to her.'

The next year, Sushma's daughter was returned to her. Yes, I say, returned. When she telephoned to give me the news, she sounded strong and confident. The thoughts I had given her for truth and healing had become a part of her. I was glad. 'Sometimes life makes us do bizarre and horrible things, doesn't it?' she said. 'We can't afford to think about it too much. We have got to be strong, to go on living the best way we can.'

'You're absolutely right, Sushma,' I replied.

And then she said, 'And why should we always be the ones to blame, if God makes us do certain unspeakable actions? He is answerable too. And so is the society He has put me into. He must share the responsibility for my actions — both good and bad. I feel strong and free when I think that, didi. And I know I can go on living in this maze.'

'Are you happy with your daughter now, Sushma?' I asked.

'I am happy with what I have become. She has nothing to fear from me or anybody else. I can protect her,' the mother said with dignity.

I looked at the crystal on my desk and it glimmered in the evening rays of the sun. I was glad that that day, when Sushma had come to me in guilt and grief, I had been able to convey to her the right philosophy through the touch of my hand and the light from my crystal. What she had said to me over the phone was what I had once written in my Book of Shadows a long, long time ago.

'Should we live all our lives in guilt and God go scot free?'

**21**

# *The Witches of Purulia*

Those were the seasons of people, and more people. Their problems, their woes, their dreams, their frustrations, their maladies of body and mind, their hurting spirits, their damned and greedy souls. It confirmed my view that most humans — certainly not all — are searching not for spiritual healing and peace, but for material abundance — more, more and more. Their greed and hypocrisy was mindboggling — even to me. Once they realized that it was possible, through me, to acquire aspirations and attain ambitions, I was in danger of becoming a wish-fulfilling tree.

I had achieved what I had set out to do. I had proved that Wicca held power which could be invoked to grant genuine needs. That was enough for me. But now I had to deal with the never ending throngs of people who wrote me endless letters, full of what they considered their woes. The phone rang constantly till I had to appoint two secretaries to deal with calls and callers and mail. I still met people twice a week and with a practised eye sifted the genuine from the merely grasping. I suppose there was some good in me somewhere, because I helped those who were in pain — physical or spiritual. I tried to infuse the magic of true strength in the weak so that they would learn to bring about their own healing. I listened to the stories of actual distress from women who were struggling to exist in a world dominated by male harshness. I gave of myself and my art to those who were being battered by God and man.

But to those who came with outstretched hands, whining with hard-luck stories, I was callous and ruthless. I turned them away or else told them to their faces that it was doubtful whether their luck would ever change. I was no fortune-teller, but I enjoyed it when their faces fell in disillusionment. It was what they deserved. Sometimes, they would try the godwoman–disciple strategy, fall at my feet and with moist eyes plead with me to help them win some petty property dispute, a promotion or lucrative marriage proposal, someone else's husband, more money and above all, control and power. They put it more insidiously of course. Clothed in words which depicted their 'needs', they wanted 'justice' they said. Such is the human race. I watched them grovel, shorn of dignity and self-respect. Anything for worldly goods and worldly gain. I shrank from their touch when they stretched out their hands to touch my feet. I hated to be confused with a miracle-peddling godwoman or guru. I felt contaminated. My power had been given me by a Source which did not stoop to doling out favours to the greedy and ignorant.

Eventually, I decided to stop my sessions with people. I had learned what I needed to know about human nature — its weaknesses, its frailties, its vices and now and then, its nobility.

I am about to make a strange statement. It is this. I have discovered that it is interesting, sometimes exhilarating to deal with the vileness but startling and disturbing when you come across the good in human nature. Because it is so rare and thus unexpected. You can tease the covetous and taunt the lustful — but you cannot turn away from the genuine heartache, the wistful face, and stoical sorrow. In the beginning I tried to tell myself that it was all sham, that it was put on, in order to wheedle out a secret from me, a favour, the aura of my special energy. But somewhere in my being, I discovered that I had a heart after all. I could not turn away from eyes which pleaded for some magic in lives gone all wrong. If God had forgotten them, the witch could not.

※

That was how I decided to go to the villages of Bengal and Orissa — the interiors, which most city dwellers chose to read about, not to visit. The roads were mere tracks, strewn with stones and white with dust. People lived in mud houses roofed with thatch and ate off the floor on large banana leaves. Their animals, as emaciated as they were, helped them tend sun-baked fields in summer and often did not live to see the next — monsoon floods having swept them away. Their bodies bloated and fetid, would float past when the water rose.

The summer that I went to Purulia, the sun blazed down and the temperature soared to forty-eight degrees celsius in the shade. That summer was a gruelling one. There would be no rains here — or so it seemed. A social welfare organization had asked me to accompany them to the rural areas of Bengal where there had been some cases of alleged witch-hunting. I was asked to talk to the women accused or to their nearest kin. My job was mainly one of counsellor and investigator.

The village panchayats were hostile and suspicious. They were glad to receive free medicines from the welfare workers but refused to let me talk to their women. What was my business, they asked. I said I could help them in learning vocational skills. They didn't need any, I was told. Cooking, scrubbing and child bearing and rearing was good enough for them. But it could help them to earn money, I tried. I would come to the village every day for ten days and work with them, and help them sell whatever they produced. Suddenly eyes glittered. Money? How much? Enough, I said. All right, one nasty looking old fellow said. But one of them would have to be present, when I talked to their women. No, I retorted. This was a private, womanly thing.

Slowly and with fear in their dark, defeated eyes, the women and girls came to see me. In twos and threes, stooped and furtive. Ever watchful of the men lurking just beyond the door of the hut where I had set up camp. I asked them their names and the names of their children. They replied in dialectical Bengali, a few in Hindi. They looked curiously at my hair and my saree. A child lifted the border to gaze at my feet. What sort of slippers did I wear? I was barefoot like them. That inspired confidence. I asked them if they would do some sewing work, like the stitching of kanthas or quilts. Their faces brightened. This was something they knew how to do. One or two said they could also embroider. I told them that the organization with which I was working would sell their work for them. They would also be given the cloth and thread to start work. They asked me why anybody should care about them. Did the organization have a motive? Was some politician behind it?

I said no. But I wanted to know more about their lives. I had heard that some months back, one of them had been accused of being a witch and was tortured and beaten to death by some men in the village. I was writing for a newspaper. They seemed to understand that. Fear darkened their eyes. But there was also anger — anger because they were afraid.

Very gradually, after the cloth and threads had been supplied and we had started sitting regularly in one of the little mud cottages, did I feel that I was making some progress with my goal. They started talking in little fragments and stray sentences about their lives. I took up a needle too and tried to learn from their fingers as they deftly wove their needles in and out of the quilts, bent over the cloth, watching me out of the corners of their eyes, when my unpractised fingers got the thread all knotted up or caused the lines of quilting to go quite crooked. Then they would burst out laughing, stop their own work and take turns in helping me unravel my mistakes, with the protective superiority a child would adopt towards a new friend. Were these the women being branded 'witches' by hostile menfolk? Did the men calling them that, really understand the meaning of the word? Were these shy, frail women, the so-called black magicians, who caused sickness amongst livestock and cast evil spells on neighbours' children?

As I worked on the sewing with my little group, Brajabala, a young mother, began sitting by me, very particular about saving her place next to me, to the chagrin and amusement of the others. She became the official bringer of my food — tasty little morsels and tid-bits from the meal she had cooked for the family in the morning and which she had saved to bring me for my lunch. I was working all the time, she said. Who would cook for me? I must take time out and eat. The act of kindness touched me. I realized the poverty they all struggled against. One more mouth to feed could mean a dent in the family budget for food. But Brajabala would come in every day with her little stainless steel bowl containing rice and two earthen vessels with lentils and a vegetable curry. She would keep them safely in a corner of the hut and we would all settle down to sew. The women came after having fed their families and having had their own frugal meals. I would have some biscuits that I carried with me in my suitcase, and a glass of tea before we began our work. But as midday came and the sun became a white hot plate outside, Brajabala would go to the well and bring cool water so that I could splash it over my hot and dusty face and hands before I started my lunch. The other women would sit around me and watch with sisterly pride while I ate. One old woman remarked that it would be a disgrace to them if I went back to the city as thin as when I had come. I glanced up from my banana leaf plate and looked at her, smiling at her concern. She put a paan in her mouth and intently watched the quickly diminishing pile of cooked rice in my bowl. When I returned from washing my hands she handed me a small, green paan, with a toothless grin.

How did the men take all this? I knew they were waiting for me to leave. It was only the thought of the money that would be paid out at the end of ten days, that kept them quiet. One of the first rules they had made was that no money was to be given to the women. But they suspected that that was exactly what I would do if I got the chance. And so they waited and watched with wary, narrowed eyes, ready to pounce on their womenfolk's earnings when the time came.

When I had just another two days to go, I collected all the quilts, now painstakingly finished. Some of the women had embroidered borders of little flowers and birds in red and blue thread on their quilts. Simple, untrained needlework but beautiful in its sincerity. The women folded up the fruits of their labour and a few went to the local paan shop to get some string and newspaper in which to wrap it. Brajbala sat quietly at my side, pensively patting her child to sleep. There was a satisfaction in the air at a job well done, and anticipation at the prospect of first earnings, even though it would go to husbands and brothers. But there was sadness that I would soon be leaving. Many came to me with small gifts they had made for me, palm leaf fans with threadwork, little clay animals and cloth pouches decorated with beads. This was the time to ask them.

'Brajabala', I said, 'last month, was one of you called a witch?' The word I used was 'dayani' — Bengali for witch. She started and turned to me with horror filled eyes. 'No, didi,' she stuttered, casting a frightened look at the door of the hut to see if anyone was listening. 'Nobody here is a dayani. We are god-loving. We worship Shiva. Please do not say such things.'

'It was in the papers. I thought you might know,' I persisted. 'There's nothing to be afraid of. The witches of olden times were learned women. They were goddess worshippers. They were like doctors and wiser than the panchayat men.'

I could see Braja's natural respect and affection for me was battling with a long and ingrained fear of what would happen if the men found out what we were talking about. Some of the others had also quietly gathered around and sat as if to shield us from the wrath that was sure to descend when the village leaders came to know what I had asked and what Braja had said.

'We have done no wrong, didi.' Braja looked ashen through her copper, tanned skin. 'Last month, Phuli had some sickness. That is all.'

'Where is she now?' I asked.

The women shifted uneasily. Some began to get up and leave. But Braja stayed where she was. 'She's dead, didi.'

'How did she die?'

'She did some black magic on Bina's husband. He left her and went away. Phuli was a widow. Everybody said she was jealous of Bina. So she did her dayangiri to make Bina's man leave her.'

'Do you believe that?' I asked the few who were now sitting around me as if turned to stone.

'Didi, these things happen,' Braja said softly. 'Please don't talk anymore about it. The men will say you are a dayani too if they find out.'

'Let them say what they want, Braja. I am a dayani. But look at me. I am not afraid of anybody. I do not believe in superstitions.'

Braja covered her ears. A few others giggled with fear. By now the string and paper had been brought. But the women were no longer to be left alone. Two men had come to the door and stood there glowering, waiting to collect the earnings. They had also been listening to our conversation.

Braja and the old woman who had fed me paan saw them at the same time. The old woman made a move as if to cover me. Braja sat stock still. 'So you are a dayani?' said one of the men. 'No wonder our women are so fond of you. What are you teaching them? How to poison their husbands, so they can take away the land and money?'

There was silence for a split second. I rose to my feet and went forward. 'If you talk to me like that, I shall really show you what witchcraft is about,' I said. I spoke softly. The man stepped back a pace. 'I'll tell the others,' he shouted as he ran into the afternoon. The other followed.

'Oh didi, go away quickly,' Braja cried. 'Tell your friends to leave. Your car will travel quickly. These men are so bad when they are angry.'

'Tell me something, Braja. Then I'll go. Who was Phuli?'

Braja spoke quickly in an effort to make me go. 'She was a young woman, didi. It was not her time to die. She was very beautiful but her own family was really poor. They were in debt because of her brother's drinking. So she was married to old Jaroo Ruyiya, because he had a lot of land and owned cattle. But he died last year of old age. She had no children. Her own family took some money from her and went away. She was alone then. She spent a lot of time praying to the gods to help her. But no one heard her, I suppose. Bina's husband tried to molest her. She fought him and bit his hand. He told the village panchayat that she was a witch. He had proof of it.' Braja had been speaking without a pause. She stopped now. I understood the rest.

'After she was stripped and beaten, her body was quickly burnt so that the devil which had possessed her would be destroyed,' Braja finished her narrative, now in a voice without emotion.

'What happened to her property?' I asked. 'Her husband must have left his land to her.'

'Yes,' the old woman said. 'She was a rich widow. But after her death, the land and small brick house she lived in, were cleansed and now the local boys' club holds its meetings there. Her nearest relation was her husband's cousin — the man you saw just now. He has agreed to take it over from next month. He will rent it out. He says not many people would willingly rent such a house.'

This was just one case of the 'wicked witch' in rural Bengal. There were many others. History somehow always repeats itself — or perhaps it is that the basest in human nature lives on. The men who tortured and burnt innocent women in medieval Europe, live on in other places, in different guises. Witch-hunting never stopped. It just took on a more deceptive mask. Of course, in my experience with thousands of women who have come to me for help, I would say that every strong woman is a witch and she is always hunted. It goes against the nature of most men to tolerate a woman they cannot dominate. Witch-hunting is present not only in rural Bengal, Bihar, Orissa, Uttar Pradesh or Madhya Pradesh. It prevails everywhere in the world where women stand up for themselves and what they believe in. It is there whenever women refuse to be the pawns or playthings of a callous society.

## 22

## *The Toast of the Town*

My story would not be complete without an account of my encounters with what people generally refer to as 'high society' — all the spicy, juicy, rib-tickling episodes that played themselves out in the drawing rooms of Calcutta, Delhi and Mumbai.

From the time that the media took Wicca to be a novel cup of brew and started featuring me in glossy colour on their pages, I began to be courted by the rich and famous. And I would be a hypocrite to say that I minded. This was one more way to observe the reactions of the human zoo, to have a few laughs at the expense of those on the other side of the tracks.

Of course, never for a moment do I deny that I came from the plush side of the tracks as well. I even had blue blood in my veins. But I was the non-conformist who had broken all the rules.

I retained my entrée into the homes of the upper crust because I had 'background', a foreign education and enough money in the bank. I had married a high ranking IRTS officer and was entitled to a bungalow and a peon, I spoke English with the correct accent and my hair was done by a hair-dresser known only to the stars and celebrities. I vacationed at the right places and stayed at hotels with the correct number of stars. I had made a mark in the correct political party. Besides which it was rumoured that people from the highest rungs in political and other circles, had not only expressed an interest in my work but had taken a definite liking to me. Who could ask for more impeccable credentials?

Why is it that the more money people have, the more they want? The greed for material possessions that rocks the so-called upper classes, is astounding. They eat, drink and sleep money — when they are not thinking of the opposite sex and sometimes their own. Their little aberrations, their fetishes and perversions would fill a book if I chose to tell all I know. I cannot mention names, for obvious reaons, but it is hard to pick and choose from such a wide array of bizarre and sinful pleasures, and their perpetrators. Ego, vanity, greed and lust — these are the essential ingredients which come bubbling to the surface when the high society brew is stirred. I do not mind the sin, but I do mind the grossness.

Actresses from Mumbai want magic mantras to seduce the husbands of others. The wife of an industrialist wants my help in keeping her husband's mistress happy. Is there any Wiccan ritual which will please the younger and better-looking secretary, so that she does not make a demand for marriage? The wife was once an air hostess and I believe when she was young, she had an earthy voluptuousness. Now she is fat, ageing, and has an unpleasant aggressiveness about her. She does not particularly care where her husband strays as long as she officially runs his home and shares his bank balance and other assets.

Then I am assailed by the erstwhile Rani of a prominent northern Indian state, who wants me to stir the cauldron so that her daughter does not run off with the chauffeur. Difficult daughters are to be found even in the highest echelons of society. The Rani comes to my apartment in Delhi late one evening, trailing chiffon and whiffs of French perfume. Her long, dyed hair is in a plait. I had met her for the first time a few evenings earlier at a dinner in Defence Colony where, I suspect, I was invited almost as a guest of honour so that she could be introduced to me. I feel sorry for her plight but I really want her to leave. My intuition tells me that the bond is strong, and her daughter is already married to the aspiring commoner. The Rani wants him eliminated. She looks offended when I laugh out loud. She takes out a handkerchief and puts on a sad expression but there is a steely look in her eye as she whimpers, 'I have done so much for her. Sent her to the best boarding schools. Now she won't listen to me at all. And her poor father. He has had a heart attack because of all this.' It is true the Raja had looked a bit bemused when I had met him the other day. But I feel he is handling the situation better. He really doesn't mind whom his daughter takes as husband. In the long run, all sons-in-law are the same when the daughter is an heiress. I agree with his attitude.

The Rani finally finds solace in the arms of a young air force officer. Her daughter gets married with pomp and splendour. The son-in-law is elevated from chauffeur to something more respectable. Now, he is on good terms with both mother and daughter. There is peace. Comparative peace.

In Calcutta, it is the well-endowed Marwari matrons or else the company-wallahs who are constantly on the phone. The wives of a certain multinational company, took to frequenting my flat in Calcutta some years back. They came not together, but individually. Each said that it was crucial she meet me alone. And each had problems. The top boss' wife was exporting crafted silver to the US and making a packet, I was told by one of the director's wives. Could there be something illegal in the operation? Could she be shipping out drugs, hidden in those silver elephant leg tables? Why was the top boss in England last week? If I could get to the bottom of it, I could help her husband to make it to the big chair. I said I could but I wouldn't. This did not deter the lady. She invited me to one of her parties, just so I could meet the crowd. She was keen that I size up the others and tell her the inner, gory vibes I was receiving.

I knew I should refuse the invitation if I wanted to end all truck with them, but the temptation to see the corporate menagerie up close was too great. I disliked her husband, the director, on sight. He was an overbearing, cunning-looking man with shifty eyes who kept on staring at me when he thought I wasn't looking. He was afraid of me for what I might 'see', and I knew he had plenty to hide. His wife took me on a guided tour of their large, well-furnished flat. As we passed their bedroom, she whispered in a conspiratorial tone, 'Guess what's in that steel almirah.' I looked at the piece of furniture set in an alcove and shook my head. 'My husband keeps stacks of cash there. He's a whiz at multiplying money. He's a genius at stocks. He'd like to talk to you.'

'But I know nothing about the stock market,' I protested.

'You don't have to. He'll just tell you certain names. You say what feelings you get from the names,' she instructed.

The corporate world obviously lived in style. The long buffet tables on the patio were piled with rolled salmon, roasted duck and mounds of strawberries, frosted with sugar and glistening with fresh cream. My host took me aside during dinner and tried to bring up the names of certain companies where he intended to buy. I deliberately fed him the wrong ones and made a quick getaway. I believe he later told his wife I was a 'crook'. Some years later the company found itself in a lot of trouble, and the big bosses, my good host included, were put on trial. I wonder what happened to his shares — and the steel almirah with all that cash.

Once when I was in Calcutta, a society called the Ladies' Study Group invited me to deliver a lecture on Wicca. The study group turned out to be a gathering of rich, bejewelled women. One didn't need to be a witch to see the boredom in their lives. They wanted some thrills. I complied. I even demonstrated some common psychological magic tricks, practised by Wiccans of old, to get the attention of their audience. The ladies nearly swooned. They had come prepared to be scared. After all, popular Hindi horror serials on television had taught them that witchcraft meant skulls and bones and candles in a dark room. Then, when I knew I had them spellbound, I started talking about what Wicca really was. This much I must acknowledge — they listened with awe, mouths agape. The prescribed one hour stretched into one and a half, and still they wanted more. They had never had another speaker who had so dazzled and yet so confounded them. They talked about their experience all over town.

A few days later, some of the ladies phoned me and asked if I would visit their houses. Why, I asked. They had told their industrialist husbands all about me, they said. Now as it happened, their husbands were having some business problems. Could I help them? What were my charges? To hell and back, I said and hung up.

Midway through this hectic social whirl I nearly got a complex. I felt I wasn't loved for myself, only for what I could divine, for what I could solve, for what I could give. I consoled myself with the thought that after all, I was having the most fun — at their expense. But still, I wondered if I wasn't having to sing for my supper. I decided to play dumb for a bit.

He was a Rajya Sabha member with a husky voiced wife, who chain-smoked and wore tight stretch pants. The capital's glitterati vied for an invitation to one of her parties because her special man friend was a former prime minister. She still did some social work on his huge farm and was generally very much a high flyer.

Soon after I met her, she invited me to a ladies' dinner at her beautiful, very expensive apartment in the city. She had invited six or seven others from her intimate circle of women friends. I was the first to arrive, being a stickler for punctuality but as each woman arrived, I was introduced in the most flattering terms by my hostess. 'Ipsita is a legend in her own lifetime,' she announced when finally we were all seated. Chairs were drawn closer round the circle and a hush fell over the room. All eyes were on me. I sipped my fresh lime and water as I read the thoughts around me. I had got such a build up, I knew there had to be a price to pay.

'Now, Rajni,' said my hostess turning to the woman sitting on her left, 'ask Ipsita anything you want to know. She has a fantastic intuition. She can actually see what's happening to you.'

Before I had time to protest, Rajni, with two husbands behind her and an export business in trouble was practically eye ball to eye ball with me.

'Ipsita, I want you to see whether my ex-husband plans to marry the girl he's going around with.'

'Rajni,' I protested, 'believe me, that's not in my line.'

'Oh, please, Ipsita. You can see if you want to. I've read so much about your powers.'

'Why won't you let your husband be, Rajni? After all, he is your ex. You are involved with someone too.'

'Oh,' she gasped, 'you saw that? Please tell me, will he leave his wife? She's a bitch, you know. Just because she has all the money, she throws her weight around. But you saw this man, no? You knew at once I was seeing someone.'

'No, my dear, I guessed that.'

Rajni quivered between a frown and a smile. She didn't know what to make of my remark. She decided to ignore the sarcasm. 'Her husband is unhappy with her but he enjoys the perks too much. It's so unfair. And he's such a hypocrite. He sees me but goes back for the luxury to that bitch.'

'But you're pretty well off too, Rajni,' I said. 'I am sure he enjoys life with you too.'

'Oh, do you see that?' She turned to my hostess. 'Oh, Ipsita is amazing.'

By this time I decided to close my eyes and take a little rest from this circus. It worked.

'Sshh,' my hostess husked. 'Now she's seeing things. Let her talk.'

There was silence except for the occasional clink of glasses or the wheezy sound of a cigarette being inhaled. I threw my head back against the upholstered headrest of my sofa and smirked to myself. The quiet felt good. I was nearly dozing off when there was a soft padding sound and my hostess' dog, a lovely golden retriever, lumbered in and with great devotion started licking my toes. I came out of my reverie with a jolt. At first, in shock I wondered if Rajni or anyone in the milieu had gone a bit too far. Then, I realised it was the dog. I closed my eyes again and kept from giggling. Everyone was urging him in whispers to go away but the dog, bless him, knew by instinct that I loved him and refused to budge. I opened my eyes slowly and returned from far away. Turning to Rajni, I murmured, 'Ah, yes. You were asking me something.'

'Please Ipsita. Will he leave her and come to me?' she pleaded.

I think only the dog understood that I was having a lark. He jumped up playfully and licked my face. 'Yes. But first his wife must have a dip in her career. As long as she keeps on bringing in the money, he won't leave her.' I think the dog snorted. Or maybe it was a laugh. 'But you were asking me about your ex-husband's girlfriend,' I helpfully reminded her.

'Yes, yes. What will happen there?' she said eagerly.

'The time will come when both the men will want only you, Rajni,' I said.

'You know, you're so right. A famous tarot reader I went to in London, told me the same thing. Oh, Ipsita, when will you come to my house? I want to show you the pictures of these two bastards. Can you make them crawl before me? Huh?'

But my kind hostess broke in. 'Come on, Rajni. Time up. You're monopolizing Ipsita. Now it's Tara's turn.'

I was saved by the ringing of the phone. My hostess went to answer it. After a few minutes' cryptic conversation, she turned back to us with a smug smile. 'Hands up, those who want to come with me to see him at the farm tomorrow. We'll have a picnic. He'll be there.' She spoke with a magnanimous air. She was sure of him, the famous man friend. He looked at no other woman when she was around. Unknown to her, he had consulted me about his chances of a comeback two days ago over a relaxed and friendly lunch at his house.

'Ipsita, you must come. We'll have a really good time. And you know, I think he'll be very pleased to meet you. He has a tremendous leaning towards the spiritual,' my hostess said.

'Oh, that would be lovely, but I'm sure your picnic needs no witchcraft to spice it,' I smiled lazily. 'And then, of what use are former PMs? You live too much in the past, darling. Wicca loves present prospects.'

The ladies giggled. My hostess gave me a suspicious glance. The dog rolled over. I hid a smile and bent down to tickle his tummy.

---

Somehow, the well-heeled set just won't accept the fact that I am not interested in foretelling their prickly futures. It is true I have done it at times, but for me it has been like a parlour game, done mainly to amuse myself. The future is best left in the hands of Isis. Why meddle with the future when the present has a lot to offer if you don't have to worry where your next meal is coming from? Where the petulant and the pampered are concerned, my patience runs dangerously low, but I credit myself with the fact that I have never revealed the secrets of one to the other or used them to cause friction between two people. At times important individuals have cajoled or threatened me — reveal or be damned. I've preferred damnation. I'm more familiar with that word. In the meantime, the secrets entrusted to Wicca remain in safekeeping.

Like the time the ambition ridden wife of a certain, very important politician from the eastern part of the country developed the habit of dropping in at my flat in Delhi. She would only say she was starved and while waiting for the food to arrive, ask for a jar of my most expensive cold cream, open the lid and start lathering her legs with it. 'Delhi winters are so dry,' is what she'd say by way of explanation. One day she burst in tight-lipped and furious. She wore a blue printed silk saree and her normally perfectly coiffed hair was dishevelled.

'Well, what did you think of it, Ipsita? Dropped. Absolutely dropped. I think it was on his wife's advice that he did it.' I knew what she was referring to for it had been in the papers that morning that her husband had not been included in the newly formed Cabinet. But I pretended not to follow. 'Who's dropping are you referring to, Chitra?' I asked innocently. 'My husband's, of course. His dropping. He waited and waited to be called but no, no call from Rashtrapati Bhavan for the oath-taking. Can you imagine it?' she ranted. 'How can the government run without my husband? This new idiot in the PM's chair knows nothing. His wife is an upstart. My husband was the best candidate for PM. But he gave it all up for this chap and now look what he goes and does.'

'Maybe one should just watch and wait for sometime,' I said.

'And then what? With people like these you have to be aggressive. Give it to them.'

'How do you propose to do that, Chitra?' I queried.

'That's why I've come to you, Ipsita. You must know black magic. I want you to finish them.'

'You mean eliminated, of course,' I said as matter-of-factly as I could. Obviously, Lady Macbeth still lived on, I thought to myself.

'Can it be done?' she looked at me hopefully.

'Evil done has a habit of boomeranging, Chitra. You wouldn't want anything to happen to me of course?' I looked at her with large, trusting eyes.

'Nothing will happen. Just do whatever needs to be done,' she persisted.

'Chitra, when you ask for something like this, you have to make a sacrifice. What will you sacrifice?'

'Why should I have to sacrifice anything? What kind of a witch are you? I just want them removed and my husband in power,' she said angrily.

Then a light suddenly seemed to dawn in her eyes. 'Well, I will pay something of course. How much do you want? Will a thousand do?'

'Their lives are cheap, I'd say,' I said with a smile. She missed the point. 'Oh yes. They're worth nothing. When shall we do the ritual?'

Finally, I could play the game no longer. I looked at her and my eyes narrowed. 'Your husband will never be prime minister, Chitra,' I said. 'So forget it.' I knew this would hurt the most. 'What kind of a low woman are you? And how dare you come to me with such a proposition?'

'So you won't do it?' she asked, nearly shouting. 'I've always suspected you're a hoax. You don't have the power. I'll get back at you,' she spat out. 'Remember your husband is in government service.'

'Yes, Chitra, you're right. I don't have the power. And you know something? Sometimes I get very tired. Weary of you all. Is there no end to your greed? Your viciousness? Just let me be. Leave me alone.'

She left. I opened the window and let the cold, clear air sweep in. It cleansed the room of her presence. I closed my eyes for a moment and when I opened them again I was strong. The room was chilly and aloof.

Today, I hear, she has become a bit strange in the head and can hardly get around anymore. I am told that she hates me with a fierce venom. But I must tell the story of how this vicious madness played itself out, and how sometimes the unbearably vicious can become unbearably funny.

Soon after her descent on me, her husband came to visit me one evening in winter, muffled in a fur cap and overcoat.

'Ipsita,' he started off, ponderously, 'I know you have certain powers. Of course we all have abilities but you may have developed your skills a bit more than others. Now, are you able to do something I ask?'

'What?' I asked.

'Work some magic so that the PM should be attracted to me,' he ordered.

'Attracted to you, did you say?' I asked, my lips half quivering with laughter. 'But in what way do you mean?'

'Any way. I am not particular about that. But he must take me into the Cabinet.'

I couldn't resist this. The witch in me bubbled over with mirth. I dived into a few drawers and took out some old papers and pored over them. They were some Wiccan love spells and chants.

'Here are the words of attraction, sir,' I told him. 'Say them thrice every morning. Keep his photograph before you. Then kiss a red rose and throw it into the garden.'

'It will work? You're sure about that?' my scorned politician asked me.

'It's worked for women in love. It should do its stuff for you too,' I said with a straight face. He took the spells and left.

Now, strange as it may sound, he and I have a lot in common. We both fancy power. The only difference is, I play with it. It is my lackey. While he kisses ass for it.

# 23

# *Sweet Revenge*

Revenge is always sweet. Anyone who says it isn't, has either never tasted its heady wine and honey or else is being a flat-footed hypocrite. I have never gone too far out of my way to bring grief to anyone for big or small wrongs done to me. I haven't had to. I have merely taken note of what has been said or done and then, inevitably, after a while, and not too long a while either — I have with regret, not rejoicing, seen many a guilty one bite the dust. I generally lose interest in my foes. It's much, much later, when I come across the shattered pieces of what used to be the grand edifice of my adversary, that I remember the dastardly deed he had tried to perpetrate against me, the vile words spoken or the wormlike intentions. And by that time, it usually is too late — for him, that is.

Many are the incidents that come to mind, of foes once mighty, now fallen in the dust. Poor mites. I tried to impress upon them the fact that elemental Wiccan power brooks no opposition and tolerates no base and petty stabbing in the back. They did not believe me, and so they had to pay. Does that sound sinister? It should not. These are the basic laws of nature that surround us and with which I am aligned. When somebody deceives or betrays me, I shake my head and know that one ill-intentioned deed or action has set in motion a hundred elemental forces of retribution. A child of Wicca is protected by the winds and waves and fires of a pristine justice which has nothing to do with our man-made sense of morality and social norms of right and wrong.

Sometimes I take a fancy to somebody. I like the way he speaks or the way he tries to please me. Or it may be a woman — someone who professes friendship. But then comes the greed or the insincerity or the hidden motives which I had chosen not to notice before. And I know that Wicca must strike as surely as an asp with which played the fair fingers of the beautiful Cleopatra.

How are the guilty brought low? On these pages I hesitate to write lest someone read them and thus come to possess knowledge which is essentially mine. But I may perhaps divulge, before other things come to occupy me, some cases of those who lost their ill-gotten power, others their wealth, money and vanity. Some came to strife with family and friends. A few were made ridiculous in the eyes of the world which they held in such high esteem. The curious have often asked me, is this what voodoo is all about? I have replied that I do not understand the names which are used to frighten people. I have never practised voodoo. But I have looked into the eyes of a liar. I have seen the darkness which creeps up in a man from a lack of inner courage and I have witnessed the writhings of greed and lust battle for a man's soul — and win. But not for long. I say this with the confidence born of one who has seen for herself the workings of a strange power.

Of a few, I have already spoken. Ranjit lost out in the end.

He became a wreck in every sense, his health, wealth and peace all having deserted him. There was nothing I could do about it, even had I wanted to. And I did not. I hope he has found some solutions to his problems now — in the dimension beyond. I do not wish to meet him again.

The others of my kith and kin who had tried to harm me in those early days, lost the battle long ago. I can hardly recall their names today.

Through the years, I have become aware of a strange fact. Wicca will not be denied. Those who come to me for help and then claim that they overcame all hurdles on their own, generally come to regret their arrogance. Those who deny that they have received my help, do not make such an ill-advised statement a second time. I do not eagerly proffer my aid, but if I do so, I insist that it be acknowledged and not denied or abused. Woe be to him or her who does so.

※

He was a prominent politician of Orissa. The fates had treated him well. He was well-liked by the populace and had reached a position of power. That summer, I was in Puri reviving myself and restoring my energies in the sea. I always go to the Elements when I wish to fill a cup depleted. The politician, who had seen quite a few summers, got to know that I was there and drove down from the adjoining town, the capital of Orissa, to see me at the BNR Hotel where I was staying. I greeted him with cordiality for my father had once helped him, long ago, when he was a struggling aviator. He sat with me on the beautiful, vine-covered verandah of the grand old building that houses the BNR, and asked me of many things as we sat listening to the sea. I told him I knew not of fortune telling but I wished him well. The sea responded with a roar — or maybe a warning.

After that meeting, he came to see me a second and then a third time, driving those long miles to Puri in order to take of my power. He said he felt the mind could focus when he talked to me and he asked for my advice. On one of his visits, he told me he had a yen for some fish freshly caught from the sea. I ordered the fish to be caught and cooked, and he ate it with relish, sitting on the verandah with the breeze playing over him. Many journalists came to know of his frequent visits and were curious. They plied me with questions but I kept silent. His affairs of state were his own. They were not for me to talk of.

That year was one of political turbulence but he fared well. Then the folly struck. A few months after he had been settled in his seat, some journalists, who had probably got to know of his visits to me, happened to ask if he had ever taken the advice of Wicca — and he taken by surprise, poor fool, said no. To make matters worse for himself, he said, or so it was reported, that I had offered him advice but he had refused it. I knew that that was the beginning of the end for him. The decline began within a few months. First his asthma began to grow worse and his energy levels fell. Then his own men in the party, started revolting against him and he began to make all the wrong moves. Finally, he lost his power and his seat. I had really thought him to be more intelligent. He should not have offended me.

Then there is the case of the actress in Mumbai whose name I will keep secret because in this country, they know her well. Like many others in her profession, she suffers from a fear that as she grows old, she will lose her charms. And then what? The people, who applaud her attributes of body and face will love her no longer, she complained to me over the phone late one night. When she was alone, the fear was worse, she said. So she tried never to be completely alone. She wanted my help. What she was actually asking of me was this. Not peace of mind. But a way to stop the clock. A way to freeze beauty so that the scars of the years would never show. That's the way people are. They demand the impossible from me. She never once considered what she was asking for. Was she so foolish that she did not know that the body and its muscles and sinews and flesh and skin will undeniably, one day, give way and shrink and shrivel and be consigned to the Elements?

The man or woman of power and wisdom, overcomes the threats of the body and goes his way with dignity and a certain arrogance. But all are not strong. This actress was very ambitious. She had risen high and was endowed with talent. Her personal life was lonely but she intended to set that right. She loved a man who was pledged to another woman and had children. But that did not deter her, and who was I to set her right? And the man, caught up in his own vanity, said he loved her in return but refused to end his marriage. He met her frequently, away from the eyes of his wife and the world thought that surely one day he would take this actress as wife too. Some of his peers in the world of celluloid make-believe, had already done that, taken a second wife — and she was hopeful. If she could somehow attain the second position, she had no doubt she could climb to the first. In the meantime, it was essential that she maintain and preserve the looks with which nature had endowed her. Her youthfulness must not fade. The roses should not leave her cheeks.

I told her to go elsewhere — to a surgeon of cosmetic arts, who would make taut the chin and firm the breasts. She said she already had — twice. Now, the tightened skin was starting to give her an unnatural look and alter the expression. No, she was determined to have my help. She had heard that the ancient and secret arts of Wicca, knew how to capture forever the lure of youth and the lustre of the hair and eyes. I looked at her and wondered at her greed. But I admired her for being able to know the difference between the youth bestowed by the cosmetic surgeon's knife and that which was promised by Wicca and the Elements. She wanted the secret formula.

I told her that we would meet after three months and I would consider.

Three months later, she called me again. This time, I agreed to see her. She said she had lost all peace of mind. The fatigue and unrest showed on her face. Beneath the creamy skin foundation, the dark lines of age and weariness were creeping in. Her eyes appeared sunken behind the fringe of false lashes. The hair, crimped too tightly, was half covered by a glittering scarf. The lips, outlined in scarlet, drooped disconsolately at the corners. I looked at her and felt a twinge of anger somewhere, deep down. This poor woman was a victim of a society that treats its players and performers like pretty dolls. There is no room here for genuine talent or worth. The skin must be forever taut, the figure ever lissom, the eyes ever shining. Youth is an obsession. No grace is attributed to the silver streak in the hair, the mellowed wisdom in a face made beautiful by the years of experience. The doll must never stop dancing. The merry-go-round of the flesh must never have rest.

The actress and I met quite a few times that year, not in Mumbai but in Delhi, where she had recently bought a well-appointed house. I would ask her to come to where I was staying and she would appear, muffled up in scarves and collars. It was lucky that it was cold in Delhi that winter. I taught her some of the ways in which to draw in energy from the earth, the ground beneath your feet, the air you breathe. She was already an adept at yoga and that helped her in assimilating what I had to teach her. I also taught her how to make the ancient brew from the buds of white roses, saffron and sandal. The concoction, steeped in crystal clear spring water, is kept in a hollow bowl of pure white rock quartz. It is splashed over face, shoulders and hands and applied to the pulse spots. This was a secret used in the ancient yogini temples of India and promised to preserve the body's energy and grace.

She was an apt student and soon profited from all she learnt. The damage done by the knife of the cosmetic surgeon, was much less apparent. The white roses had given some of their dew to her, and her natural glow returned. Her skin looked fresh once again and her hair began to recover its shine. She no longer kept it tightly combed back or covered with artificial curls and tresses but let it fall naturally around her shoulders. Above all, I noticed that she was more confident and ready to fight for what she thought worth having. I did not ask her about her private ambitions. I considered my work done.

But folly, alas, cannot remain in hiding. Back in Mumbai, her career started an upward climb. Her man, I read in the papers, was more than ever besotted by her. She was hoping, it was hinted, that he would leave home and hearth to be by her side. People wondered at her secret of perennial beauty. She just did not seem to age. But then she got into a tangle. Her plastic surgeon who resided in the US came down to India on a private visit. Word got around that he was the one who kept this screen goddess in good shape. The papers loved this bit of information and played it up. He was asked by journalists what the secret was. How had he managed to impart this spectacular look to the actress, now in her forties? She of course was livid and in panic. She wanted him to leave and go back home immediately. She called the press and dismissed the surgeon's statements as absurd. In fact, she disowned him completely, saying she had never met him. Her regular yoga regime, her careful diet, her inner calm, was responsible for her wonderful youthfulness. Then somebody suddenly asked her if she knew Wicca and if she was a witch. He was a journalist from a Delhi based paper. She went into a tizzy and retorted that the thought was preposterous. Of course she knew nothing of witchcraft or Wicca. She was completely the mistress of her own face and fortune. She was a special person. A chosen one. Nobody else had ever helped her achieve anything.

That was when she ruined the magic. Her man's love never culminated in any sort of deeper commitment. She kept on using the Wicca formula for beauty, but I do not feel it worked anymore, for during her frequent 'holidays' abroad, she had to visit the same cosmetic surgeon she had pretended not to know. Wicca had given her much but it would give her no more. Weakness and betrayal of this kind is not tolerated.

If any doubt me, do so at your own risk. Take not your chances with a power you do not understand. The Elements are not to be trifled with, especially after you have taken of their favours.

The third incident of Wicca revenge happened in the spring of 1998, during the twelfth Lok Sabha elections. It is a long story and involves many people. It seemed like a trifling thing when the wheels of wrong first started rolling. A petty prank perpetrated by a minor politician in a fit of rivalry against me. I had been asked to stand for the Congress party from the 27 Hooghly parliamentary constituency. Next door to me was the constituency of Serampur and then came Arambagh. All the three constituencies are part of the district of Hooghly and are often subject to confusion. That general election promised to be a wild and turbulent one in West Bengal. The Congress in West Bengal had just suffered a split leading to the emergence of the Trinamul as a separate political entity. The Congress workers were in disarray. Always a neglected lot, they now veered from this side to that in search of direction. Both sides campaigned vociferously but the common people were confused. Which was the real Congress, the poor, illiterate people of the villages, asked their local leaders and workers? There was chaos in Bengal. Betrayal and blackmail. Who was loyal, and to whom? It was hard to know. Political self-seekers, fishing in troubled waters swarmed around.

In the midst of all this, I was asked to take on the Hooghly constituency. I had worked with rural women and was known as a champion of their causes. The Congress was going through troubled times. I was never one to refuse a new experience, and so I agreed.

In the meantime, things had taken a sudden positive turn in the Congress party with the entry of Rajiv Gandhi's widow, Sonia, onto the scene. She agreed to campaign for the party and Congress workers all over the country heaved a sigh of relief. Now there would be an anchor. A person with popular charisma, who promised the return of the old ideals and values, which seemed to have been temporarily lost. Bengal looked forward to her visit to campaign for the party. The rally at the Brigade Parade Grounds in Calcutta, was a grand success. Sonia Gandhi spoke of why she had finally broken those long years of silence after the tragic death of her husband. Her love for the country she had made her own, and where she had spent long years as wife, mother and now widow — moved people to tears. She said that now she had nobody left but her children and the people of this country, who had given her so much love and affection. She had come now to do her duty by the party and the people, for whom her mother-in-law and her husband had sacrificed their lives. She recalled the affection Rajiv had always had for Bengal and his love for Bengal's famous sweet delicacy 'mishti doi'.

Sonia and I shared an understanding which was not based on politics. I admired her for maintaining her dignity in the murky milieu in which she found herself after Rajiv's death. Her detachment was obvious but not many understood it. Most people clamour for temporal power. Here was someone who was shying away from it. She seemed to want no position or chair — even when these things were being thrust upon her. She just wanted to be left alone with her children and her memories. When she finally entered the political arena it was because certain Congress leaders literally pleaded with her and painted a picture of a Congress torn and tattered, mauled and mutilated by a lack of direction and leadership. I think she also admired my non-attachment to power which came through in the course of our talks. I never asked her for anything — favours, or posts of power. When we had occasion to talk I would tell her about the craftsmen and women of Bengal, and show her the simple earthen crafts the poor village women I was working with, had sent her. I felt rewarded by her simple joy when she held the rough, clay lamps or toys in her hands. Once, when I gave her a clay diya, she said, 'I have never seen a lamp like this before'. It was a lamp with a shallow, false bottom which held water to cool the oil on the part above. As a result, the wick lasted longer and the flame burnt for many hours. Sonia Gandhi held it in her hand and put it on the table beside her. 'Ipsita, thank the woman who made it, and thank you for bringing it to me,' she said.

One day, while discussing the tribal people of Bengal and their customs, I showed her the crystal skull Carlotta had given me whose movements I had once demonstrated before my village friends. She looked with interest at it as it twirled before her eyes on her coffee table at No. 10, Janpath. 'My goodness,' she exclaimed as it did a little spin. She knew about my work and my research into Wicca, and my years spent in painting. What moved me was her simplicity and her open mind. As a Catholic, she could have been shocked by my name in 'witchcraft' but she wasn't. People said that her 'inexperience' in politics went against her — but I always felt that she had a shrewd insight into people. She understood me — the hard sides, the brittle sides, but also the side which cared for people, almost against my will. And that is the part of me which entered politics that spring when Sonia asked me to stand for elections from Hooghly.

In turn, I asked her to come to my constituency to speak to the people and she agreed. Her private secretary, Vincent George, said he would talk to the security personnel and the pilots about the course of her tour in West Bengal so that it included Hooghly. But petty rivalry and envy which had been brewing in the state unit for some time, started playing games with me. I suspected something was amiss and watched to see how far my own partymen would go in order to provoke me. As soon as her itinerary was announced, there was a scramble among Congress candidates to get her to visit their constituencies. I kept silent, wondering what the plans would be for Hooghly. Sonia kept her promise and included Hooghly on the itinerary, but unknown to her, those who were out to do mischief, manoeuvred things so that the plane would land not at my constituency but next door at Serampur, which technically was also Hooghly, being the district but not the constituency. It was a subtle deception. The leaders also chalked out a programme where she would visit a number of other neighbouring constituencies but completely ignored mine. When I found out, I did not protest. I waited for the day to come.

Arrangements were on in Serampur on a war footing. On the morning of Sonia's visit to South Bengal, there was tremendous excitement in the Congress rank and file. I had heard that the candidate in my adjoining constituency, Pradeep Bhattacharya, who was also then a general secretary of the West Bengal Pradesh Congress Committee had gone to considerable lengths to organize a rally which would impress all and sundry about the extent of his influence over the Congress leadership. I knew his efforts were childish and petty but I sympathized with those candidates, who through not having grovelled enough before certain powerful and vindictive state functionaries, had been overlooked in the scheme of the programme. Such is the cesspool of human nature when running the rat race. I could have contacted Sonia and warned her of what was happening but I knew that Wiccan revenge was at hand. I wanted to relish it.

All the past month and more, the weather had been perfect. Campaigning had been conducted under blue February skies, the sunshine had been pleasant on one's skin as one made one's speeches in little market squares in the old town of Chinsurah or in the green potato fields of Dhaniakhali. The wind was bracing on the face as the open jeep sped through the long and often bumpy roads of Polba and Haripal and Singur — the different segments of Hooghly. The sun would glint on the Ganges while I stood speaking at a street corner meeting in the beautiful little town of Chandannagore, and the people milled around waiting to give a bunch of flowers from their garden or some sweets from the local sweet shop.

But when I woke very early that morning of Sonia Gandhi's visit to Bengal, I knew that the powers were afoot. And they were about to show certain politicians that they were displeased. I had my usual frugal breakfast of porridge and a piece of toast and went and stood on the balcony looking onto the narrow lane in Dhopaghat, in Bansberia where I was staying. Streams of people were already winding their way towards the station on their way to Serampur. The polling was just a day away. Today was the last day for campaigning.

Somebody glanced my way and waved. 'Didi, we promised Pradeepda we'd go to his meeting for Sonia Gandhi today. Are you coming?'

'No,' I smiled.

'Why?' he asked confused.

'Well, for one, Pradeepda has not asked me to be present. The other reason is that you'll soon be back. We should wind up the campaigning in our own constituency.' The poor man smiled, nodded a bit vaguely, and walked on. I returned to my room and waited.

As the clock struck eight in the morning, the first mists started to rise from the grounds of Hooghly — my Hooghly. They rose in swirls and strips and waves. Then they covered the land of Serampur where Pradeep and his friend Abdul Mannan waited with mobile phones, for the message to come that Sonia's helicopter was on the way. The dias was large and decorated. The crowds from neighbouring areas started to pour in. The skies had suddenly lost their azure softness and turned a hard slate colour. It even began to drizzle in some places. But the startling thing was the fog. It came in layer after layer and would not leave. Serampur lay shrouded in its white and grey folds. My part of Hooghly was sunny and bright. I drove down to Dhaniakhali where scores of workers waited with posters and flags, to help me round up my campaign. I got the message from one of them, sometime in the afternoon. He had heard it from a friend who was coming back from Serampur. The rally had been cancelled. The pilots of Sonia's helicopter had refused to take the risk of landing in that fog shrouded area. In fact, Sonia had called off the entire itinerary scheduled for South Bengal.

I believe Abdul Mannan, one of the prime organizers from the West Bengal side, had been frantic with the phone, begging and pleading with his counterparts at Dum Dum to somehow get the helicopter off its wheels. But it was no use. Pradeep, it was reported had finally burst into tears because his victory depended on being able to show his clout with Delhi. Later on, when he lost, he acted like a bad sport and told me that Sonia Gandhi's proposed visit had done him more harm than good. It should never have been planned. I smiled. I usually did when another one bit the dust.

## 24

# *Some Witchy Diplomacy*

It was an afternoon in summer that Sonia Gandhi called me to see her at No. 10, Janpath. I entered the drawing room and found her engrossed in arranging some yellow flowers in a vase. She was wearing a printed cotton kurta and her brown hair was caught back by a hair band. It flashed through my mind that the flower stalks looked something like corn. Ruth amidst the alien corn. She had not yet entered politics formally but even then she seemed out of place, in a strange land, trying to cope.

Ram Lakhan, the young man who ushers people in to see her after they have been approved by Vincent George, had just received a bag of groceries at the door and handed them over to the concerned bearer. A long loaf of French bread and some vegetables were quickly hustled in. A tin of tomato puree had got held up in the X-ray machine and was handed in later. My instinct told me she missed the foods of home.

Why didn't she leave it all? I am sure she had the inner strength to have done so at one time, but I do not think it is possible any more. The people around her will not let her. Because as long as she is there, they have a say. As long as she is there, they are important. There is no doubt that she was devoted to Rajiv and still misses him. One can see that in her eyes. But I have always felt that she is trying to mould herself in the lines of her mother-in-law, Indira. She feels that there was the more successful politician. And today, she gives success a very high priority. So she tries to keep men and women around her who will do her bidding. She prefers it if they have no individual standing, or a base amongst the people. Perhaps she is right in doing this. It is a move which will keep her secure for a time. Popular leaders can wrest power from her but the losers and those without grassroots support cannot afford to rebel. Today she is afraid of rumblings which have started within her inner fold.

On her birthday, she had asked me to be present. I was there observing, as she went around the lawns, meeting well-wishers, favour seekers and curiosity addicts. It was December but the sun was hot and she was hard put to keep a smiling face. But with her two women aides, Archna and Anuradha close at her heels, she managed to do the right things. She patted the cheeks of one or two children and posed for photographs with them and was particular about cutting a cake with a Sikh group. That was before the BJP government fell and the Congress was left in the lurch by Mulayam Singh Yadav. And that was before the betrayals by three senior Congress leaders. That was before the Congress debacle at the hustings. After all these events, I think she is more determined than ever to hold on to her position in her party.

That is one change I have noticed in her. The detachment is no longer there. Even her closest aides say that her priorities have taken a beating. I do not think that that is for the best.

Power games should always be played with a bit of unconcern. That is the way to win.

There is one point on which I would like to set the record straight. I am not teaching her Wicca. I pick my own students. Nobody forces me to do anything.

If she has profited from any advice of mine, that is a totally different matter.

Like the time when the then Youth Congress president of Bengal, Paresh Pal, created a very sticky position for himself and the Congress party by indulging in acts of vandalism at the beautiful, old Victoria Memorial in Calcutta. A certain very rich NRI had rented the spacious lawns to hold a musical soiree to celebrate his son's wedding, having got the approval of the CPI(M) government. The next morning, Pal and his retinue arrived on the scene and created quite a furore, burning and damaging property. The public and the press did not take kindly to his actions. Certain influential and rich industrialists complained to Sonia, insisting that Pal be removed from his position. He was already in disgrace being well over the age of being considered an 'youth'.

When all human agencies fail, they come to me. The West Bengal PCC President, A.B.A. Ghani Khan Chowdhury, Barkatda to his friends, sent me an SOS. Could I meet him immediately at his 12 Akbar Road residence. Paresh Pal was his special protegé, and he had been summoned to Delhi to tender his resignation or else be thrown out by a very peeved and angry Sonia. Ghani Khan is an old man who had been in the political wilderness for many years. His memory is failing and he commits blunders. But he is devoted to his family, whose stranglehold he cannot seem to shake off. He looked flustered when I arrived. He called me into his sitting room and set out to explain to me as best he could why Pal should be retained. In his halting way, veering between Bengali and English he said that the boy, (of forty-five plus) had meant no harm. At this point Pal entered the room and took the floor. He is a compulsive talker, and now he was hysterical about his impending sacking. I said I would do what I could and left. Khan's secretary told me that Sonia was not meeting anyone who wished to sponsor Pal's case. There was gloom all around. As I came away the only sound was Pal delivering a lecture to Khan on his own greatness and how unfair it would be if he had to go. But as I started to get into my car, he came running up behind me, waving his hands.

'Didi, at least tell Soniaji to let me stay for two months, till the rally in February,' he pleaded. 'Then I promise, I'll go. I'll resign. But let me do the rally.' This was a youth rally he was planning on the Brigade Grounds in Calcutta. He had already made a lot of noise about it and roped in various sponsors.

I came home and put in a call to 10 Janpath saying I would like to meet Sonia Gandhi. Her secretary said he'd ask her and get back to me immediately. That evening Pranab Mukherjee told me over the phone, 'I don't know whether it will do any good — your going. In the first place, she most probably won't see you. In the second place, even if she does, I hear she is extremely angry about the whole matter. You might suffer the consequences. I think Barkat is making use of you.'

The call from 10 Janpath came at about ten p.m. Sonia Gandhi and I would meet the following day at noon. When I entered her sitting room, she was pleasant as always and asked me to sit down. I think she suspected I had come to discuss the case of Ghani Khan's protegé, and I think she knew me well enough to realize that I wasn't part of the various cliques and counter cliques. I had come to prove a point. After casually discussing one or two matters, I brought up Paresh Pal and waited for the brow to frown. Instead she looked helplessly at me. 'Ipsita, why don't some of these Youth Congress presidents resign of their own? They are so old. I believe this Pal also is well beyond in years. We'll put them into some other constructive work.'

I sighed. She was right. But I had to fight this losing battle. I only took up cases that were lost. 'Well, Soniaji,' I said, 'that's true, but he has a good command over the youth he heads. Besides he's a street fighter, and that often comes in handy.'

'But he's got himself into a big mess now, hasn't he? What has he done at the Victoria Memorial? He's burnt and destroyed property and given the Congress a bad name — just when we are trying to build up our image.' As she got more and more perturbed her Italian accent grew more pronounced.

'Well, I suppose he was doing it for a cause,' I replied. 'Saving our national monuments from people who feel they have the money to buy it for a night.'

She paused. 'No, no, I appreciate that. The motive may have been valid. But look at how he has done it. It is so embarrassing for the party. It has to answer for his very irresponsible actions. I think he should go, Ipsita. We must replace him.'

I had to think of something that would save the useless blighter. 'Soniaji, Bengal is a very class conscious state. It is constantly aware of who is "rich" and who is "poor". If they feel that you are throwing him out because he fought against the rich NRIs, then they won't take kindly to it. The common people will start looking upon him as a champion of the poor. You must not allow that to happen. Let him stay for now. When you formally appoint the PCC Committee, they can take a decision and appropriate measures against him.'

It had worked. I could see it in her expression. When something struck her as worthwhile, she looked very intently at one. She was looking intently at me now. By no means was she going to displease the masses. 'Yes. All right. Of course I could do that I suppose. Yes. Yes.'

We went on to talk of other things. When I came away, I knew Paresh Pal and his mentor had been saved much embarrassment. But human nature! When I informed Ghani Khan about the success of the mission, he sounded relieved but said that he was planning to send a note to her anyway. And she always gave a lot of weight to his views and requests. I smiled and nodded with understanding. That night at about ten, Paresh Pal and a friend of his rang my bell.

'Didi, I understand from Barkatda that Madam has seen the light. I knew it. What I did has full public support. Nobody in

Bengal can stand up to me.' He paused for breath. 'I believe I can stay on?'

'Yes,' I said wearily. 'Soniaji has very kindly consented to let you continue.'

'Didi, now there's something else you must tell her to do. She must come to the youth rally in February. I'll have a huge crowd anyway. But naturally if she comes, it will be a bit more.'

'Paresh,' I said, 'be grateful that you're still the youth president. I refuse to ask her for anything more on your behalf.' I yawned deliberately. I do not like to keep late hours. He finally took the hint.

'Anyway, I'll be returning to Calcutta tomorrow. I must inform the papers that Madam has requested me to stay on. But I have one thing to ask, didi. Never let anybody know that you went to Madam on my behalf. It isn't right for us in Bengal. I'll tell the papers that Pranabda and Barkatda spoke to her. But anyhow, that's a small matter. She would never have removed me. Not with the mass support I have. Still, please make sure that she comes to the rally. Didi, I'm counting on you for that.'

I shut the door quietly after him. I sent a message to Sonia that the rally would be a farce. It was. She never went. It served Paresh right. He needed a lesson in manners — and gratitude.

# IV
# Myths, Mysteries, Miracles

*'You look up into the heavens when you want to be exalted.
I look down because I am exalted.'*
— Friedrich Nietzsche

**25**

# A Witch by Any Name

So who is a witch? Or more important, what does she do? As she is a Wiccan, it would be fair to say that she practises Wicca or wiccecraefte or the skills of the wise. She was the original wise woman, the shaman, the healer, the counsellor, the lawyer, the stateswoman of her community. Her power became a threat to men, to organised religion — and hence the persecution, the witch-hunts and the slander.

I wonder how many people have the scholarship to realize that the first witch was the Mother Goddess of old. Wicca is a part of the universal, animistic paganism, as old as the human race itself. The beginning of Wicca goes back to the dawning of man's awareness when he began to personalise and deify the various manifestations of nature. Twenty-five thousand years ago, our ancestors were worshipping the female deity. Statues and carvings have been found in France, in Czechoslovakia, in Austria, Siberia, Yugoslavia, Romania, Hungary, Greece, Egypt and in India. She was the strong one, the total woman, daughter, wife, lover and mother. Her roles were many — enchantress, stateswoman, warrior and scholar. Benevolent and unforgiving, stern yet seductive. The way of Wicca, with its permutations and variations, spanned the world. The names of the Witch Goddess were as many as the aspects she presented.

In the twentieth century BC, in Egypt, Isis was worshipped, and in the fifteenth century BC in Turkey, Arinna. She was called Ishtar in Babylon from the eighteenth to the seventh century BC. From pre-Vedic times, India has worshipped Durga and Kali. Tibet knew her as Tara, and the ancient Mayans as the Goddess Ix Chel. In Africa, they revered Yemaya, Goddess of the Sea. In Rome, Fortuna held sway and created abundance whichever way she glanced. To the Japanese, Amaterasu Omikami was the great Sun Goddess who brought life and light to the world. In China, Kuan Yin was the Goddess who brought things to completeness. In Sumeria, the protectress was Inanna. In the Navajo tradition, the source of all was the Changing Woman.

In Baltic lands, the grand old witch or goddess was Baba Yaga. Pagan Ireland worshipped Sheela Na Gig, the Goddess of Good Fortune. Celtic society took to themselves the Lady of Flame, **Brigit**. She was the Goddess of poetry and medicine. It is significant that she was seen carrying a cauldron, representing her divine powers of creation and transformation. The Libyan Amazons worshipped Medusa, who was afraid of none. In Ancient Mexico, Coatlicue was the mother of all who lived atop a mountain in Aztlan. Known to be the five-fold Earth Goddess, Coatlicue guided when one was lost. In Greece, Hecate, a Witch Goddess, was the guardian of the crossroads, who granted her followers wisdom. She gave a grandmother's guidance. Minoan Crete is said to be the last of the goddess-worshipping civilizations. Some authorities extend the worship of the Great Mother or Witch Goddess as far into the past as 50,000 BC. Society began as matriarchal and remained so for millennia. The Wiccan way was a way of life.

Wicca was more than just a worship of the Goddess as the all-pervading strength. It was a realization that there are forces and Elementals surrounding us at all levels. We are actually very small specks in an inconceivably huge place. To know this and to be aware of this, is the beginning of the knowledge we are trying to probe. What does the cosmos consist of? What are the unseen powers which are there? How can we reach them? Is it possible to invoke them?

True Wicca never worked against nature. It worked with it. It accepted the laws of nature and through this acceptance strengthened itself. But Wicca was a form of revolt too. Revolt against suppression and the hypocrisy of society. It had the strength to speak out against exploitation and abuse. It was the craft followed by highly individualistic, thinking men and women. It was a poetic, aesthetic, cerebral way of life.

Who were some of the famous witches in legend and history? In India I have mentioned the seeress Khana. Many say the Empress Noorjehan of Mughal times, had the true qualities of Wicca. Exemplary wife, mother and stateswoman, she knew how to rule and control turbulence. Gentle without — steely within. In France, we have the famous Wiccan, Joan of Arc. It is claimed that her designation, 'La Pucelle' or the Maid of Orleans, meant in actuality that she was the Maiden of her coven or second in command to the High Priest or Priestess. She came from Lorraine, a district famous for magic and paganism. It is said that she had her first clairvoyant experience at the Fairy Tree of Bourlemont. She was a healer and had a huge following. The strangest part remains that after her death, she was rumoured to be still alive.

Her story illustrates perhaps more than any other the extent to which men have always feared independent, free-thinking women. She refused to say the Paternoster. She said she did not need a middleman for God spoke to her personally. She dressed in men's clothing when she pleased, an act that annoyed her prosecutors the most. The history of witch-hunting has been tied up, without a doubt, with the male fear of strong women.

In legend and story, there are the most alluring Circe, Medea and Oenothia. There is also the Arthurian enchantress Morgan Lefay, supposed to be the mistress of Merlin and an astute weaver of magic herself.

Amongst the men, a very famous Wiccan was said to be none other than Robin Hood. He lived in the green woods, a lover of nature. He had around him a coven of twelve members, he being the thirteenth. He was certainly anti-establishment and fought against all forms of exploitation of the poor and helpless. He was also against organized religion. The woods were his church.

Unfortunately, by the end of the Neolithic and the beginning of the Bronze Age, the people worshipped two deities — the Witch Goddess and the Horned God.

Detractors of Wicca have called him the Devil. I would say that this was the God Pan who was certainly not dark and sinister. He was a God of nature, and the protector of all living things. There is evidence of the Horned God from Paleolithic times. In the Caverne de Trois Freres in Ariege in France, there is a drawing of a man clothed in stag skin and wearing antlers. In fact, horned figures started appearing from the Bronze Age. In the Near East, the gods and goddesses wore horned head dresses and this was a sign of divinity as in the instances of Isis and Hathor. In India God Shiva was often shown as horned, since he was Pashupati or the Lord of the animals. Even the crescent adorning his head can be taken to be a form of horns. In Europe, apart from Pan, there were the horn sporting Minotaur and Dionysus. Cernunnos was the Horned God of Gaul and wore stag antlers.

It is quite clear that the Horned God had no connection with the Christian version of Satan, the evil one. Why then, did the pagan religions put this emphasis on the Horned God or Goddess?

One interpretation can be that this was their way of presenting a nature deity — the master or mistress of nature. The woods and fields belonged to them. It could be that there was a clue here on how to draw down the energy from the Elements. A kind of antennae. The same reason why places of worship have spirals, minarets and domes. The same theory as to why pyramids were built the way they were. To bond the terrestrial with the heavens. To receive and transmit from and to the beyond.

Whatever the reason, there is no doubt that organized religion used the horned figure to represent evil. The gods and goddesses of old were turned into the devils of the new manmade paths. The power seekers wanted control in their own hands. Control over the populace, control over laws and governance. Those with independent, free thinking ways and minds, were a threat. Hence the persecution of Wiccans. Specially if they were women. They became the 'evil witches' who always tried to harm people, specially children. Folklore and fairy tales abounded equating witchery with wickedness.

I often used to ask questions about this. What is wicked? Evil is so relative. What is wrong today, may not be considered so tomorrow. Besides right and wrong are such personal, individual things. I have always set my own standards, keeping only one thing in mind. I do not willingly and purposefully harm another in body, mind or spirit. I do not initiate mischief. However, I do not tolerate any form of nonsense from another. My honour is of great importance to me. I admit I am exceedingly proud. I can and will strike if any attempts are made on my dignity. In such instances I judge about when and how to retaliate. Past cases have proved that, and I am unrepentant.

Over the past decades I have delivered innumerable lectures, written articles and columns for papers and journals, and met people, generally referred to as the intelligentsia, in an attempt to clear up the myths and superstitions surrounding the subject of Wicca. I think I have made a breakthrough in India, where the word witchcraft is now no longer as negative as it was in past times. People, specially women are taking a keen interest in learning more about it. I continue to receive countless letters from them asking to be 'witches'. I have conducted workshops around the country, which have experimented with Wiccan ways in dealing with mind improvement and problem solving. I believe that in India, the Vedic system and the yogini cult had a great deal of similarity with Wicca, as it was known in the west.

Now, I have other things to do. Other vistas to view. My work with the people is nearly over. Wiccan work does not prolong itself in one area only. It moves on, experiencing and experimenting. But, before I turn to other horizons, let me set right a few misconceptions about Wicca.

### Witches in flight

Somehow, eastern yoginis never 'flew' but western witches were supposed to ride the broom over hill and dale. I have often wondered about this. And this is what I have discovered. Both African and European witches were said to fly as well as shift shape. This has figured prominently in children's stories as well as adult imagination. What did the broom symbolize? It stood for hearth and home to which a woman was tied by male domination. As she 'flew' away on it, it meant that she was breaking the bonds. It symbolized her freedom. It might as well have been a flying carpet. Colourful stories abounded about how a long-suffering wife would fly away into the night on this piece of domestic bondage, while her husband slept snugly unaware in his bed. She would revel all night long under the moon and return only at dawn to sweep the hearth with the very broom which had carried her off to her secret trysts. It has been said that witches were women who were never afraid to 'fly'. Maybe that is why they had to be burnt.

### Controlling the weather

It has often been said that witches can control the weather. People believe that they can create storms and tempests for weal and woe. Sailors feared women who could whistle because of the sympathetic magic which 'whistled up the wind'. Magic believes in a connection between the microcosm and the macrocosm. After all, witches did call up the storm that defeated the Spanish Armada in the sixteenth century and also the fog that prevented Hitler's invasion in the twentieth century. It is known that the yoginis, sometimes called 'dayanis', of India could remove clouds from the sky by offering the Sun God at Konark one large ruby and by chanting the Gayatri Mantra.

**The witch's pointed hat**

Has it ever struck you why the witch was believed to wear a tall, pointed hat when she could have worn any other shaped headgear? The witch's hat is connected with the cone of power with which she is so associated. This certainly makes sense if there is some aspect of electrostatics that links with psychic ability and the pineal gland. It is an established fact that a pointed object, like a church spire, or a minaret attracts electrostatic energy. Perhaps the horns on the headresses of Wiccan gods and goddesses were supposed to be similarly charged.

**Satanists and Wiccans**

It is really a pity that the pagan craft of Wicca should even be mentioned in the same breath as Satanism. As I understand it, Satanism is an inversion of Christianity. It has nothing to do with the magic of nature or the mind. It is merely trying to draw attention to itself by rebelling against the rules of an organized religion by holding up Satan as a guru — not Christ of the Christian church. It believes in the pro-establishment duality of good and evil. A pagan sees the world and the universe as beyond all man-made terms. Everything is relative. As long as you do not deliberately and wilfully hurt another being, anything goes. It lives life on its own terms. It is a cerebral way of life, not an exhibitionist one. A Satanist indulges in just that. He holds what he calls black masses. He turns the cross upside down, spells the names of deities backwards and generally makes a nuisance of himself. He wants to be called bad. That's where his thrill lies.

## The witch's wand

The witch's wand of power was identical to that which belonged to the healing priest of antiquity, from whom it had in reality been borrowed. The power of the wand is no more than the extension of that of its owner. The original magic wand was the healer's hand and only later did the wand emerge as a separate instrument. It is interesting to note that right down to the end of the eighteenth century, the hallmark of the English physician was his gold headed cane, which originated in the staff, carried by the healing priests of Asclepius.

26

# *The Tools of a Witch — And a Few Secrets*

onjuring, sleight of hand, ritual, magical objects, flowing robes, ambience — these were all tools of the trade, at one time. They were used to aid people who came for help to the Magi, to alter consciousness. Sometimes they shocked like an electric jolt to regain lost mental balance. Often they provided an anchor for the insecure, that served to calm, before actual Wiccan treatment began. They fanned the imagination and acted as a catalyst to the mind, so that it could catapult itself into its own power. These provided some of the poetry and visuals of Wicca but the real secret of its power lay in its link with the mysterious forces beyond. I have always referred to it as the X-factor. The factor which cannot be denied.

That inexplicable something in life — which is not coincidence. Which is that mysterious quality which cannot be explained or analysed, by believer or sceptic.

However, here I must make a confession. By nature, I am what sceptics are made of. I believe, as must be obvious by now, in very few and very little. No matter where I have gone, and whatever I have done and experienced, I have been analytical — sometimes overly so. My eyes have been like those of a hawk — watchful and piercing. My rational mind has time and again, questioned the obvious explanation. To my own disadvantage, I have often turned away from the extraordinary because I wanted tangible explanations to that which was too marvellous for common equations and theorems. I have sometimes whimsically tried to marry magic to orthodox science and found that while now and then, common ground can be found, there are areas too startling for words. How many whys can one answer? How many answers are there? None to define. Many to experience and know.

There is very little literature handed down to us regarding the true tools of a witch. A woman who was truly wise, gave away very few secrets. In those days she burnt for it. Today's witch may not go to the stakes — but what the heck, who wants to share the goodies? The truly diligent witch wrote and maintained a kind of diary called A Book of Shadows which recorded her thoughts and experiences throughout her career. Today's witch, if she's worth her salt, keeps up the tradition. I have done so. What's written there, could help make you rich, keep beauty preserved, hair lustrous and sanity intact in an insane world. It could throw down people from high chairs and raise a few ghosts. It could show you the road to personal peace — but it could also start a war. It could also make your ears burn and your stomach turn if your nerves are delicate. I have written of things unspeakable and completely true. Ancient brews and people's follies. Of green herbs found only on the highest mountains and human scum found behind the masks of power and position. You could come upon the results of Wicca's research into the famous mandrake, henbane, basil, and rosemary.

You could also read about the young woman journalist who joined my group of Wicca in Calcutta. She wanted to learn the words of power so that a certain ageing actor, very much married, would fall under her spell, enough to marry her. He wasn't your conventional, good-looking star — but he was certainly successful. I liked her. She had a certain freshness about her and was struggling her way up in a world where women generally had a hard time. Her father had died many years ago and she and her mother were alone. She brought her gentleman friend over to meet me, when he was shooting in Calcutta on a much acclaimed film. Afterwards, he was going down south to start work on a movie with esoteric undertones. He wanted a few tips on how to project his occult role. He was basically a good man, who had risen the hard way from a life of poverty. It was quite obvious he wasn't in love with his wife, who may have been too sophisticated and demanding for him. However, she was holding onto him for the reason most angry wives hold on. She hadn't found a better deal. I would not like to divulge their private lives. Suffice it to say that he was able to get a divorce even though, at first, his wife kicked up a holy row. Today, he is married to this bright young thing, who learned her spells well. They even have an heir to his flat in Mumbai.

Why did I help them? Not because I believe in coming to the aid of spring and autumn romances. In fact not that I believe in coming to the aid of any romances. But I repaid her because at one time she had written a very attractive and accurate article on Wicca for a prominent daily. She never whined about her hard lot in life. She showed tenacity, not tears. I was pleased with her and her talent. And as I will so must it be.

But I digress. I was writing about herbs. Hemlock was at one time a witch's herb. It is associated with Socrates, who it is said died of a drink of hemlock, laudanum and wine — a 'pleasant' death reserved for important criminals. Henbane is famous in witch lore because it was used by the famous sorceress Circe, who allegedly used it to turn Odysseus' men to swine. The priestesses of Delphi, burned henbane seeds and prophesied under the influence of the fumes.

Such is the poetry connected with the herb. In Book X of *The Odyssey*, Odysseus arrives at the hall of Circe, where 'wolves and mountain lions lay ... mild/in her soft spell, fed on her drug of evil.' And evil she was. A beautiful witch. She enthralled men, made them weak and helpless, took away their manhood 'in her flawless bed of love.' Many a strong woman has done that, in times past and present. Were they all witches? Of course. Every strong, beautiful, powerful woman is a witch. Hail to them. I have never used henbane, but then red rose petals in white wine is just as effective. He will forget every other woman he has ever loved. It will be only you — as it should be.

What are the other tools of a witch? Firstly remember, they should be handmade whenever possible and shared by none. They take on a power of their own and impart it to their owner.

*The Athame:* A double-edged dagger with a magnetized blade. It was used for healing, for attacking predators and for drawing the magic circle around one.

*The Crystal Bowl:* Wiccan tradition used a dugout rock quartz bowl which was filled with clear water and left out in the sun to absorb its beneficial rays. Later, witches floated various coloured rose petals in the water to impart special properties therein. The water was never drunk but splashed on special nerve points on face and body to heal, energize and rejuvenate. This perhaps, was the original magic cauldron.

*The Cape of Black:* In many myths and traditions there are stories of a cape or special coat conferring magical powers. At one time, witches emblazoned their cloaks with magical designs and pentagrams. In many ancient religious and esoteric traditions certain clothes are worn only during prayer or ritual and kept aside later. This is true of both the east and west. In fact, Egyptian and Hebrew practice says that robes worn in the presence of the deity must be washed thereafter. The sacred aura must not go into the world. It is reserved only for the inner sanctum. Fortunately, the witch's cape does not share this rule. It is exclusive but also practical. And it is said that while wearing a cape you may perform magic in the kitchen. Of course if you are strong of will you may perform magic anywhere and you need no cape. But it certainly has its own dignity and beauty. The regal cape of Athena. To show everybody that you are a queen among queens. And why black? Because that is the colour of mystery — inscrutable and enigmatic. A witch is not one to talk or gossip or reveal too much. Just enough to keep one thirsting for more.

*Gloves:* Sometimes gloves were mentioned in Wicca lore as part of the witch's garb. They were to be made of catskin with the fur inside. The choice of fur is significant. Why the cat? This no doubt comes down from the cat's history as a sacred animal in ancient Egypt. However, during the era of orthodox religion, the cat was associated with the Devil. This is a perfect example of how the gods of old paganism, became the devils of the new religion. The wise women of old became the evil witches of the next generation.

*The Crown of Diana:* When meetings were held outdoors under the moon, the head priestess often wore a thin band of silver with the silver crescent moon in front. This was to honour Diana, one of the important patron Goddesses of Wicca.

*The Will of a Witch:* I would say this is the most important tool of a Wiccan. This is that part of herself that makes the magic work. That draws down the power, that bends circumstances to what they should be. The other tools are mere stars which revolve around this central sun. How can a woman acquire this will? First and foremost, she must want it. She must not quaver before the temptations of the flesh or the weakness of the heart. Compassion in moderation is part of the Wiccan personality, but certainly not sentimentality and emotional frippery. She accepts the pleasures of body, heart and mind — when and where she chooses, not because she is slave to them but if and when she wants them. She controls her world and the Elements acknowledge her power. If at any particular time, her destiny leads her to suffering and trial she takes it like a warrior — bloody but unbowed.

**27**

# *The Mystery at Konark*

At one time, Wicca ruled the world. How else would one explain the similarity in theories between say, Wicca as it flourished in Egypt in 3000 BC, in India, when the Vedas were composed from about 1500 BC and in France from about the same time. It is fascinating to note how the Vedas which invoke the Elements, do so in practically the same way as the witches of Isis invoked them centuries before.

The Egyptian Wiccans believed in the magical properties of the sun's rays, the water, earth and air. Thus were they invoked and worshipped. Thus ran the magical chants:

> 'A Re Neb Satetu'
> Hail Ra, Lord of Rays
> 'Anet hra k Tefnet'

> Homage to the water
> 'Anet hra k Geb'
> Homage to the earth
> 'Anet hra k Atum'
> Homage to the Fire
> 'Anet hra k Shu'
> Homage to the air.

The yoginis or dakinis of Vedic times worshipped the Elements too, personified and deified. Vayu is the chief Element pervading space. It is born of Agni, the fire and due to Agni gives out a lustre. The Vayansis are the shining heat waves. Heat has become immortal due to them and due to the electric effect in them, can heal and energize.

There are forty-nine cosmic rays born out of heat, rotating in different fields and giving rise to different shapes. The Marichay are the most uniform. These rays, mentioned in the Rig Veda, are similar in effect to the solar rays and move in electric fields. They are the maruts and are the sons of Rudra, the Sun God. His horses, which so powerfully pull his chariot are actually these electrically charged maruts. In fact all electromagnetic power in space is due to them.

The Rig Veda also indicates the direction taken by these beings. The eighty-seventh hymn is the marut hymn and they have been referred to as Ishaan therein pointing to the northeast. Wicca always invoked its powers from that direction.

The Egyptian Wiccans believed that Ra, the Sun God gave us unending energy. The Wiccans of Britain, France and Germany worshipped the sun, invoking his power near huge megaliths at dawn. The dakinis of India similarly worshipped Aditya, the indestructible source of power. He possessed seven magical rays and was called Saptarishay.

> 'O Effulgent Lord
> May the person who enslaves us
> Be crushed under thy feet
> Whether he is near or far.

May'st Thou be with us
For our progress and prosperity'.

Rig Veda 1.79.11.

Many have said that Wiccans were predominantly feminists fighting for the Goddess. That may have been so, to an extent. But worship of the Elements and giving them male persona would prove that they were striving for the perfect balance in their lives.

They were immersed in nature — the stars, the moon, the fields and mountains, the sea and the winds. They were intoxicated by them. Thus this special verse from the Atharva Veda was frequently read out to us at the chalet.

'O Lord of the vast universe, grant me capacity to receive and absorb the strength of those innumerable divine forces such as the sun, the moon, the stars and nebulae who are travelling around in the cosmos assuming various shapes and forms.'

And that reminds me of Konark, and the extraordinary Sun Temple there. The Elements I had learnt to invoke, proved to me there, that it was not just imagination. Not an empty exercise. Carlotta had once said that the results of some of our experiments were 'startling'. I was brought face to face with the truth of this, many, many summers later at the little town of Konark in Orissa.

After returning to India I used to make frequent trips to the beautiful, little temple town of Puri, with the extraordinary deity, Jagannath, who I have always felt is an old pagan god. His body made from the wood of the neem tree and his huge, hypnotic round eyes like vortices of power, are from another time, another thought dimension. Surely it was a wise, knowing people that fashioned the stumps of his arms, held up towards his worshippers to transmit energy and strength. The town sits next to the heaving green sea, the Bay of Bengal with its tempestuous waves and the roar of the waters reach you long before the dazzling sands suddenly burst upon you as you turn a bend in the narrow, old road, leading to the beach.

That part of the country seems to possess amazing vibrations. I have mentioned the Konark temple as being the place most probably referred to in the prophecies of Luciana in the sixteenth century. Konark is a few miles from Puri and the crumbling temple there, dedicated to the Sun God still holds intact its ancient mystique and power. The edifice there, conceived as his chariot, with twelve wheels and seven rearing horses is a masterpiece of architecture and art — but I realized one day that it was much more than that. The site emits tremendous earth energy. A compass has been known to behave strangely there. A watch may stop. Ofcourse it is true that the building rocks there contain chlorite. That can be one reason why compass needles sometimes spin uncontrollably. But what about the watches? And it doesn't happen all the time.

Temple history provides interesting facts. This was once a place for healing afflictions of body and mind. That was when the gigantic, magnetic capstone still rested at the top of the pyramid shaped roof, before it was allegedly removed by the Portuguese because it pulled alien ships off course, causing them to founder.

Today, the Sun Temple is a mystery. History books say that a massive image of Surya once stood in the inner sanctum on an intricately carved pedestal. Local lore says that the image was not fixed to the pedestal. It retained its extraordinary balance because of the magnet overhead. The stories are many. I draw my own conclusions.

During my last visit there, about four summers ago, I had a strange experience. I had decided to spend a week there, virtually living in the temple and writing my notes. Nights were spent in a nearby guesthouse. But each dawn would see me climbing the massive rocks on the eastern face of the pyramid. As the sun cast its last, lingering, orange glow across the calm but tired visage of the Lord Surya, I reluctantly returned to my room.

I remember the day. It was just after noon when it happened. My daughter, who had accompanied me, and I were sitting on some rocks leading down to the inner sanctum when I suddenly became aware of a strange and powerful energy field. My daughter had come to help me with the photography. I pointed to some rocks and urgently asked her to shoot. She started clicking. Something told me that we must descend to that innermost room.

The sanctum sanctorum of the Sun Temple is awe inspiring. The original entrance to it was blocked off long ago, when the roof started crumbling. Today the only way to access it is by climbing up some steep and unguarded rocks and then descending down a flight of steps, till one arrives at this fairly large room open to the sky. Walls climb up darkly on all four sides. It is something like being in a well. The pedestal stands at the head of the sanctum. An oval shaped slab marks the place where the towering image once stood. I believe that this is the point from which the energy is received and transmitted. I would also say that this is the point from where the earth forces join some greater power. A strange idea came to my mind. I wanted to experience that fountain of power. I climbed onto the ancient pedestal and stood on that very spot where the Sun God had once stood. Presumptuous? Perhaps. But is there not a little bit of divinity in each of us? I wasn't playing God. I was experimenting with the gigantic forces of nature.

I stood feeling the tingling cool of the rock slab under my bare feet. Then I slowly sat down, closed my eyes and waited. The Gayatri Mantra, that ancient Hindu chant dedicated to the Sun God came to my mind. I softly chanted it, invoking the power of the sun, then I fell silent. Slowly ripples of warmth started playing around the pedestal. Maybe five minutes passed. Perhaps fifteen. The ripples increased in strength and power. Wave upon wave of light and space seemed to be playing about me, bringing with it an enhanced alertness and energy. I use these words for want of the right one. Through my closed eyelids I could visualise some power within that pedestal rising — but it was descending from somewhere above me also.

When I had the photographs developed in Delhi a few days later, I realised that something amazing had been captured on film. The descending force had appeared as a mist on either side of me. It was not there when I first sat down. Somewhere along the way an old Elemental power had been tapped. This was a manifestation, a proof.

Can this phenomenon be explained in so-called 'rational' language? The well-known psychic investigator and writer T.C. Lethbridge was fascinated by the subject of earth forces. He wrote that they are largely responsible for the 'sacredness' of certain sites. He even pointed out that many Christian sites are built on ancient pagan spots. It had obviously been recognized by early builders that certain places had powers which could not be explained. The Ancients had known how to track down and attune themselves to these lands. That was where they conducted pagan ceremonies.

Stonehenge in England is one such place. So is the Cornish circle of standing stones, known as the Merry Maidens. When Lethbridge placed his hands on a stone at the Merry Maidens, he felt a tingling force, very much like a mild electric shock. He believed that ancient priests had recognised this earth power and had ordered the stones to be put up there — to conduct the force. This theory is plausible. Konark definitely emits earth power. But it also attracts energy from other sources. I had succeeded in invoking them, and they manifested themselves in a marvellous way.

**28**

## *And at the End*

And now many winters and summers have passed by. Have I changed with the passing seasons? No, for as I have already said, lifetimes do not change one. I am the same. There is a streak of silver in my hair but the smoothness hasn't left my brow. I stand just as slim and tall as when I climbed those stairs to the chalet and felt the wind in my hair blowing in from the mountains. However, there is a certain quiet in me, because I have completed part of the work I had returned to accomplish. I also know that I have set certain forces in motion which will do the rest.

Today, many people — men and women, young and not so young, come to me and want to learn about the ancient craft of Wicca. They have heard about it and read about me. Some, I suspect, think it is fashionable to say one is a 'witch'. They say they want to be like me. I smile and shake my head. Not that I am cynical. It's just that my teaching days are over.

Sometimes when I am tired, I go to the sea. For renewal is there. The waters have always known how to revive me. They froth and fume as I dive into their depths. I am a creature of the deep. I mingle and mix with the turbulent energies of the waters. The churning sea wraps itself around me and we are one. I feel the sensuous, sensual power of the ruthless green and white waves in every sinew and nerve. They tear at my loose flowing hair and whip my head back and draw me under, under into the heart of the thundering waters. The essence of me draws life from this pristine power. I, Ipsita, the Elemental being, revel in the mountains of water heaving and carrying me to the crest and then sucking me into their translucent tunnels. It is a strange and ancient ritual. I am free. I belong to none. I emerge from the waves, recharged. And I look at the world again — with interest. My eyes sparkle. I run my fingers through my wet hair and shake out clinging golden sand. My skin tingles under the warm fingers of sun. As I start towards the shore, a teasing, but unyielding wave creeps up from behind and encircles me, pulling me back for one last embrace. I laugh and surrender.

What of my old group?

Carlotta passed on many summers back. Karen and Mrs. McComb looked after the chalet, till the time that it was considered that due to changing times and circumstances, it would be expedient to sell the place. I heard that it was bought by a well-to-do family, who turned it into a small hotel. The society had been run by a trust, started more than eighty years back, by calendar time. Most of the trustees, four in Canada, the rest in other parts of the world, decided to let go of a shangri-la which had been there... for a time. I never went back to the mountains, even on a subsequent visit to Canada many, many winters later. Trying to find the chalet as it was, would have been maudlin sentimentality. I was a Wiccan. A warrioress.

And the others? A few I lost touch with. We weren't really taught to write warm, newsy letters to one another, full of personal gossip. However, Jean continued to be a popular film star and was successful in both Hollywood as well as in England. I think she brought a lot of charm and charisma onto the screen. Yes, she did marry her English actor boyfriend and they had a wonderful marriage. She passed on a few years before him, after both had lived to a ripe old age. I wonder what happened to her sensitive dog who loved TV. Maybe he's with her now, bullying her all over the place. I wonder if she's looking for someone to sit with him while she shoots her next movie. Sounds strange? Well, it shouldn't because we carry on with our work in the next dimension and it often gets mingled with the work of our friends being carried on here. Maybe that's why we, who are working on this plane, are suddenly 'inspired' by forces beyond our ken and knowledge.

Cindy and Jessica. No, I haven't forgotten you. You were friends and so much fun. Even today when I have chocolate cake I remember Cindy and the cake she baked me for my initiation. Is that being sentimental? Perhaps, but a little sentiment is permissible. Talking of which reminds me of Cindy and her boyfriend — and the little love affair which nearly cost her her place at the chalet. Well, she did lose interest in him after a few weeks. She said it had nothing to do with Carlotta finding out but I wonder. Anyhow, in later years Cindy travelled to New York and became a Wall Street broker. An extremely successful one too. And she did marry. No, you won't believe me. A boy called Derek. He had waited for her after all. Such is the allure of Wicca. I met her about six summers back, quite out of the blue at Crab City in New York. She was as slim and freckle faced as ever. We both recognized each other at once. She looked with wide blue eyes at me and asked me if I ever lived in Canada. When I said yes, she threw her arms around me screaming 'Ipsita, Ipsita.' I wondered with amusement what Carlotta would have said at this show of emotion. Cindy took my hand and wanted to take me across to her apartment which she said was just two blocks away but I said that we should sit down right there, have some lunch and talk. She was too excited to argue.

She has two boys and a girl. I believe the daughter has her red hair. Derek is a lawyer. After lunch I said goodbye. Memories of Shangri-la should not be disturbed.

As for Jessica, extremely intelligent, quiet and reserved — she went into the family business in Montreal. She never married. The essential career woman. I once heard that she was engaged to a boy from Illinois but he was killed in Vietnam. I think Wicca has helped make Cindy into that warm, vibrant person. A wife and mother who juggles home and stockbrokerage with intense energy. I think Jessica has coped with her loneliness and her loss with philosophy and faith because she was basically a strong person and also because Wicca taught her that there is no end to the soul.

A long time ago, Carlotta had said that the soul lives on. Energy is never destroyed. It is there. She would remind us of Aldous Huxley who had said that we change but we do not die. She had talked of Spinoza who had believed that the human mind was a thing apart from the body. 'Something of it remains which is eternal,' he had claimed. This continuity of the conscious agent cannot be explained by any physical or chemical law. We also read Vedantic theory which emphasized that thought, feeling and intelligence can never be produced by any mechanical or molecular motion. In the same way, consciousness cannot be extinguished by the molecular destruction of the brain and body.

So is there a heaven where you go if you have been 'good'? I think we make our own heavens (and hells?) right here — and we continue living in them with those we want near, even after we pass on from our physical bodies. The dividing line between the two dimensions is exceedingly fine. I have come to believe that returning to this dimension is a matter of choice for the soul which has passed. I chose to return. That is all.

Today, I know that just as I have blessed many with my mere presence, so also I have wreaked revenge where it was deserved. I have no qualms of conscience about that. I have no sense of misplaced morality. I have written of the way I chose for myself, because it is the way of power and power is needed in this life — or in any life. The fount I stooped to drink at, was sweetly spiced with hemlock, and henbane and deadly nightshade and I have relished it — even as I offered the cup to my foe.

Carlotta had once said that one should shun no experience in life. Life was the greatest school, the best laboratory for the most interesting experiments with the human species. Look at them, listen to them, mingle with them and learn. Wicca would teach you how. I believe I have followed that advice.

My parents were very strong individuals. I realize that more now than ever. They allowed me to walk on roads which were relatively uncharted and delve into worlds fascinating but unknown at the time. My father, inspite of being an important part of the Establishment, as we would call it, believed in the worth of individual freedom and conviction. He gave me the liberty to tread the path of my choosing because he had the insight to see the vistas of knowledge that it might lead me to and because he believed in me. My mother, the aristocrat from the very discriminating blue blood of Bengal, could have made things difficult for me if she had so wanted. She came from a line which looked critically at anything new and alien before stepping into it. But, in spite of her initial qualms about the 'safety' of her daughter, she let me go ahead with the boldness which was a natural part of her character. 'Do what is right for you as long as it hurts nobody,' was all she said. 'Open up new avenues. New ways of thinking. The women of India should be proud of you one day.' For her, that was important. I think she was always something of a feminist at heart. And what they both believed in wholeheartedly was dignity, pride and honour. As long as one walked with those, the road was right.

I have looked into unknown worlds and studied the ways of forgotten civilizations. I have learned how the minds of men and women work, and the mysterious ways of the Elemental powers.

I have stepped into the dark caves of the unknown which men have been scared to enter and have not cared what the world might say. I have stood alone — often risking personal safety. My values have been different from the world's. My priorities separate. People have often wondered why. But a few have understood. Those whom I have recognized as special and who have known me and have touched hands in friendship.

In Canada and Europe there were people in my youth whom I have talked of. There were and are others. Men and women, some whose names I cannot mention too openly, because of confidences I must keep and honour. Some have passed on to better dimensions. They are there I know, because I believe the soul does not pass into extinction. Its strength and beauty remains.

In the present, so many lives touch mine and I watch their ways and purposes with interest. Rivers, running towards the sea. People doing their work in many areas, in so many directions. Some who are known throughout the world and are celebrated in their chosen professions. Others who tread their lives' course in anonymity but are important to me and I to them. Senior politicians with old values and ideals, with whom I have discussed certain matters of late; the hard working but neglected Congress workers with whom I worked in the 1998 general election campaign; writers and editors who suddenly will say something which startles me with their depth and sincerity — and they and I have forged a bond. Doctors and lawyers who cross my path — and whose dedication to their work makes me pause and reprove myself for my hardened cynicism. Women who come to me for strength and advice — and I recognize the Goddess in them. And lastly, all those men and women who work on against all odds, all reason — because they must. They have no option, no way out. They are the ones who know injustice and pain. They know the drudgery of trudging on. They know pain without cause and despair without hope. But they do it with head held high. They are the ones whom I really know and understand. I belong to them and their souls belong to me. That is a powerful bond. And we bow before none.

In the course of time which seems to be endless, many have come to me for help. I have befriended — sometimes because they needed me, and often when the fancy struck me. Then I have wished to see them no more. I have wandered through the world in high places and low. I have sat down to sup with princes and prime ministers and have also called the poor peasant, my brother, my own.

I was born with extraordinary assets and I have worked to enhance them. I have told you the story as it is. I neither ask you to believe it, nor do I fear your scepticism. I have crossed and climbed many mountains and finally stand at a point from where I can survey the land I have left behind me. I look upon it with pleasure and satisfaction. The secrets I have studied, have enabled me to hold back the years so that my appearance is as I will it to be. I know how to draw from the well of energy. Time has no meaning for me. I feel that I have done the first part of my work and now my time is my own ... for some time. I contemplate the powers I hold in my hands. I have plans for the future.

www.ingramcontent.com/pod-product-compliance
Lightning Source LLC
LaVergne TN
JS040420805026

V000458/3448